Saltlands

Population Series Book Two

Elizabeth Stephens

Published in the United States by Elizabeth Stephens.
www.booksbyelizabeth.com.

To request authorization, and for any other queries, please contact Elizabeth by email at
estephensauthor@gmail.com.

LCCN 2016905318
ISBN 978-0-9991305-8-2
eBook ISBN 978-0-692-70111-9

Printed in the United States of America
Digital art and cover design by Amygdala Design

Second Edition

Table of Contents

To those who seek out other worlds,
you're welcome here.

New Rules for the World After

Rule 1 *(aka the only rule)* — Never give up. Not even when you're dead.

~~Rule 1 Never hope~~
~~Rule 2 Pack light~~
~~Rule 3 Don't get personal~~
~~Rule 4 the BIGGER the badder~~
~~Rule 5 Run~~
~~Rule 6 Always trust your gut~~
~~Rule 7 Never drop your weapon~~
~~Rule 8 Don't help strangers~~
~~Rule 9 No talking in the grey~~
~~Rule 10 Don't start a fight you can't win~~
~~Rule 11 Double tap~~
~~Rule 12 Don't talk to the Others~~

Chapter One

My chest burns. Mikey's mouth is on mine and I try not to touch his tongue with my tongue. It's awkward. Made worse by the fact that we're waiting for the deluge Notare Elise caused to stop. Waiting for the mountain to settle. Waiting for what feels like years. For what feels like freaking ever.

Kane is all I can think about. Where is he? Why'd she take him? That isn't even allowed from everything I've heard. What does she think is gonna happen? They have some structures in place. Somebody called the Lahve is supposed to protect Kane and if not him, then I will.

I'm going to get him back.

I won't let him down.

Not now. Not ever.

He's the man — well, the alien — I never knew I wanted. The one I didn't know could exist, so I didn't know to dream about. Now he's all I dream about. All I think about.

And I'm trapped and he's taken.

I start to squirm as rocks slip into our little alcove and claustrophobia makes my anxiety even more potent. Mikey has my face in a vice, his lips locked around mine as he exhales oxygen into me. I can practically hear him shouting at me even though we're underwater, trapped in a darkness that's near absolute.

I fidget but he holds me in place until most of my panic subsides, and it's in the dark calm that I find clarity as I recognize what I'm going to do next, the only thing I'm going to do next:

I'm going to get Kane back.

Whatever the cost.

Whatever the cost.

Eternities later, Mikey exhales a little more deeply into my mouth. Something's different. He's filling my lungs all the way up, and now he's pulling back. Cool water claims the space where his warmth had just been, and in its absence, I'm anchored to nothing. Swimming through a vacuum in the dark.

I windmill my arms and hit rock hard enough to grate the skin off my knuckles. I kick out, hitting Mikey, but when I reach for that heat, Mikey presses his hand flat against my sternum and maneuvers my body entirely behind his so that I'm wedged between his broad back and the smooth stone walls. It's a tight fit.

Air bubbles from my mouth and nose explode against my cheeks as more rocks pour into the alcove. I slice my knees and palms as I fight my way through them. What is Mikey doing?

My straining lungs are set to burst. Pressing my palms forward, I find shoulders. I feel my way down his back and take a hold of his belt loops at just the right moment, because when he surges forward then, I do too.

He drags me through an opening in the rocks, which slash and cut at whatever's left of Tasha's dress. The one I seduced Memnoch in.

Remembering Memnoch's impaled body hacked to pieces in the tunnel adjacent to this one fills me with a satisfaction that I need right now when everything else feels like it's gone to shit.

I break through some kind of surface and cough up a lungful of water. My hands grab for rocks, and though most of them fall away, some of them hold.

The problem is the chain. It's still strapped to my body and is dragging me back. "Mikey," I croak, slipping back under.

An intense pressure around my shackled wrist makes my whole arm feel like it's ripping from the socket, and suddenly I'm hurtling up and out of the water. My torso and chest hit something warm, and while the tips of my toes still tickle the water's surface, I'm out. I'm safe. Mikey's underneath me and we're both alive.

I'll have to take that as a win.

His chest rises and falls under me while and I can hear in the heavy way he breathes that he's hurting.

"Do you see a way out?" I cough, spitting up half a lungful of water.

Mikey makes an annoyed sound and pushes me off of him.

I hit the stone hard and it's chill comes as a shock. I jolt. Frustrated, I try to kick Mikey in retaliation, but my bare heel hits stone and I yowl.

"You're an idiot," Mikey grunts.

I can hear Mikey moving around me, breath hard and heavy, footsteps labored and short.

"Abel," Mikey says and his voice is a mangled snarl wrapped around another snarl. I can feel, rather than see, as he moves towards me when his heat draws closer. "Get up." His hand tugs at the heavy chain at my back, but right now I don't want to stand up. And it isn't just because the floor is oh so inviting. It's because I can *see.*

"Wait." There's light. I don't know where it's coming from or how. Everything is so disorienting. But it's there, nestled in between the crack separating two stones.

I reach a hand forward and push on the first boulder I find, but it doesn't give way, so I tug on the smaller rocks beside it.

"Careful you don't bring the mountain down on my ass…" My. Everything is *my, me* and *I* with him.

I roll my eyes, though he can't see my face from that angle. "I'm in here too, you know."

Lying flat on my stomach, I push aside enough smaller rocks until I hit boulders. Their sides are smooth and rounded, but between them is a jagged mess of smaller stones. I paw my way forward, throwing them behind me into the pool. Light spills over my fingers and I've never seen anything so welcome or so beautiful.

Mikey drops down to his knees at my side and reaches forward to help me clear the rubble. His hand is pale but strong, lined in blue-green veins. His hand is the first part of him I've seen. Funny that we almost died together, but I still have no idea what he looks like. I tense a little bit, worried that he'll look too much like his brother. That it'll be a constant reminder that I failed him.

"This leads back to that place with all the tunnels," I say. "But that room collapsed."

"It's our only choice at the moment, and there's light."

I nod at that. Must be a good sign.

"I can't fit," he grunts, warm breath near my cheek as his shoulder presses against my own. "But you can."

I nod. "I'm not going to leave you."

"You're damn right you're not," Mikey says, "but maybe you can move the rock from the other side."

He doesn't sound convinced himself, but I don't argue. Instead, I kick my way forward through the opening. The chain slows me down, ripping at my wrist as I wriggle through the tight space. Two frost-flecked rocks come together against my sternum and my spine and I start to panic. "Mikey, you gotta push me."

He places his hands against the backs of my thighs and shoves me hard enough that the shoulder of my dress tears, taking skin with it. Tasha constructed the thing to be indestructible. The downside of that is that nothing is truly indestructible, including me.

I clench my teeth through the pain, curl my fingers into the stone, chipping all my nails and pull, pull, pull.

"How's it looking?" Mikey shouts, though his voice is muted now. I can't feel his hands on my legs anymore. I must be almost there…

My hand hits air. I grab the rock beside it and heave, finally dragging my body into the cavern that once had all the exits. The last place I saw Kane right before he was dragged down that tunnel by Elise.

"Dusty." I cough, as if for emphasis. "Dust everywhere."

"That isn't fucking useful. What about the exits?"

I rub the back of my wrist across my mouth as I squint around, trying to make sense of the rocky world around me. "You know, I could just leave your ass in this rock prison."

"You wouldn't be the first." Mikey's voice is bitter and I feel a momentary guilt that I'd even joke about that after he spent the last three years locked away in here by Memnoch, being experimented on by Notare Elise.

"The exits have all collapsed. There's enough room for me to kneel, but there isn't much more than that. The ceiling is lower than it was, which probably means it's not stable." Mikey curses but I speak over him. "There's got to be an opening, though. I can see in here."

"Fuck. Find the source."

Unfurling my legs hurts. Everything is stiff and sore and tired, even with Kane's blood in my system healing my superficial wounds so fast water would be jealous.

I shake out a cramp in my right leg and gather the chain to my chest as I start inspecting the rocks, careful not to touch any of them until I'm sure I won't be buried alive, at best, and at worst crushed to death. Or maybe the former is worse.

The tunnel entrance that claimed Kane and Elise is well hidden now, as is Memnoch's mausoleum. He'd be trapped forever, even if there had been the slightest chance in hell he'd have survived what I did to him. To save myself and avenge Ashlyn, I'd impaled and decapitated the bastard.

The more distant corners of the cavern disappear into darkness, except for a small ray of pale grey light that filters into the chamber through a small fissure high above the rocks piled up in front of the exit tunnel where Kane and Elise went.

"I found the opening," I say with a grimace. "But it's too small to get a body through, though. Not even mine." I tilt my head to the side and squint while Mikey says something behind me.

"Wait..."

I approach the rocks, pushing on a couple larger boulders to test their stability. They don't budge. Slowly easing myself onto the larger of them, I duck beneath a protruding sheet of stone and climb towards the place where the light filters in. And as I get closer, I notice something that brings a smile to my face.

Tree roots.

I grab at the roots growing by the fissure and pull. Rocks and dirt shower me. I'm greeted by a rush of cool air.

"There's a way out!" I press harder, a tiny stone avalanche sliding back to cover my stomach and bury my feet until the darkness breaks fully and I'm left looking up into a sight I never thought I'd be so happy to see.

The grey.

I laugh up at the grey ruined sky and edge up, up, up, sliding and slipping over the scree in order to be able to stick my head all the way out and up.

The cold air freezes the moisture to my skin and I shiver, teeth clacking together already. Looking down, I see the mountain from the outside for the first time. The surface is solid stone. It curves down to meet a ledge about twenty feet across and four feet wide, on the other side of which is absolutely nothing.

"Shit, Mikey. We're high up." I pull back into the cavern, which feels suddenly so much smaller than it had before. Smaller, but also safer.

I return to the crevice that I crawled through and can hear Mikey shuffling around on the other side of it. I ask him what he's doing. "Trying to get the fuck out of here."

"Hold on a second. Let me help." I drop to my knees only to feel hot pain slice into my shins as I kneel.

"Shit," I curse, jerking back. I reach down to swipe at the stones that are in my way, but as my fingers move, they come back bloody. There's something shiny and *sharp* down there.

Grinning, I dig and keep digging until the familiar hilt of Kane's sword comes into view. It takes a little maneuvering, but I manage to free it. I close my eyes and wrap my fingers around the well-worn hilt and for a moment, it feels like Kane is here, telling me to keep going, to keep pushing, to never give up.

Tucking the sword under my arm, I slide down to the opening. My body blocks out the light, so I can't see anything.

"Any luck on your side?" I say quietly, like I'm afraid that the mountain will hear us and try to keep us inside if it knows how close we are to freedom.

He grunts and I can hear rocks shuffling and sliding against one another uncertainly. A few smaller stones fall, but the big ones remain in place.

"Nothing's moving over here," Mikey grumbles. "I'm going to have to come through the same way you did."

"You won't fit." I pause, then consider, "And if you could fit, then why haven't you?"

He doesn't answer. Then there's a crack followed by pained grunt bordering on a scream. I call out to him, but he still doesn't answer me. There's shuffling. Time moves slower now. Then finally, after my third plea for information, I see his hand clawing through the small space I'd just barely fit through myself. I squeak.

"Pull me through," he rasps, and I don't hesitate.

Carefully bracing my feet against the rocks on either side of the space, I lock my fingers around his right wrist and wrench him straight towards me. It's slow going. My biceps and shoulder blades burn and rocks shift precariously beneath the pressure of my feet, but eventually his head comes through, and then his torso, and then the rest of him.

It's like the mountain is giving birth to a fully grown alien. Eeew. Or just taking an alien-sized shit.

I collapse back and when he falls directly on top of me, I'm crushed by his weight. Thick, wiry hair brushes against my chest and arm — a beard, maybe? He drops forward and his forehead lands square on my right tit but there's nothing at all sexual about this. His hot breath fans over my ribs and he just stays like this, without moving.

"Mikey, are you okay?" I reach down and touch the back of his head, trying to be comforting, but his hair is *gross.* It's one solid sheet of filth and the *smell.* Oh god, the smell…There are no words to describe it.

I laugh a little, hoping to break the tension. "I'm taking it hot showers weren't readily available to you down here, huh?"

"Shut the fuck up. I just broke my own arm and shoulder to get through that fucking hole. I haven't seen hot water in three fucking years. And you're here trying to crack jokes? You're a bitch." He snaps and I know he's in pain and that he's lashing out and that it's for this reason alone that his words are meant to hurt.

But they still do.

Bracing my arm against his throat, I heft his torso off of mine. "Get off me, Mikey."

As he chokes, I catch my first glimpse of his face. Well, what little of it that there is. Mostly he's covered in a course beard that I think might have started out blonde at some point. Now it's just a dense, matted mass flaked with black dirt and brown blood. So is his hair, which tickles my chin as it hangs down towards me in thick, uneven clumps. He smells like shit and sulfur, and he must catch the look of unsympathetic disgust that crosses my face, because he grins.

"My good looks aren't cutting it for you?" His voice is a sarcastic jab.

I raise my tone to match it. "To say the least." I give him one hard push, fingers slipping through blood. He winces, then falls onto his side off of me.

Mikey drags his flaccid legs through the opening while I struggle up into a crouch. My lungs catch when I look down at him. "Holy fuck." I point. "Mikey, your arm." It looks to be broken in half a dozen places and hangs from the stump of his shoulder like an empty sac. "Christ, Mikey…"

"I told you I couldn't fit. Not whole anyways." He coughs blood onto my legs. "I'll heal soon enough, though." He freezes with one ear cocked.

"Oh fuck, what is it?" The mountain groans and I don't wait for Mikey's response.

I shove my shoulder underneath his one remaining arm and haul him to his feet. "Nothing wrong with my legs," he mumbles, but I can still feel him leaning on me.

Keeping a fierce grip on Kane's sword, I scramble onto the boulder and squeeze through the opening in the side of the mountain. Carefully, I drop down onto the ledge nearly ten feet below, pain rattling through my shins and heels when I land hard on the stone.

I glance up at Mikey, who emerges from the opening with fervor, like he's scared something will go wrong now that he's so close to the light. Out under the grey, that low-hanging sheet, Mikey maneuvers awkwardly beside me onto the stone outcrop.

He's barefoot too and though he limps on his left leg and favors his right, mangled arm, he still towers over me. As he ambles stiffly by, chest pressing close to mine, I can't help but compare him to Kane. They couldn't look less like brothers and I'm a little relieved that, looking at him, I won't have a constant reminder of my shame.

His skin is pale where Kane's is olive, hair light where Kane's is dark. His eyes are black where Kane's are hazel and full of light. Despite being cut leaner than his older brother, he has an air of desperation that surrounds him like a stink and makes him look just as lethal.

In Population, I learned to trust things by the look of them and watching Mikey scale down the side of the mountain, moving from this ledge to the narrower one beneath it, I decide that I don't trust him at all.

The only thing that binds us is his brother and I get the feeling that his brother is the only reason I'm alive right now.

"What are you staring at?" He says without looking at me.

I shrug and swing down onto the precipice beside him. "Nothing." I cling to the rock wall to keep from slipping.

He shuffles a few steps forward, leaning heavily against the rock as he tries to keep weight off of his right leg. He peers over the edge before crouching down onto his haunches and scaling his way down to the next rock protrusion.

"Well, fucking quit it. It's weirding me out. I get that I'm ridiculously good-looking but there's no need to make me feel self-conscious about it."

I roll my eyes and follow him, step-for-step.

"It's a quarry," I say, half to myself. "Makes sense why everything is so smooth. Even these protrusions aren't too difficult to scale." I tell myself these things to distract from the height, because the smooth curve of the mountain leads straight down to a hole in the earth full of smooth rocks a hundred plus feet below,

A more gradual slope ahead of us leads to forested terrain off to the right, and that seems to be what Mikey's headed for.

He pauses to rest, or perhaps simply take in the sight of the sky. His eyes crinkle at the corners as he slumps against the mountainside. He tilts his face up to the grey and surprising tears streak through the black filth covering most of his face.

I look away, giving him this moment in peace. I might not like him, and he might hate me, but he deserves to process this moment anyway he needs.

I move past him quickly, heading down, down, down until I finally reach the place where there are no more ledges and smooth stone has transitioned to clustered boulders. At the bottom of this incline there's dirt and soil. I feel like sprinting for it, but am aware that moving too quickly would probably kill me. So I don't.

I take it slow and eventually, earth finds its way beneath my feet.

I squish my toes into the moss-covered soil. There's no grass here. Grass is a bit of a tricky thing in Population. It grows like a weed in some spots, but in a lot of areas around here, it's almost like it's too wet for it.

And it's wet here. The air clings to my skin like a blanket and I shiver when goosebumps break out over my skin. I firm my grip on the sword I carry and take a deep breath, then close my eyes.

"Kane," I whisper.

"What?" Mikey's hard voice snaps and I turn to see him jumping down off a boulder to squish into the soil beside me. He takes the same deep, assured breath I did as he lands.

I meet his gaze and am a little thrown by its intensity. I'm even more thrown by how crazy he looks. He's white under there, I'm sure of it, but right now he's all red and black.

The clothing he's got on…Jesus Christ. It's just a pair of pants, if you can call them that, but I have no idea what color they were before. Right now they're just wet black rags clinging to his legs. They don't fit him, and are definitely too short. His stomach is the cleanest thing about him. Dirt outlines his muscled torso, which clenches the longer I stare at it.

Drawing my gaze back up to his face, I say dumbly, "You don't really look like Kane."

Mikey scoffs, gaze darting away from mine. "Did you expect me to?"

"People always said that I looked just like my brother."

"Was he as ugly as you are?"

I roll my eyes and take off towards the sparse tree line decorating the brow. "Charming. Another thing you and your brother don't have in common."

"Stop fucking comparing me to my brother," Mikey shouts after me, voice and hackles rising. "Heztoichen don't have to resemble their kin, and Kane and I were born two hundred years apart. The only thing we share are parents, and now they're both dead, so just forget it."

"Fine," I say, pitch flat, moving on. I look instead to the desolate world surrounding us while the chill from the mountain numbs my toes. I hug my arms and walk faster.

Is there anything I can use to make shoes? The bark on the trees is pine — not malleable enough — and I can't fashion the needles into anything useful.

I clench my teeth together, grateful for Kane's blood in my system, knowing that it's likely the only weapon I've got at the moment against hypothermia.

"Are you fucking listening to me?"

"No. What?"

He stands on high ground looking down at me. Haggard and blood-drenched and glaring at me like he wants nothing more than to rip my heart out through my chest, he's a nightmare with a face.

"I'm nothing like my brother."

"Yeah, I got it. I heard you the first time. I'm sorry for comparing you," I say, not at all sorry.

"No," he says, staggering towards me. "You don't get it. You don't understand anything. You don't know anything. And now I'm stuck with you." His face takes on a murderous glint that I'm unprepared for.

"What is your problem?" I lift the tip of the sword and the sight of it distracts him.

He glances at me sharply, embers glittering in the black jewels of his eyes. "Do I really need to explain it to you?"

When I don't answer he roars, "Everything! Everything is my fucking problem. I've been waiting for a rescue for three years only to get you instead of my brother and you drag Notare Elise and Memnoch along with you.

"And now I'm out here in the middle of nowhere with nothing to eat and I'm tired and I just want to go back to my fucking house, but instead I've got to go on a wild goose chase to save my brother from a psychopath even though he's probably dead already and I'm going to die trying to save him, and for what?"

He throws out his arms. "For you? For an ugly, skinny, stupid human?"

"You were rescued," I say, heat flooding my face and funneling through my arms. "You let yourself get kidnapped by a human woman and an idiot like Memnoch," I scoff. "You don't have anybody to blame but yourself."

"You fucking…"

"And," I shout, voice rising over his, "I'm the only reason you're even here. Without me, Kane would have *never* found you in the first place and you'd still be rotting away in that cell."

Mikey's rage is reaching a peak that I know I should be afraid of, but I'm pissed off, too, and incapable of being the voice of reason. He stomps towards me, dirt squishing under his big, stupid feet with every step.

He screams, "Yeah. I'm out. But for how long? I can't get Kane back. Not on my own. I'm only a hundred years old and the Lahve won't believe anything I tell him and he definitely won't believe you. So now I've got to walk to my death for Kane — probably gonna get imprisoned again — and it's because of you."

"Are you entirely forgetting that I'm here? That I killed Memnoch, your jailer? The guy who kept you prisoner for three years?"

I lift the sword with conviction now, even as the slack on my chain holsters my movements. It's gonna be hard to take him down. I shake my head. Take him down? This is Kane's brother. We're on the same fucking team! What are we doing here, screaming at each other like this?

"You got lucky," Mikey sneers, but I hear how his voice dips. Nervous, maybe. Or maybe even more pissed. "Memnoch wasn't even that old. He was barely older than me..."

"So that must be why *you* couldn't kill him." I laugh in a horrible way I've never heard before as this creature brings out the monster in me. "No. Why don't you just go home, find a nice drink, and let me save Kane. You're fucking useless anyway. The useless, shitty brother."

Underneath the filth streaked across his cheeks, there's red. A very dangerous red. A red that reminds me that he's actually an alien — not a human at all — but that even an alien is capable of being hurt.

"I...I shouldn't have said that..." I start, but Mikey doesn't hear me.

He roars, "I told you not to compare me to my fucking brother!"

Mikey lurches towards me in a move that's frighteningly fast. I jerk my blade up, nicking his left pec, but he jerks back before I can do any serious damage. Not that I'm trying to. I'm not trying to...I think...or maybe I am.

He shouts again, this time in Other-speak, before he seethes, "Give me the sword."

"It's mine!" I glance towards the trees behind me, wondering if I can make it that far before he rips my head off my neck. "Kane gave it to me." And it's the last piece of him I've got left.

"He had no right to give it to you."

Mikey slaps his chest twice — thwack, thwack — and I canter back, reminded suddenly of a movie poster for some title called *King Kong*. Aiden had it in his bedroom when we were little. Though he'd always been little. He'd died little.

"That is my father's sword. Kane's gone now, so that sword is *mine*."

Mikey moves brutally and without grace. Still, he's fast and manages to punch me in the shoulder *hard*. He isn't holding back.

I switch the hold I have on the sword when he comes at me from the right so that I hold it with both hands. I cut down into his exposed thigh while my feet sink further into the muddy ground underneath me.

"Mikey, quit fucking around. We're on the same side!"

"We aren't! We aren't on the same side. You're a fucking human."

The irony is that, he's absolutely right. We *shouldn't* be on the same side, and two months ago, I would have agreed with him wholeheartedly. Now look at me? Who am I?

I'm a queen among the aliens.

Hah.

How wild is that?

I'm panting, exhaustion making it harder to fight. I hit him again, this time with the flat side of my sword and hard enough to knock him back. His left knee collapses inwards, as if it's made of cardboard rather than bone.

He shouts words in alien that are unintelligible to me, but I don't stop to interpret them. I turn and run. I race for the trees, and as I duck past the first copse, the whole world darkens.

Thunder chases me while branches try to pull me back. I don't make it very far before a soft tugging sensation lights across my left foot and wrist. My feet leave the ground as Mikey grabs the chain I still wear and throws me by it.

A blitzkrieg of heat ripples across my spine as I hit the soft, squishy forest floor. I'm down for a second before the back of Mikey's hand hits my cheek — not hard, but hard enough to shock me — then he rips the sword right out of my hands. A light push and I collapse back into the dead leaves and mud beneath me.

Placing a tree at my back, I struggle up into a seat. I swab the inside of my mouth with two fingers and taste the metallic tang of my blood mixed with Kane's.

"Asshole," I shout after him while hot tears sting the back of my eyelids. I'm not hurt, but I'm angry, frustrated, and cold, made colder by the blood, residual quarry water, and cool, soft soil stuck to my skin.

I'm pissed. I'm pissed because he took the sword away, even though he had no right to take it. I'm pissed because when I was fighting him, I showed a restraint that he didn't. He's Kane's *brother.* He should be like kin. But instead he's this...this horrible jealous thing who hates everything. Including him.

"We're on the same team," I croak.

His back to me, Mikey misses his next step but he continues forward, away from me. Eventually, I get up and follow the muddy tracks he leaves behind into the grey.

I find myself constantly flexing the fingers of my sword hand, wishing I had it back. Wishing I could swap one brother for the other. Wishing I could undo time and make Kane a set of new promises.

To accept that some fights aren't fighting and to forgive his brother for this. But I can't. And I won't ever forgive him.

Chapter Two

It's dark and my stomach is rumbling in a way that's uncharacteristic, my abdomen twisting in my belly like water snakes. Maybe I'm hungry… That must be it.

I've known hunger before though, and this isn't it. It hasn't been *that* long since I left Kane's and I've got his blood in my system giving me the illusion of fullness.

Must be something else.

I stop for a moment and brace my hands on my knees. "Mikey, hold up a sec. I've got a cramp." Breath puffs up in thick white clouds against the blank backdrop before me. "We need to find food and water."

Somewhere in the darkness up ahead, Mikey snorts. "Sounds like a people problem."

Frosted pine needles tickle my bare toes. I want to build a fire, but I don't. In Population, there's always the risk you aren't the biggest or the baddest thing out there. "You don't want to eat?"

"Don't ask me what I want to eat."

I trudge another dozen steps forward until I spot Mikey's charcoal silhouette. He's found a seat and collapsed against the trunk of a massive moss-covered tree. His eyes flash to me and stand out bright white in the shadows.

I frown down at him. "Don't be nasty."

His upper lip twitches and his lids fall shut. I stalk towards him and quickly snatch for the sword propped up against the tree just out of his reach. He's quicker though, and keeps it from me.

"I will take my sword from you eventually," I say, kicking and scattering some damp leaves across his outstretched leg.

He tucks the hilt under his left arm and crosses that arm over his abdomen. "And then I'll just take it right back." Mikey grunts, groans, and shifts until he's nearly prone against the forest floor.

I shiver as I stare. It's cold. But as I step closer to him, that chill wavers. If I weren't so pissed at him, I'd snuggle right up to his side — smell, be damned. But I am, so I don't.

"So this is your plan, then? You want to sleep here?" I look at the trees clustered around us. They're patchy and the bushes are thin here with barely any leaves on them. Everything is just a moss-covered stick. We're totally exposed.

Mikey doesn't answer. Like he doesn't hear me, or is too stupid to care. I wonder if he'll even bother waking me up in the morning, or if he'll sneak off while I'm asleep. Standing over him, debating whether or not sleeping is worth the risk, I decide that I hate this blonde brother before me. I nudge a lonely rock with my foot and again find myself debating…should I bash his skull in?

"You going to do it or not?" Mikey says, voice slow but otherwise alert. He doesn't open his eyes.

I shake my head, though I know he can't see me, and for just a moment I picture his blood on my hands. That blood makes me think of Memnoch and then of Ashlyn and then of those other girls, of Kane the first time I saw him lying broken on Population's unforgiving city streets.

"No."

A flash of white appears in the dark and I move away from it. His eyes. I feel a pinprick of rage. A pinprick of fear. I lie down in the hollow at the base of a tree far enough away from him that he won't be able to get up and find me immediately should he wake in the middle of the night debating the same thing I just did.

Though my eyes are shut, I don't really sleep, and reality comes for me well before daybreak — greybreak. As I get up, my concerns about Mikey abandoning me transition to concerns about Mikey waking up at all. He looks like he died several days ago.

His too-white skin looks grizzly in the soft light and the blood and black filth crusted too him looks even more pronounced. It streaks down his neck and over his chest. His hair is black on his face, on his head and under his arms. It's not supposed to be black, I'm sure, but I'd have to guess at what color I think it's supposed to be right now.

"We need to move." I kick his leg. No response.

I say his name several times, then call him all the insults I'd been dreaming about. I'm still flat-lining. Rolling my eyes, I turn from his corpse and trudge through the trees. The forest floor surrounding our sleeping spot is uninterrupted, soft soil covered in thick, dry foliage that crinkles under my feet.

Huzzah for the small blessings…

I siphon water from the large oak leaves, collecting dew and rain. It's not enough to slake my thirst, but it's better than nothing and helps calm the knots in my belly. Then I set to work.

Frustration and physical exertion have me sweating nearly five minutes in as I try to break free of my shackles.

Because Mikey's right — I can't even free myself. How am I supposed to free Kane?

I try rocks, sticks, and lots of wriggling and eventually manage to smash the heavy iron weights down my wrists and over the broad of my hand. The effort covers my fingers in a crimson glove, but the pain is only fleeting and already I can see the shredded skin there mending itself anew — another gift from Kane. One of so many.

Massaging my arm, I turn to my bare feet. Together, the shackle and chain must weigh thirty pounds, and no matter how I bend and twist and smash, I can't wrench my ankle free.

"That's not going to work."

I jolt at the sound of Mikey's voice, and look over my shoulder to see him standing just a few feet behind me, arms crossed, sword tucked into a beltloop.

I bring the rock I'm holding down against the iron shackle again. Again, it clangs and makes a small scratch in the surface. At this rate, I'll have the thing off by the time I'm eighty.

"Any…other…suggestions?" I grunt between strokes.

Leaves crunching precede Mikey's arrival. He lowers down in front of me and touches my ankle. His fingers are gentle, so I know not to trust them. I flinch. He meets my gaze.

"I'm not going to hurt you," he grumbles.

"Hm."

"Why haven't you tried the sword?" He pulls my leg out straight and I feel my face heat — both because of the question, but also because of what I'm wearing.

Tasha's dress is tied to me by a few resilient threads at this point. There are huge holes over my stomach, and if I twist my hips the wrong way, I'm pretty sure Mikey'll get an eyeful.

Shoving one flapping shoulder up to more fully cover my right tit, I snap, "I would have if I'd known I was allowed to touch it."

Mikey doesn't respond, though I see the tightening of his jaw, letting me know that this docility only lasts in brief bursts. Very brief.

"Plus, I'd more likely saw off my own leg than get this stupid thing off."

Mikey narrows his eyes as he stares at the shackle. Clearly thinking, but I have no idea what odds he's weighing until he says, "Let me try."

Pressing the sharp edge against my metal cuff, Mikey very carefully leans his weight into the blade and begins sawing back and forth.

As he bends over my calf, I watch him closely. Begrudgingly, I notice that he no longer looks so bad. Maybe he really did need those few extra minutes of sleep.

Or maybe he just laid there to piss me off.

Either way, some of his color has returned and his shoulders seem fuller than they last had. Perhaps it's only how close he is to me. Close enough to smell him. He smells like crap. Actual human crap.

"What?" Mikey barks, stalling for a moment. His eyes flash to mine and I grimace.

"Nothing. Just…loving your look. The mud locks, the caveman beard, the smell of boiled eggs and urine, a little bit of shit and vomit mixed in..."

Mikey's lips twitch like he's going to smile, or trying to restrain the impulse. He doesn't, in the end. But he doesn't hit me, either, which I think may be a step in the right direction for us.

"Yeah, we make quite the couple. You look like a zombie prostitute."

Laughter bellows out of me and Mikey's smile breaks. He grins as he keeps working at my cuff, trying just about everything to get the damn thing off — sawing, hammering, slicing, pulling, ripping, gnawing, tearing. The sword puts a crack in it, but even with Mikey throwing his full weight behind the blade, he doesn't get far. He doesn't get far *enough.*

"Mikey, it's not working."

Mikey spits out a host of what I think are curses in his alien speak and falls back onto his ass.

He tosses the sword into the mud while the swollen muscles in his arms flinch in small pulses. He's got about as much control over his anger as I do. Not a great combination.

Trying to be the voice of reason, I say calmly, "It's alright. Thanks for trying. I'm just going to have to deal with the chain until we reach a city where…"

"I can get you out." He kneads his jaw, which is entirely invisible beneath the thick blanket of beard covering his chin, his cheeks, and some of his neck. It makes me wonder what his face actually looks like under there.

"You can? Why are you telling me this now?"

"I can get you out, but you're not going to like how."

"Is it gonna kill me?"

"No."

"Then it's probably worth a shot."

Mikey grunts and grabs my leg below the knee, making me flinch. "What?"

"That hurts," I complain, trying to shrug him off.

"I'm hardly touching you."

"I mean, it tickles."

His face scrunches up. "It hurts or it tickles? Which one?"

"Why can't it be both?"

"If it tickles, it can't hurt. They're like opposites."

I laugh lightly then and shake my head.

"What?" Mikey says, and his expression is softer than it was. Unlike his brother, who has some sort of unearthly aura about him, Mikey looks so crazy human. So human.

"Nothing. I just happen to disagree with you and with your brother." I smile, lost in the memory. "He says the same thing."

Mikey grunts and tickles the back of my knee, sending my whole left leg into spasm. "Ow," I howl, falling onto my back and clutching my left thigh. "That hurts," I say, but I'm laughing and there are hot tears in my eyes.

"Goddamn, you're weird," Mikey says, but I can hear the smile on his tone and I feel hopeful as he straightens my leg out that maybe we can come together somehow, and this won't be so bad traveling together after all.

I'm still mad at him.

I still don't trust him.

But maybe *hate* was a strong word.

Maybe with a new day things will seem more possible, including friendship.

I decide then to try a little harder.

"You ready?" Mikey's hand is warm and firm around my left ankle.

"I don't know what I'm supposed to be ready for."

"Bite down on this."

He hands me a stick. "Oh fuck." Understanding dawns on me and I quickly shove the stick in my mouth, bear down with my hands, and shout around it. "Go quick!"

In one quick motion, he crushes my heel with nothing but his hand. I scream around the stick, pulverizing it to shards in my mouth, which I then struggle to spit up.

Pain radiates through my whole left side and I fight my way through it, like I've been buried and have to claw my way back to the light.

Hacking out thorny spittle, I roll onto my stomach and lay my forehead on my hands. I try to breathe as I feel heat work its way through me. Kane's blood to the rescue. Hallelujah. I could get used to this…

"Abel? Are you…" Mikey coughs, his throat catching. He doesn't say more. I just lie there and as I lie there, Mikey pats me once on the right shoulder.

I laugh, mad with fever and pain. I sound hysterical, even to myself, but when Mikey asks me what's wrong, I say, "I'm just loving your bedside manner."

"I guess I'll have to work on that." He stands and puts space between us. When I open my eyes, the entire world is fogged over, a warm breath against a clear pane. All I can make out against the ashen background of the forest are his arms folded over his broad chest, his one bare calf visible through his shredded pants, his fingers twitching.

I roll onto my back and drape my arm across my eyes, waiting for Kane's blood to do its work. Even as that funny heat makes its way down to my heel, I know that I won't be able to put weight on it for a while.

As Mikey looms over me, I can sense his impatience. His feet are tapping restlessly and his hands are fiddling with the sword.

I suggest that he goes and finds us something to eat. He stomps off and returns half an hour later with a handful of mushrooms. Most of them are poisonous, but I pluck out the few good ones and we chew in silence. He stares into the forest with flat, black eyes. They are utterly vacant. I wonder what he's thinking, but don't ask.

I tilt my last mushroom towards the pale light above my head and smirk, "So what, you don't know how to hunt?"

It's got dark red spots on the cap and when I check the stem, it's full of dozens of microscopic holes. Lovely. I toss the mushroom over my shoulder and dust off my hands.

"Why would I?" Mikey's tone is harsh but he doesn't meet my gaze, and I can see just beneath that hard, condescending veneer, that he carries a very real insecurity with him. Something I never saw in Kane.

"Because it's a sort of useful skill."

"Perhaps for humans."

"Or for anything that likes eating." He's only a few feet from me and I still can't run anywhere, so of course I bait the beast. "I could teach you some tricks sometime."

Mikey's bottom jaw juts out. "Don't flatter yourself."

I roll my eyes. "Fine. We'll just keep eating poisonous mushrooms until one or both of us drops dead. Sounds like a super plan. While we wait for that one to work out, do we have an actual plan?"

"Get Kane back."

I fight the ever-present urge to chuck something at Mikey's head. "How? Do you even know where he is?"

"No." Mikey steeples his fingers and looks at me over the tops of his broad, flat hands. His nails are crusted in onyx, as are the seams of his knuckles and knees, the laugh lines around his eyes. "But you do."

"I don't even know where *we* are."

"We're just outside of the Diera." Back in Population then. Oh goodie. "And you're wrong. You know where Kane is. You're the only one who can find him."

He answers my curiosity with a groan and punches his fists back through his hair, fingers tangling in the matted locks.

"Have you not been listening? You're Kane's wife. The Sistana. His queen. Your blood bond works two ways. He can sense you, just like you can sense him. You know where he is. You're the map. You just have to find the key."

"You're telling me that I can *find* Kane? Like in the world?" I know that's how he found me, I just thought…I guess, I assumed it was an alien thing. Sounds too much like magic to me.

Mikey nods.

I suck in a breath through my teeth as the pressure in my leg explodes in several simultaneous crescendos. I force myself to ignore them so I can concentrate on what he tells me.

"How does it work?"

"How should I know? I've never blood bonded with anyone before." Mikey flushes for reasons I can't interpret.

"Is that a bad thing?"

"No," he barks, pivoting away from me. "It's just a thing. It only means that I don't know how a blood bond works from the inside so I can't guide you. You should be able to figure it out."

"That's helpful," I mumble.

He points a finger at my chest. "You are so lucky that you have Kane's blood flowing through your veins." I can tell that if it were up to him, I'd have already died a thousand times.

Pushing myself into a seated position, I knead the tender skin around my ankle. It's swollen and stinging and pink but I can feel the bones shifting and the meat and muscle filling themselves up, like a salamander regenerating.

"Can you at least give me the theoretical?"

"Try thinking of Kane." He pauses, then slams the point of the sword into ground and crouches beside it. Only a few long strides from me. "Think about him and what reminds you of him. Think about where and when you last saw him. Where you think he might be. How you think he might be feeling.

"I don't know," he blurts out stormily, and the desperation in his eyes seeps into his tone. Still, he's trying to keep it cool. He's failing. But I can appreciate the effort because I'm failing, too.

I frown.

If Kane were here, he'd know what to do.

I nod once, close my eyes and picture Kane in my mind. I picture his face reflected in the strong glow of his chest that was so much brighter than Elise's. Elise…

I feel a tightening in my rib cage, a ripple of effulgent pain, and wrench myself away from the thought of what she might be doing to him. I can't meet Mikey's gaze as the sudden sense of rejection blows through me.

Mikey curses. "Try harder."

I don't have the heart to be mad. Instead, my shoulders slump forward and I say softly, "Why do you think she took him?"

Mikey shakes his head and tries to ruffle his hair again, but it doesn't move at all, just hangs there like a thick sheet. "I can't be sure, but I have a bad feeling about her dying light. Maybe she's…" Mikey's dirt-crusted eyebrows pull together over his straight nose. "It's not possible, though."

"What isn't?"

He straightens and shakes his head. "It doesn't matter. We just need to find him."

I know he's right, but I hate the sudden responsibility I feel, and with no other outlet, I throw both arms up into the air. "Don't you think I know that! But what am I supposed to do? I'm not an alien! I don't know how this works, and even though you *are* an alien, neither do you. Yesterday, you talked about going to get Kane on your own." I wait for a response, but his face just gets redder and redder.

"Did you forget that? Well, what was your plan? You can't fight. You can't find him… What good are you?"

Mikey roars and surges across the short space between us. He grabs me by the sides of my arms, and the moment he touches me, my heart jumps up into my throat…but my chest isn't empty without it…no, there's suddenly a second kicking…

And then comes something harder. Something scarier. A pounding, like the pressure of a heel against the underside of my sternum is followed by a ripping heat. The tug of Mikey's large, damp mitt against the back of my scalp is firm and heavy, but in slow succession, I cease to feel it.

Instead, I remember the weight of Kane's body atop mine in the darkness of his bedroom, I see the light reflected off of his high cheeks. I think of the easy way he lifted me from the floor, and from disaster, on the dance floor in that monstrous ballroom, and I think about all the ways he was monstrously devoted to me.

Air wrenches into my lungs as I touch the place where my chest heart is trying to jam its way out. My eyes shut when a horrible burn torches my sternum but that darkness is interrupted by a pinpoint of light, far away. It glows like an ember, stagnant at first, and then it's rushing. Or maybe I'm rushing. We're both rushing towards one another like two trains on the same track, headed for collision. I hold up my arms to ward away the blow but it doesn't do any good. Something sharp jams against my forehead. I can hear the crack and feel the blood drip over my cheek and nose. I can taste it on my lips. *It tastes like sulfur.*

Everything goes dark. I can't move. I can't breathe. Everything shatters around me and then a dark chasm opens up like a mouth under my feet. I fall through a world…through a city…one with streets, and buildings…I fall through the roof of a building and land in a room full of metal tables and grey tiles and I'm not alone here. Inside, there's a person with a voice and they're whispering…

"Abel? Abel!" Mikey's hands are on my shoulders shaking me and when I open my eyes and look up into his face, he exhales, and manages to sound almost relieved. "Jesus fuck. What was that? Are you sick or something?"

"No, I…" I blink a lot. Many times. The foreign feeling in my body is still there, but it's fading away. "I think I did the thing."

His eyes round. He grabs my shoulders and shakes them again with purposes. "Shit! What did you see?"

"Stop that." I bat his hands off me and struggle up into a seat.

"So? What happened? Where'd you go? Where is he?"

"I…I can't be sure."

Mikey looks down at his hand. He's holding the sword, but he looks like he wishes he were running me through with it. In a piss-poor attempt to calm himself, he speaks through clenched teeth. "Try."

I shake my head and knead my chest, wondering about the heat I felt and still feel. The backs of my legs burn, and so does my stomach. Foreign pains of unknown provenance. Implication with no meaning.

"Seattle?"

"Seattle? You're sure."

I hesitate, then nod. "I saw the…the needle thing."

"Yeah, it's still there."

I pause, surprised, "You know it?"

"Fuck. Yeah, I do. That's not even two hundred miles from here."

"Two hundred miles?" Mikey looks west, as if hoping to catch a glimpse of that infamous skyline from here and I scoff, "That'll take us weeks."

He rips his sword from the ground and continues to pace. "Not if we drive."

"Drive?" I use the tree behind me to stand, wishing I didn't need it. I want to appear more aggressive because Mikey isn't listening to me. He's already hundreds of miles from where we are.

"Mikey, you don't know anything about Population. Driving is a sure-fire way to get yourself killed. We're a long way off from anything recognizable. Could be scavengers out here, other gangs, or worse."

"Worse than me? I can take on any humans that come for me."

Frustrated, I stomp my injured foot, only to squeal in pain. "Ouch. Dammit. Mikey! You're not hearing me. There's worse out here than you. Trust me." Much worse.

He clicks his tongue against the back of his teeth and shakes his head. "We'll get a car and get to Kane as soon as possible."

"Mikey…"

"You're not in charge here!" He points his sword at my chest and snarls, "I say we drive, so we drive."

I take a step forward onto my injured foot, which screams beneath me. I hope my face doesn't betray the agony that ripples through the sole of my foot and burrows into my bones. I want to appear strong. Not sure it's possible since I look like a zombie prostitute, and feel like one.

"Today alone I've stopped you from eating poisonous fungi and found your brother *with my mind.* You need me a lot more than I need you. I say we walk, so get your fucking head out of your ass and start fucking walking."

Mikey struts towards me, ever the peacock while I just stand there. I'm not sure what I expect him to do, but I don't expect him to lift his fist and slug me right in the center of the forehead.

Right where I felt imagined blood earlier. *Kane's blood.* What is she doing to him? I think to myself, and as my feet slip out from beneath me, a second thought follows this one.

His brother and I make the worst team in history. We're never gonna make it.

I'm out before I hit the forest floor.

Chapter Three

I hear mumbled words long before I'm able to make sense of them. Groaning, my head rolls on my neck as my face is tilted to look up.

"You bastard…" I groan as I stare up at Mikey's unwashed beard.

I want to punch him, hurt him, bite him, hit him, but what I manage instead is simply another groan.

"I shouldn't have hit you," he spits, and it takes me until then to understand that he's carrying me, my legs and arms bumbling along at regular intervals in time with his steady pace.

"Eff," I moan. Licking my lips, I try again. This time I manage a mostly coherent, "Fuck you."

He snorts and remains silent while my eyes trace the spindly lines of the boughs above Mikey's head. Their faint emerald outlines hang suspended against a ceaseless charcoal sea. Endless monotony. Warmth surfaces in my right cheek and left ankle where Kane's blood is doing its work. I kick my legs and when they react for me, I force my hands to twitch.

Softly, I stutter, "Put…put me down."

"It's fine." Mikey repositions his arms so that he holds me flush against him. "I don't mind holding you."

I make a face, and when his returning expression flickers scarlet, I frown.

"Besides," he shrugs, looking ahead. "What do you weigh? Like six pounds?" He smirks, and I can tell that he's trying to be funny. A strange reaction from him. I wonder what changed while I slept.

"Where are we going?" Syrupy spittle coats my tongue and I cough. I'm dehydrated.

Mikey hoists me higher so that my head hits his shoulder, which is at least better than lolling about as it had been. "Seattle. Like you said."

I lay there for a while in silence while the rest of my senses come back to me. Sight first, then taste, then touch, then sound. There is no wind whistling through the treetops, no birds, no bugs. There is only the sound of Mikey's footsteps crunching over dead foliage, and his heart beating. Thump, thump, thump.

Clearing my throat and trying to dislodge the oppressive weight of Mikey's arms wrapped around me, I say, "Why'd she pick Seattle?"

"It's in Population, for a start. Outside of the seven regions, so outside of any turf owned or monitored by the other Notare. It's harder to track activity in Population."

"Still seems awfully close to Kane's territory. Wouldn't he have found out about it?"

"I guess not." Mikey shakes his head and shrugs. "Maybe his informants have gone sour. Maybe they're corrupt. Maybe Elise is just too careful. She's crazy smart and manipulative and ancient." He clenches his front teeth together and I get the feeling that he's lost in thoughts. Unpleasant ones.

"Hmph." I kick my injured foot a little and watch the way it bobs. "What about the Council or the Chancellor or whatever sort of police force you have? Can't they do something?"

Mikey looks down at me, eyebrows knitting together over his strong nose. "How do you know about the Chancellor? Have you met him?"

"No." I didn't even know it was a he. "But I heard a few people talk about him." Kane, I think. But also Memnoch. "Who is he?"

Mikey scoffs and doesn't look at me as he answers. Instead, he veers sharply to the left and narrowly avoids crashing into a thicket of shrubbery. Not quite as graceful as his brother. Tree branches scratch the bottoms of my bare feet and I shudder.

"He's called Lahve and he's not *really* Heztoichen. He's over three thousand years old and he's actually from a tribe that considered themselves above Heztoichen, and above our politics. Because of that, they've always taken this weird, impartial role as watchdog, judge and, if needed, executioner.

"Their job, above everything, is to keep the Notare safe. And if there are ever issues between two or more Notare that the Council can't resolve, he decides."

"The Council being…"

"Comprised of the seven Notare. They outrank everyone."

"And the fact that one of them kidnapped another is not a big deal?"

Mikey grimaces. "Do you see a phone out here anywhere? Who would I call to tell that Kane has been kidnapped? And even if I did call, there's no way that the Lahve…"

He bites back what he would have said next. But it doesn't matter. I already know.

"He wouldn't believe you?"

Mikey laughs and it's a bitter, awful sound. "I'm dead, remember? The Lahve won't hear words from a corpse." He exhales, warm breath touching my forehead.

"What about me? Aren't I Sistana, or whatever?"

"There's no way to prove it without Kane."

"What do you mean?"

"Unless the Lavhe tasted your blood on his tongue, how would he know you're Sistana? And it's illegal to taste your blood. Hell, *I* could be thrown in jail for taking from you."

"You didn't know, though."

"Of course," Mikey grumbles, but I'm not sure he's convinced. His fingers tighten around my shoulders until they hurt a little bit.

"Kane would never let you go back to jail," I say.

Mikey hesitates, then nods. "I know. But still, the fact that your blood is in my system is a risk to him."

"How so?"

"Because if you got my blood in you, I could bond to you, too."

I cringe. "Then you would be able to feel Kane, too?"

"No, but I'd be able to feel *you.* It's the worst kind of violation for a Heztoichen to do to another. Worse than cheating, if it's willing. Worse than rape, if it isn't. Double bonding doesn't happen, unless it's in covens."

"Covens?"

"Polyamory. Where everybody shares blood." He shakes his head at that. "Can't imagine, though. It'd be overwhelming. Or so I'm told."

Mikey sighs again. "So no. Getting Kane back is all up to me." He pauses, even in his stride, and glances down at my face. "To us."

A shiver rakes its way through me and Mikey watches me with confusion as I flinch. "I think my foot is better now," I say quietly. "Put me down."

"Just a few minutes. There's a road up ahead." Mikey gestures with his chin and I look right, unable to see anything. "I forgot. You've got those lousy human eyes."

I roll my eyes. "First you punch me in the face, now you're trying to crack jokes? Seriously, put me down."

He lets me drop but doesn't let me go. I squeal as I fall a foot, landing back in his arms. He laughs, but still, gently sets my feet on the ground. I swat his shoulder and stomp away from him, my foot mostly healed by now.

"You've got jokes."

"Do I ever." He chuckles and follows me towards the road which, sure enough, appears in front of me some ten-odd minutes later.

At my insistence, Mikey stays off of it and we stay in the trees, following the road's graveling shoulder as we move past street sign after gratified street sign towards the next city.

"It's a ghost town," I say, as we reach the first building we've seen in miles.

It's a trailer park that looks as if it was abandoned overnight. Portable grills and spits turned on their sides are overgrown with weeds and tall grasses. The doors of the first RV are propped open, screens half-hung from the rusted metal lintels.

In the center of a grouping of three RVs stands a huge television with a fifty two-inch screen, perfectly placed on a high black table. The fact that it's got very little decay is a little freaky.

"Come on," Mikey says when I pause, skirting bits of broken glass hiding in shin-high grass.

He reaches back, palm outstretched. I hesitate, finding the thought of holding hands with him weird. *Don't overthink this.* I begrudgingly take it.

Some miles later, we crouch in the shadow of an abandoned house — an actual house this time, built with some kind of foundation. Blue paint peels off under my fingernails at my light touch and when I press a little further, the damp siding crumbles around my fist. Maggots rain down around my feet and Mikey makes gagging noises in the back of his throat.

"Let's get the fuck out of here."

"I'm following you."

We've evidently reached what was once the more affluent part of town, though now this suburban hellscape is characterized by overgrown lawns, stripped cars, and rotting white picket fences.

Mikey tries to stop me from moving forward from around the back of the house into the next lawn, which is way more exposed and abuts the main road. I shake my head.

"Nobody's been here for years. I think we're okay."

He considers, then nods and leads the way into the yard, past the driveway and into the yard of the next house. I lift my knees towards my chin in order to avoid sticker bushes as I follow him, and I still trip over kids' stuff as I walk — a deflated soccer ball, blonde Barbie dolls with earthworms in their eye sockets, a pink plastic princess castle that's still perfectly in tact, some kind of oversized orange squirt gun.

I pick it up and aim it at Mikey, who snarls then snickers when the trigger locks up. I stick out my tongue, toss the plastic weapon into the grass and move towards the rusting bicycles at Mikey's feet.

"You think these work?" Mikey says, fingers picking apart his beard.

I scratch my neck. "Except for having bald, flat tires and being big enough to fit a four-year-old, sure."

Mikey swipes the pink bike from the ground and takes it out to center of the street. He mounts it like some storybook knight might mount a steed, checks his balance, then places his feet on the pedals.

He scrunches his neck down into his shoulders, brings his torso to meet the handlebars, then kicks out onto the road.

I laugh, and it's the only sound in the world other than the rusting chains of Mikey's bike, squeak, squeak, squeaking. His elbows jut out wildly to either side and are framed by tassels that glitter silver and pink.

"You coming or not?" Mikey shouts over his shoulder, struggling to revolve his knees around the tiny pedals. This isn't going to work. But I'm too entertained to tell him that.

"Right behind you," I say, laughing.

Mikey's *actually* covering some ground and, on a downhill, he's moving faster than I'd thought possible.

"Wait up, Mikey."

I grab the blue bike Mikey left behind, kick up the kickstand and push it out onto the street, finding it a little bit sad that, even though it's a kid's bike, it almost fits me.

I speed past Mikey who somehow manages to keep those thick thighs churning, and soon the houses start crowding closer together and I start to feel nervous of the unknown.

It's been a while since I've been in Population, the land of razorblades and fire, of aliens and madmen, of loneliness and deprivation. My glorious, gluttonous home.

It was different on Kane's turf, in Memnoch's place, because facing up against him alone I knew where the danger was and because I could see it and touch it and anticipate it, I knew I could kill it. But out in Population, the enemy is never certain.

We ride through a small city center, short wooden buildings rushing by on either side, all abandoned. Mikey shouts when we reach the next intersection and I skid off my bike, taking skin off my knees as I hit the ground.

I'm on my feet in an instant, fists up in the air, prepared for battle, but when I turn it's to see Mikey standing, bike thrown to the side, both hands stretched above his head. He says something in his own language and bows at the waist, giving respect to the large, brown building on the corner.

"Mikey, we need to keep going. We've got ground to cover," I bark, struggling to mask my irritation as I coddle the fresh scratches on my knees and palms, not to mention the litany of healing cuts on my feet.

"Since I'm not a rabbit, I'm going to need more than six mushrooms to eat." Mikey doesn't look at me as he kicks open the crumbling front door and steps into the restaurant.

I curse under my breath, but reluctantly drop my bike and follow him. As I step into the space, I pass a sign on the wall. Faded brown and grey — like everything else — it reads: WE NEVER CLOSE, in blocky, Wild Western letters.

I smirk at the irony while my gut begins to gurgle unable to decide if the nausea is physical or mental.

Glancing around, I don't think I would have wanted to eat at this place even *before* the world ended. To say it's dingy would be an understatement. The air lays against me in a thin, wet veneer and the carpet squishes under my feet every third step. Shuffle, shuffle, squish. Shuffle, shuffle, squish.

Faux wooden tabletops stand above blood-colored carpet and the torn plastic seat-cushions lining the benches around them spew black and yellow foam. A menu sits open on one of the tables. Only one. It gives me the chills as my fingers drag through the dust lying thick on top of it, and I wonder what the last person was doing when they placed this menu here. Where are they now? How long did they make it? What killed them?

The words HORSESHOE CAFE are written in the same tacky lettering that hung crookedly off of the sign outside. The same words that Mikey is muttering under his breath.

"Horseshoe cafe, come on…" He says.

Behind the bar against the far wall, Mikey's flung open all of the cabinets. He's throwing everything he finds onto the floor. Plates and glasses smash, utensils clatter, boxes of straws tinkle as they spill and the remnants of disintegrating paper napkins flutter lazily to the tiled floor, landing in silence.

"Can't find what you're looking for?"

He only grunts as I come closer and lean against the bar.

"What are you looking for? Tell me and maybe I can help." I drum my fingers across the tacky, peeling surface. Still nothing.

"There's not going to be any food in there. Why don't you try the kitchen?"

When Mikey remains silent and fixated on the cabinets, I roll my eyes and move on. Following my own advice, I head through the swinging silver doors that lead into the kitchen. A faint smell gives me pause.

I know that smell.

I know it well.

There aren't any weapons nearby, but I'm not afraid of the dead. I hold my nose as I wade through the room, but even then, I can still taste death on my tongue.

Ignoring it for now, I flip open cupboards and drawers and look under the sinks.

The kitchens have been cleaned out. Pots and pans and empty wrappers litter the floor. I kick metal bins aside and pick my way through the broken glass until I come around a huge metal island built into the center of the room and see him against the back wall.

Slumped against the white paint, the scent is overpowering. I cover my mouth and nose and blink back the sight. Half his head is missing and there's a gun lying nearby. The rats have been at him, and there's not much left of his torso or legs. Lucky for me, because it makes it possible to reach the stainless steel freezer door to his left and open it without disturbing him.

I fling it open and half a dozen rats charge me, but when I kick at them, they know not to fight a bigger opponent and scurry past me. We're all just rats out here.

I cringe as I try to move forward into the darkness, but the smell of death is even *worse* in here. Worse enough to make me choke.

I stagger back, falling into the island, and I get lucky that it's got a sink in the middle because I retch. I don't have anything to give up, so nothing comes, but the sound must be enough to draw Mikey's attention.

I hear the kitchen door open and then Mikey's voice say, "Yikes." He walks into the room and when I finally stop dry heaving, I look up in time to see Mikey press his bare foot to the dead guy's shoulder and push the corpse aside. Chunks of brain stay matted to the wall, and I start dry heaving all over again.

"No wonder our friend here took himself out. You took the gun, right?"

I nod, not wishing to concede to it. "Yeah." I don't mention that I had to break three of the dead guy's frozen fingers to do it.

"Any bullets?"

"Two in the carriage, I think, but maybe there's more inside," I say, pointing to the open freezer door behind him. "I couldn't though. Wouldn't be mad at you if you can't either."

I've got my hand on my nose and mouth still and my eyes are watering, but Mikey plunges forward. "Hell…"

"What is it?"

"Looks like missus here died trying to give birth to a baby. Oh…but hey! Check this out." There's clanging and then Mikey curses again. "Aw Jesus. Baby's leaking."

An even *worse* smell comes from the freezer and as my stomach hurls up into my throat, I grab the gun and stagger out of the kitchen.

Holding the heels of both palms to my eyes, I slide into the booth closest to the open front door. I only lower my hands when Mikey slams a cardboard box down onto the table in front of me.

"Check it out," he says, a grin on his face and a sparkle in his eye that makes him look like another being.

My stomach sinks even further. "You found booze." My thoughts flit back to what he told me about how he was captured by Memnoch. He was drunk. That's how they got him.

"A hell of a lot of it." He pulls out bottle after bottle of clear and amber liquids. Some are half empty but most are full and all of them make me uneasy.

"We hit the jackpot," he says, holding up a bottle of a clear liquor. Vodka. I look up at him, wondering what the hell he wants from me. What kind of reaction could he possibly hope for?

"Don't worry, I think there'll be enough for the two of us." He unscrews the top and upends half the damn bottle into his mouth before handing it over.

I take the vodka to my nose and wince as I sniff it. It smells like nail polish remover and battery acid and tastes like something you'd sterilize wounds with.

In fact, that's the only thing I've *ever* used alcohol for.

Mikey beams. "Good. More for me."

I frown as he takes the seat across from me and continues to drink in easy pulls, like it's water. I wonder what expression my face betrays, because he rolls his eyes.

"Don't worry, I found a present for you too."

He kicks something under the table and the hard, dry edge of a cardboard box scratches my shins.

The box is full of food.

"Hallelujah," I mutter.

"Gotta thank your human god for the small things," he says, and I know he isn't talking about the same thing I am.

Ignoring him, I crouch under the table and start sifting through the goods. Canned fruits and veggies, dried meats, about every kind of bean known to man, pasta and even spices…

"Mikey, you did..." I start to say before catching myself.

He pauses, bottle halfway to his lips. "What?"

I shake my head, pick out a few items at random and head back towards the kitchen. I open the swinging silver doors with my ass and as I look back at him, nod once.

"You did good."

As I polish off my second plate of spaghetti topped off with some dicey tomato paste mixed with water and a bunch of spices, Mikey finishes his first bottle. It's only then that he turns to the food. He rubs his hands together and twirls spaghetti around the tines on his fork. He takes a bite.

"It beats hunger," he says with a shudder, "but not by much. I guess Kane didn't marry you for your cooking abilities."

"Who needs food when you're drinking your calories? You going to polish off another bottle for desert?"

"Damn right, I am." His voice is slurred, but only slightly. Meanwhile, that quantity of alcohol would have easily killed me.

I snort and clear my plate, even as my stomach rebels, but I don't let that intimidate me as warmth from my bowl wafts up to my nose, carrying the scent of tomato with it. Well, *sort-of*-tomato.

"You eat like a maltron," Mikey says, one eyebrow raised.

"What's that?"

He lowers the bottle of Jack Daniels he's holding and drops his head so that we're at eye level. "You don't know what a maltron is?" His elbows spread across the table, filling its width.

I shake my head.

He laughs. "Big ugly animal. Fifteen feet tall, black tusks the length of my arm. No? You don't have those here?"

I shake my head again and he looks down at the bowl of pasta in front of him. A tendril of steam dances up from its surface to touch his cheek.

"What?" I say. It looks like he wants to say something.

"Nevermind." He draws lines in his tomato sauce with his fork. "Just thinking about maltrons."

"Thinking about home?"

"Fuck off."

"Geeze," I say, wiping my lips with the back of my arm. Can't get any filthier. "Better stop while I'm ahead.

Who knows, my next attempt to get to know you could end with me getting punched."

I toss my bowl onto the table and it clatters against my fork. I can't be around Mikey anymore. Standing, I check out the rest of the food I sorted out meticulously on the next table. Three jars of canned beef sit closest to me and, curious, I pick one up.

"I wouldn't do that if I were you." Mikey pushes his empty plate to the edge of the table. It falls but doesn't shatter when it lands.

I shrug and dig a finger into the mysterious brown substance. "It's protein," I say, glancing at the ingredients list on the back. Barely protein. I slide my finger across my tongue and immediately start to cough.

"Aw fuck," I lean over and spit up onto the threadbare carpet.

Mikey laughs. "I told you."

"Yeah, yeah, yeah…" I can still taste the crap on my tongue, and in this second, I prefer the alcohol. I swipe Mikey's bottle and take a sip before handing it back.

"There's other stuff there too," he says, eyeing me appreciatively as I hand the bottle back. "Check under the food."

Digging beneath the cans, I find a pile of neatly folded men and women's clothing. Baby clothes too. I wince when I find a pair of pale pink shoes, never worn, and quickly place them — and thoughts of the bodies in the kitchen — aside.

I pull out a white long-sleeve tee shirt, a pair of army green cargo pants that look like they might fit me, and two sets of sneakers that are both only a half-size too big. I even find clean-looking panties and a few miscellaneous bras.

I feel a little guilty in the instant where I'm grateful for the stuff because I wouldn't have gotten any of it if they were still alive.

Stepping back into the kitchen, I find a knife, cut myself out of Tasha's dress and don the spare clothing. When I come back into the restaurant, I see that Mikey's done the same. He's wearing a plain blue tee shirt that's too small and khaki pants that are way too big. He's busy cinching an electrical cable around his waist. I laugh.

"Yeah, yeah. If you humans weren't such gluttons this wouldn't be such a disaster."

I roll my eyes, unable to argue with that. "There aren't any bags. How are we gonna carry this?" I look down at the stuff, frowning at the thought that we might have to leave it behind.

Mikey nods once towards the bar. "There are a few. At least one backpack and a few purses."

I scoff. "I'm not carrying a purse."

"Why not? You'd look cute with one." He winks at me and sticks out his tongue.

I stick out mine, trying to keep this light, but inside I'm concerned. "So booze makes you pleasant to be around, does it?"

"Makes you pleasant to be around too."

I roll my eyes — as I've been doing every other second today — and retreat to the bar. "Let's just go." I grab the bags I find, and we do.

Chapter Four

The next few days are warmer, and for that I'm grateful. Even in the tattered coat I found, the influence of Kane's blood in my system isn't as robust as it once was. The winds cut into me sideways and my best guess is that it's winter or maybe even fall, but I haven't owned or seen a calendar in nearly a decade. Time is a vacuum in the grey.

As we walk, Mikey tries to coach me on how I might be able to better access Kane, but each time I reach out with my thoughts, I feel pain. After the first few times he asks, I finally tell him that I can't feel anything anymore. The nothingness is better than the truth and though I know he doesn't believe me, he nods and doesn't question the lies I know he knows I've told him.

"Augh," Mikey says, collapsing down in an office chair in front of a fake wooden desk.

Making a similar sound, I slide down to the floor against the wall opposite him. "How far do you think we've come?"

"What city are we in again?" He tilts his head towards the windows, and I wonder if he sees anything outside of them but blackness.

I snatch a piece of paper off of the floor. There are piles of it everywhere. "Everett," I read, eyes skimming the stationary. "The place is called Honeywell."

"Where's the kitchens?"

"What?"

Mikey yawns. "Honey or wells. Can't draw water or keep bees in here."

I can't tell if he's joking or not and smirk. "They don't make food." I shake my head and stretch out my legs, feeling my knees creak at the hinges. "Probably a tech company. No cubicles. That's why I picked it."

Just big empty spaces filled with toys and slides and all the things software geeks dream about late at night — at least before it was looted. Now it's just an empty room full of broken gadgets and fading paper.

"Why is that good?" Mikey says, glancing around the edges of the desk behind him, as if expecting monsters to jump out at any second. "Kind of feels like open season."

"No cubicles in these offices. No places for scavengers to hide."

"Scavengers aren't what concern me."

"What does concern you?"

Mikey glances up at me only once. His face is mean, but also cautious. "Humans may be stupid…but sometimes they have numbers."

I remember the story Mikey told me in the cave, about how he'd been captured by Memnoch's band of human mercenaries. He'd been too drunk to hear them and distracted by some woman. Three bottles in, I wonder how drunk he is now.

"We're on high ground," I say. Windows are clear. There are six exits on this floor alone. "We'd see them coming and we'd have a lot of options to get out of here."

As I turn to my pack and begin rifling through it, he whispers, "I hope you're right."

We dine that night on apricots and chickpeas before finding the office showers. Water still runs through the pipes and though it's rust-colored and freezing, it's also welcome. I take the risk and when I come back, Mikey's got a fire going right there on the office floor, nestled in a bed of dismembered file cabinets.

He heads to the shower while I draw the blinds and yank on clean clothes. I even wash the old ones in the bathroom sink.

I try not to think of the mother as I hang the cotton by the fire to dry. It squishes between my fingers, reminding me painfully of the sound of a dead baby sliding across the tiled floor…

"Oh shit, Mikey, you scared me." I jump when fingers tap me hard on the shoulder.

Orange light from the fire illuminates his skin and his hair and I start with a laugh. "What?" He grumbles, shifting from foot-to-foot.

"No, you just…I've had no idea what you looked like this whole time. It's nice to see you. I wasn't even sure you were blonde."

Mikey smirks and as I rake my gaze over him he seems to become even more uncomfortable. "Yeah yeah, laugh it up," he says, tugging up his pants. They're the same ones as before and hang so low around his hips, I can see the trail of blonde curls leading down from his belly button to meet his pubic hair.

"Got another towel?" He says, louder than he needs to. I'm standing right here. His gaze darts away from mine like he's nervous or something.

"Yeah. Give me just a second." Hanging my wet shirt over the edge of a chair, I toss him a towel from my pack and take a seat in front of the fire.

I watch him as he tugs on a shirt as takes the place across the fire pit from me. His blonde hair is blonde now. It's clear he didn't bother trying to comb it, even with just his fingers, but the lack of black gunk all over him is a start.

"Trying to make me self-conscious?" He mumbles.

I smile. "Just happy to see you looking more human — or alien. Whatever you are."

He snorts and continues rummaging through his pack until he reaches another bottle of booze. I didn't get the final count from Horseshoe Café, but he must have taken upwards of a dozen. His pack is overfull and clinks every time he touches it.

"What are you staring at?"

"Nothing. Just wondering if you were up for sharing that."

Startled, Mikey looks from the bottle of bourbon trapped in his fist to my face and back again. "Seriously?"

"I mean, I'm not going to fight you for it or anything. I just thought it might help me sleep," I lie. I don't really want to drink. I want to make peace.

Mikey smiles at me very slightly and edges around the perimeter of the aluminum filing cabinet pit — the only thing preventing the embers from burning straight through the floor. He slides the square bottle into my open hand. It's warm from where he held it, and when I take a drag, the liquid itself is fire.

I hiss. "Damn. I feel like I could breathe smoke."

"I thought so too when I first got to this piece-of-shit planet."

Ignoring the jab, I take another swig. "You guys don't have booze on Sistylea?"

Mikey shakes his head and stares at me too intensely as I take another swig, letting the booze burn. Letting it ride. "What?" I prod. "Trying to make me feel self-conscious?"

Mikey picks at his beard, which hangs down past the collar of his tee shirt. "You even pronounce it right." He shakes his head and laughs. It's a sad sound. "Nothing fazes you, does it?"

Warmth settles in my belly though the desolation in his black gaze makes me shiver. Some things do still throw me. The good things. Everything that was Kane. But the bad things stopped fazing me a decade ago.

"I guess not. At least not anymore," I say.

He runs a hand back through his hair. The first time he's actually able. Without the mud and blood matting his locks, it actually looks quite soft. Soft and, like his beard, almost dandelion yellow.

"What about you?"

"What about me?"

"You still surprised by stuff?"

"Every day," he says. "Every day."

I smile, feeling unsettled and hand him back the bottle. "Tell me about your planet."

"Sistylea?"

"No. The other one." I roll my eyes.

Mikey surges towards me and I wince, but the blow I expect to feel never lands. Instead, he wraps his hand around my neck with one arm and grinds his knuckles down onto the top of my head.

"You've got some lip on you," he says, but the humor in his voice catches me off guard and I laugh.

I jab him in the side with my elbow and he curls in around the blow, releasing me. "And you are a madman." I shake out my head, damp curls swatting me in the face and clinging to my cheeks.

Mikey passes me back the bottle with hooded eyes that grow increasingly distant. "Kind of like Earth. A lot of greenery, but our water sources are more dispersed. If you look at it from space, the whole planet looks like an emerald."

He holds his hands in two circles and lifts them to his right eye, like peering through a telescope. "Even though we don't have any oceans, there are rivers, lakes and streams everywhere, and cities are built around the natural habitat."

"Sounds beautiful." My head is turning ever so slightly and when I try to picture Sistylea in my mind, the images that come to me appear fuzzy around the edges.

"It is. I mean, it was." Mikey pauses. "Our house had a river flowing straight through it. Straight down the middle. I used to play in it when I was a kid," he says, talking animatedly now.

"Once, before my mother built the dam, I fell in all the way and got carried straight out of the house. Whoosh." His raised hand falls into his lap and begins picking at the fraying strands of his tee shirt.

"That was the first time Kane saved my ass. Jumped into the river after me, pulled me out. He's been saving my life ever since."

Mikey stares intensely at the bright yellow flames and I would ask him what he's thinking about, but I'm scared to ask. Scared of what will happen if I disrupt this moment.

"Did he tell you that I was supposed to die back on our planet? On Sistylea?"

"No." Chills break out across the back of my neck. I scratch them away and give the booze in my hands needless attention. I take another draught and swirl it around with my tongue.

"There were only enough pods for every family to get two. The Council decreed that each family would supply one male and one female to go into the pods and that not even the Notares' families would get an exception.

"Hell, even the Lahve's thirty-person tribe decided that they would give all of theirs up, choosing only one from their entire race to continue on the new planet. The Lahve was the youngest member in their leadership, so he got picked and he made sure that there was no contest between the Notares and their families on who would get sent. The Notares *had* to go.

"So there was no contest between my dad, Kane and me on who would get a pod. He didn't want to go. Members from the Lahve's tribe came to our house and physically had to strap him in. He fought like hell. He wanted me…" Mikey chokes.

His eyes are still unfocused as he stares directly into the flames. I wonder what he sees. Who.

"He wanted me to take his place, but they were stronger than he was — tens of thousands of years old between them — and they knocked him out and strapped him down and sent him here."

With his knees bent and his arms draped over them, he doesn't look like he'll say more. Then he inhales deeply. "My mom should have taken the last life pod. Our family had no other females. But when it was her time to go, she offered me her place and I took it."

His whole body shudders and a physical pain rolls off of him, slides over the ground, and wraps its fingers around me. I shiver.

"She said she wanted to stay with our father. That she wanted to die with him. It wasn't her choice to make though. There was a reason we were supposed to send a female and a male. We don't birth kids at the rate you humans do. We're going to die off and that rule was mandated for the benefit of the species.

"My mom could have had more kids. I could have had more brothers and sisters. They could have carried on our family's legacy. I could have sacrificed."

His throat catches and he stretches his open palm towards me. It's only after I hand him the bottle that I wonder if he hadn't been reaching for something else.

When the bottle breaks from his lips he gasps, "But I didn't. Because you're right about me. I'm just the shitty brother."

He finishes the bottle and tosses it across the room where it shatters, then he finds another.

I don't know what to say to him. I don't have anything to say. He's right. He was a coward. And anything I could try to say to soften the blow would just be a lie.

"Tell me more about Sistylea," I say, breaking the tension between us. "Something nice."

Mikey cackles. His eyes are glossed. "I don't have many *nice* stories about Sistylea…"

"I didn't ask for many. I just want one."

Mikey sighs and closes his eyes. I don't think he'll answer me at first. Then he speaks all at once. "There's a region where mountains grow upside down. They're small at the bottom, then when they get hundreds of feet tall, they form plateaus that all connect and overlap with each other.

"Huge, ancient castles were built upon them and served as the meeting place for the Council. There's a rainforest where it's rained every day for a millennia. Another cluster of islands exists on Sistylea and never experience darkness. We have two suns."

"Do you have two moons too?"

"Seven. You can usually see as many as four at once."

"Incredible."

Mikey smiles ever so slightly then before looking away. "We don't have deserts or plains — those are new for us — no oceans either. Only streams. We have more stars though. Infinitely more constellations. And our animals are mostly all different — there are some similarities, but different shapes. The types of edible plants we grow are different too."

"Really?" I say, growing more fascinated now as Mikey's face lights up.

His cheeks are red and I wonder if that isn't the booze in his bloodstream or the boy caught in the river's riptide, emerging from its depths.

"What kinds of animals?"

He whistles. "I wouldn't even know where to begin. I can tell you that they're bigger, though. Far bigger. Much smarter too. Would you believe me if I told you that we weren't the animals at the top of the food chain back home?"

I shake my head. "I can't even imagine."

He taps the side of the bottle in a soothing, rhythmic way before, becoming aware of it, he hands the bottle over. I take it and though I know I shouldn't, I tip the base up and my head back.

"There are creatures just about as smart as we are that have their own lands. They look kind of like really ugly horses," he says, and I laugh.

"We stay out of their way and they stay out of ours. They don't eat meat. The other ones are more problematic. The Tolta are hard to describe, but they regenerate even faster than we do and hunt us for our blood."

"Seriously? What do they look like?"

"Kind of like massive bats with bears for bodies. We had a standing peace treaty with the leaders of their kind in place for centuries. Stupid, prideful things, though. They never saw the collapse coming. It wiped them all out."

"That's absolutely insane."

Mikey nods. "We were supposed to have one ship, an ark, with animals on it headed for Earth as well — no Tolta, though."

"What happened to it?"

Mikey shrugs and picks at the carpet. "Probably hit by an asteroid on the way over. Either way, it's gone. Just like everything else." Mikey lapses again into a momentary silence. "Guess we got lucky that human flesh and blood works as well as the creatures we ate back home."

I flash him a smile that seems to surprise him. It surprises me, too. Maybe it's fatigue or maybe it's just the booze, but getting riled up right now seems exhausting.

"Don't forget," I say with a wink. "This is your home now, too."

Mikey smiles and he looks like a child, only larger. He shifts as if to turn towards me, but looks to the fire instead. "I guess that's true."

"Of course it is," I say, setting the bottle down as I struggle to stand.

My goal is to head to the bathroom but the room spins and my stomach bubbles like its angry at Mikey on my behalf. I take a step, but trip over my pack and my hand misses the table when I reach for it.

"Whoa there," Mikey says, suddenly surrounding me. There's so much of him. With my back to him, he steadies me by the arms and lifts me into a standing position. "You alright?"

I let him take most of my weight, but still turn around to face him. I cling to his shirt. "I'm seeing double. Is that normal?" I shake my head, trying to shake off the sensation.

As Mikey chuckles, his breath tickles my face. It smells spicy and saturated with booze. "Have you drunk before?"

I shake my head.

"Christ." He bites his back teeth together. "You gotta pee?"

I nod.

"Let me help you get to the bathroom."

We half-stagger, half-fall to the bathroom and back and when we return, the fire's died down to embers and soot. We're laughing, though, and trading hushed, minced quips as the darkness comes around us like an embrace.

"Come on. Get into your sleeping sack." Mikey fans out his own to my left so that we form an L around the embers with our heads joined.

"Sleeping *bag*," I correct.

Mikey roll his eyes and hits me with the tail end of his sleeping bag once, in the face. I laugh as residual dust rains over me.

"Tell me," he says as we settle down into the dark, quiet warmth, "what is Kane doing right now?"

I inhale deeply and close my eyes, and this time when I think of Kane, I remember the time he came and found me with Mikey in that cave. He looked at me and told me that Ashlyn was alive, that the other girls were safe. He touched my cheek, and I imagine that I can feel his fingers as I felt them then.

Then the fire comes.

Like it crawled right out of those filing cabinets to sit on my face, I gasp at its blistering heat. It hurts. So much pain. My pectorals sear, as if my skin were flayed and a great hand reached inside and yanked out my lungs. I'm melting. The whole of me is melting except for my heart, which continues a faint, irregular thump.

But for how long?

"Abel… Abel?"

I gasp and am wrenched back into reality at the sound of Mikey's voice. His hand is touching the top of my head and I glance up to see him propped on his right side. "What is it? What did you see?"

"Nothing," I breathe, "nothing…"

"He's my brother." Mikey's fist clenches. "Don't lie to me."

I shake my head and try to disassociate myself from my own muddled thoughts. "She's torturing him," I wheeze.

"She's what?"

"I don't know." I clench my hands and pound on my forehead. "I don't know anything. But I can feel something here." I lay my hand over my chest. "And it hurts like hell."

Mikey quiets, and after a long pause, finally says, "We should get an early start tomorrow." He lies down and glances back at me, lines crinkling his forehead as he's forced to look up.

"Thank you."

Shock. I nod and, not knowing what else to say, whisper, "Goodnight, Mikey."

"Goodnight, Abel."

He lies onto his back and I stare into the embers, watching them cling to light before dying, one-by-one.

Chapter Five

We wake when it's still dark out, and my head is *still* spinning. I groan as I haul my pack higher onto my back and step into the frigid early morning air.

"Jesus Christ, Mikey, my stomach is in knots and my head is pounding. Is it always like this?"

"What? Drinking?

I nod. Mikey laughs and trudges ahead of me across the parking lot, heading towards the rusted green sign that reads I-5 South.

"I wouldn't know. Human tolerance is different than ours, but for one of your size…" He sweeps his gaze up from my toes to my crown. "Yeah, I imagine the recovery would suck."

"Some warning would have been nice."

"I thought you knew." He shrugs.

"Not all of us are alcoholics," I grumble and there it goes.

All pleasantness is gone between us and it only took five minutes into the trek.

"You're a bitch," he says.

"I know," I tell him.

Hours pass as we weave in and out of trees as we follow the line of the highway. After half a bottle of alcohol, Mikey's in the talking mood again and we make light chatter.

He asks me about Population and I ask him about Sistylea and he asks me about my family and I tell him about my brother and I ask him questions about the animals and plants on Sistylea and am surprised and intrigued by the variance between his planet and Earth.

I even ask him about Kane's former lovers…

"Kane could have had his pick of any woman." He squints in my direction as I rub the back of my hand across my forehead, streaking dirt. "And he picked you."

"Maybe I picked him," I tease as we maneuver carefully beneath a highway underpass.

Mikey starts to laugh until his gaze drops to his feet, and he holds out an arm. "Careful here. Looks like some people had a good time."

"People? Try gangs. This was a big brawl."

Glass shards litter the asphalt, sprinkled across a slick, wet ground. I'd thought it was water from a distance — maybe oil. I was wrong. It's all blood.

But where are the bodies?

An upside-down cross was spray-painted in black on the wall of the underpass. Huge, I'm still staring at it when I slip on blood and glass.

Mikey's there, catching me before I get myself drenched. "Thanks," I whisper, dusting off my hands.

"Any time," he says, but as he starts to move past me, he leans in close and sniffs my hair. "You smell good."

"Okay, weirdo."

Inhaling a second time, his eyes widen and he puts distance between us.

"What is it?" I say.

"Nothing," he barks, but his cheeks are red and his voice cracks. He rubs his palm off on the seam of his khakis and, the minute he's able, moves off of the highway and into the woods.

We break for lunch at a rest stop. These kinds of rest stops have always looked the same — even before the Fall — and this one is no exception.

Whatever fighting that took place on the road didn't make it here and I'm glad to find it empty. A few abandoned trucks sit in the parking lot where an empty QFC bag titters across the asphalt.

I eat a can of pineapple quickly and suck on some dried beans.

"Come on, let's go." I stand up from the stone bench but Mikey doesn't move. He only stares at me.

"What?"

"You're really ready to move? You've been holding your stomach like it's about to burst for the past two days."

I look down, caught in the act, and brace my hands on my hips. "I'm fine."

"The hell you are."

Mikey snatches up a bottle of mostly empty black liquid, the color of tar. I'm no longer surprised by how quickly he finishes it.

"Go take care of yourself." He belches and I can smell the anise on his lips from a dozen paces away.

I groan, "Okay, fine. Just wait a second while I go puke or shit or something."

"Lovely." Mikey snorts. "Are all human women like you?"

"The ones still breathing."

I wade through the crispy brown grass until I reach the toilets. With my hands still on my hips I debate openly with the dented blue door that has a lady in a skirt on it. I don't go inside though. The odor is enough to deter me —

not because it smells like human waste but because it smells like wasted humans — so I move around to the back of the short, red brick building instead and yank down my pants.

I blink down at my underwear. I blink a lot.

My pulse starts to thunder at the sight. I'm stunned. I'm horrified.

It's blood.

I touch between my legs, sliding a finger between my lips to be sure. They come back all red. I'm dying. I'm fucking dying!

And then I remember…healthy women used to get *periods* before the Fall. Before every meal was a godsend. Before aliens hunted us like sharks and devoured us like candy. Before before before.

And now I'm out here bleeding like a fucking sieve in a world of sharks.

"Mikey?" I cough into my fist as I remove my pants and pull off my badly stained panties. "Mikey, can you throw me my pack and my canteen?"

My voice is deceptively calm, though my thoughts are screaming. Fucking fuck. This can't be happening. I haven't had a period since…no. I haven't had a period. I punch my fingers — the clean ones — back through my hair and brush the filthy ones off on the grass beneath me.

"So it's true."

"Christ!" I jump and turn to see Mikey standing there *staring* like a creep. The redness in his cheeks brings heat to mine as I turn to face him and shield my crotch with my hands.

"Jesus, Mikey. What are you doing? Don't look." But he doesn't look away. "For fuck's sake, Mikey, hand me my pack."

"Your sweetest blood." He licks his lips and throws my pack to the ground equidistant between us. In order to reach it, I'll have to move closer, though something in the parsed way he speaks makes me want to shuffle in the opposite direction.

Not shuffle. Fucking sprint.

"I thought I smelled it earlier."

"Are you a fucking douche bag? Why didn't you say something?"

"Your sweetest blood. I could smell it on you this morning. Right now you reek of it." He gulps, like a thirsty man standing before a glass of water he can't reach.

My skin boils and I lurch towards my pack, landing hard on my knees while tufts of dry grass tickle the insides of my thighs. My hands are fluttering uselessly as I struggle to unlace the ties.

"Let me help you," Mikey says and I start when he appears directly in front of me.

He drops into a crouch, pushes my hands out of the way, unlaces the leather ties and hands me a pair of fresh pants and a towel.

"Mikey, you're freaking me out." I snatch the items away and use them to cover the space between my legs. The *leaking* space between my legs.

He licks his lips in a way I find totally disconcerting and balks, "You should be fucking freaked out. You're a walking target. Every Heztoichen in a fifty-mile radius will come crawling for what you've got. That's your sweetest blood. It's sacred."

"Stop calling it that. It's so weird." I toss the fresh pants aside for now and bring the towel to the blood between my thighs.

"Mikey!" The single word is a garbled scream as Mikey lashes out and grabs my wrist hard enough to make me drop the towel.

Falling forward onto his knees, he tosses my pack out from between us and yanks my legs out from under me. I yelp as I land on my back and before I know what the shit is happening, Mikey's *mouth* is down there, licking the space where only one other male has ever licked.

And it's his freaking brother.

"Mikey," I gasp, hips bucking as pleasure shoots through my lower back.

He holds my hips down and I should tell him to get the fuck away from me, but my eyes are fluttering and I'm distracted by the climb up, up, up.

Oh my god. What is happening?

"Fuck," Mikey whispers, his cool breath against my core making my head spin. It was already spinning. I can't…this isn't…what is…

"I've never…this is…" And then he says the word that doesn't belong to him. "*Heaven.* This is heaven."

He buries his tongue *inside* of me and I gasp as an unwilling desire scrapes its nails down my body, like fingernails on a chalkboard. And it isn't a desire for Mikey, no. But it *is* a desire for him to keep going.

I gasp, my head kicks back and my body collapses onto the grass. He licks me from the inside out, his lips coming into contact with my clit and I'm too new at this to control my reaction — I come immediately.

Pleasure shivers through me, but it's followed by a ripping sensation somewhere deep.

It starts in the pit of my stomach and then pulls up and out of my throat. My forehead pounds and my stomach tears itself to pieces.

He has to stop.

I have to stop.

My body says to ignore that thrashing pain and keep going, but whatever this is *inside* doesn't feel like heaven at all. It feels like death.

That rotten smell from the kitchens assaults me and as Mikey attacks my wet and bleeding slit with his tongue, I try to *focus* and untangle myself from the web of pleasure making my legs shake and making it so hard to think.

Almost…almost…there!

I lurch up just as a second orgasm sweeps me and the death sensation cuts so, so painfully deep.

I slug him at the same time that a delirious scream strangles me.

My knuckles rake his cheek and toss him to the side. His head hits my inner thigh and I lurch out from under him. He shakes his head and when that doesn't work, he shakes it again. He heaves into the grass under him while I scramble to pull my new pair of pants on and shove the towel into them.

"Oh my god, what *was* that?" I shriek.

Mikey doesn't speak. I don't speak. But I put distance between us.

I grab my pack off the ground and my hands shake as I redo the laces.

"Abel." He coughs. He shakes his head again and when he looks up at me I know that no amount of alcohol could have had such an effect. He looks *wasted.*

"I don't know," he says. "I don't know. I never…" He clenches his eyes shut tight.

I run my hand back through my hair. I'm sweating all over.

His eyebrows scrunch up, pulling together. "You liked it. Tell me you liked it. You wanted it. I felt you…I tasted you come. Tasted almost better than your sweetest blood…"

I don't say anything. I don't have anything to say.

Instead, I turn and walk into the woods without caring that he follows.

Chapter Six

Darkness descends right after we pass the sign that says we're less than twelve miles outside of Seattle.

So close now, I just want to plow ahead, but I know that I need to rest if we're going to face off with Elise. *And probably be killed by her.*

It's the first time that it actually occurs to me what lies ahead and the challenge it will bring. It's the first time it occurs to me that I probably won't be alive this time tomorrow. I've seen her in action and I don't stand a chance. I glance up at Mikey, remembering the last time he faced off against her.

She's going to kill us both.

We need to come up with a battle plan, but I can't bring myself to speak. We haven't spoken all day.

I polish off a can of peas and Mikey doesn't look at me over the crackling embers as he picks dried apricots out of a bag. Not even as he says, "You look sick."

He tosses a packet of dried meat at me. It's hand-wrapped in baking paper and twine. Must be something the family hunted. I catch it with one hand.

"You need iron."

I feel my cheeks warm, but I don't thank him.

"Don't mention it," he grunts anyway, looking away from me.

He tosses the empty apricot bag aside and picks out an emptying bottle of amber liquid, marked Hennessy. It's the second lid he's cracked in the span of an hour. He's red in the face and wobbly on his feet and I wonder how he continues to function.

"Eat," he says and I do.

I fidget where I lay against the trunk of a tall tree. It's hard against my back and the ground is icy cold underneath my layered pants despite the low embers that are just enough to keep us from frosting over. Couldn't light anything bigger than this. We're too close to a city for that and have to worry now about avoiding detection.

My eyelids are heavy, but I fight to keep them open. I don't know why. Maybe it's because I'm scared to dream, scared to let my guard down, scared of Mikey sniffing after me in the dark.

He's seated facing away from me, but in the low light I get a good look at his profile. High cheeks, coarse hair covering the same strong jaw Kane has. Neck thick with muscle. He looks stronger than he did when we woke up this morning. Ironic, when I feel like I'm falling apart.

"How is Kane?" he says, eyes on the bottle between his feet.

It glistens when he moves it, silver light shimmering against it like the earrings Kane gave me that one time. They belonged to his mother. A female who would have lived if only the bastard across from me had had the decency to die.

I wince, surprised at the horrible direction of my own thoughts. I don't mean it. At least, I shouldn't…

"I don't know," I sigh.

Mikey shifts his weight around but doesn't manage to look very comfortable sitting there with his arms wrapped around his knees. He rocks back and forth very gently.

"You can tell me. I can take it."

"I said I don't know." My voice is louder now, though I try to marshal it.

Mikey must hear something change in my tone because he stills and doesn't respond right away. "What do you mean?"

"Are you deaf?" My voice is more spiteful than I intended, but I'm on a train to self-hatred with no brakes. I'm taking Mikey with me. "I said I don't fucking know. I can't feel Kane anymore."

"What?"

"How many times do I have to repeat myself? I. don't. feel. Kane. I don't feel anything from him anymore."

"How is…how is that possible?"

"Has it not occurred to you that Kane felt what happened earlier? You said this works like a two-way radio, jackass. Well, he's turned off his end. Rightfully so. His *brother* was eating out his *wife* while he's fighting for his life." I can feel the tears behind my eyelids, but I don't cry. I don't have the energy.

Without warning, the glass bottle in Mikey's hand hurtles some place far away and shatters. He follows it, stalking off until the light no longer reaches him but I can tell that's where he stops because I don't hear anymore footsteps.

When he doesn't return, I try to force myself to calm down and get some sleep. It doesn't work. Not really.

Tossing and turning, I think of Kane and dwell on what he must be thinking and feeling. *Betrayal.*

"I didn't mean for it to happen," says a voice in my sleep. "You should have known better, bleeding all over like that..." So many words, but no apology.

It fades and I wake with words on the tip of my tongue, but as the world sharpens and the face looming above mine comes into focus, the words change.

"You're not Mikey."

The alien looming above me has a narrow face and pale skin that looks shockingly clean when compared to the alien I've been traveling with.

He's well-armed and his gaze is raking over me appraisingly in a way that I don't like at all because it reminds me of the hungry look in Mikey's eyes right before... *Betrayal.*

Behind him, the sky is pale and the light is harsh. I'm cold, too. Colder than I was the night before, though that hardly seems possible. Plus I feel a wet spot on my pants that's either dew or blood and a gaping hole in my chest where Kane's presence should be.

Hope seems distant, especially when I notice four other aliens in the clearing and only one of them is the one I was traveling with.

I look across our pitiful patch of embers and see that Mikey's still sleeping, arms crossed over the bottle he's got trapped to his chest. I growl out his name, but he doesn't so much as wince until one of the Others approaches him and kicks him in the ribs.

Mikey lurches to life, eyes blazing red. Lord. How much *more* did he manage to drink during the night when I slept? He lurches towards the sword on top of his pack, but an alien with a long braid surges in his path and kicks the sword behind him.

They look organized, these aliens and organized aliens are the worst kind. They've all got on heavy black vests with black shirts underneath, black cargo pants and are armed to the teeth.

I squeal as the one standing over me grabs me beneath the armpits and hauls me up to standing. Pangs and pains groan over my body, none worse than the one in my lower back.

Mikey snarls something I don't catch as he lurches towards me like he's going to try to stop the thug. The one with the braid holds him back.

"This is your human?" The one holding me says. He sniffs the air around my head. "She's got Heztoichen blood in her."

"And I can clearly smell her sweetest blood on you," says the one with the braid, sniffing towards Mikey too.

A third interjects, "You claimed her? Married a human?"

Mikey hardens in a way I didn't think he was capable of. He looks like a different man — I mean, a different male — and for the first time, actually looks mean and ready to war against someone or everything.

"Yes," he snarls, surprising me for a second time. I didn't expect him to claim me *ever*. Not even when it meant my life.

Like it does now.

Guess I was wrong.

Maybe this is his way of apologizing.

Does he know it isn't good enough?

"Interesting," the slightly taller one says while the one with the braid spits, "Fucking pathetic."

"I'd consider bonding her too if it meant I'd get to taste that sweet, sweet nirvana…" The taller one sucks his teeth in my direction and takes a casual step towards me.

Mikey lurches towards the alien, which gets him a swift gun to the ribs.

The one with the braid is practically foaming at the lips. He says, "No reason we can't open her up, Trocker."

Mikey bowls over, spittle flying from his lips, while the one above me says, "Have a smoke, Ramil. It'll help mask the smell and stop you from eating her before we get her to the master. He'll want a word."

"But the blood," Ramil grits. "We could just take it and the master wouldn't even have to know…"

His eyes lock on me and I flinch as Ramil lunges, but the contact I expect to feel never lands as Mikey surges into his path. He roars when their shoulders connect and punches Ramil in the stomach and then in the face.

Ramil hits the ground and I shout Mikey's name but he's too slow to avoid the arc of Trocker's weapon. It connects with Mikey's right cheek.

When he doubles over, he spits out blood and two words that surprise me for the third time in as many minutes. "She's *mine*."

The conviction in his tone makes my heart pound while a dark pall falls between the five of us. Someone's going to die.

Probably me.

"Of course," Trocker says, while two of the others grab Mikey by the arms and the hair on his head. "Don't worry about your things. You won't be needing them where we're going."

When they all chuckle over some shared joke, I know with a fair degree of confidence that wherever we're going isn't anywhere I want to be.

Leaving the sword behind hurts, but I try to stay focused on the present as we're led south. I don't know how long we walk. An hour? Less than that? Are we headed towards Seattle or away from it?

Are they planning to kill us?

Will I ever see Ashlyn again? Will I ever get a chance to tell Kane I'm sorry and that I love him? Or will I die with him thinking that I wanted his little brother? I may not know Mikey well, but I know that, with me dead, he'd never admit responsibility in this.

That anger fuels my determination to live as I glare at the back of Mikey's head while we're led through the woods, which eventually open up before us.

I trip over unexpected gravel and gawk up at the castle that juts out of the ground like a mountain in the middle of an enormous field. Its navy towers punch towards the sky in megalithic spindles. Wide windows reflect the grey above and at the end of the long driveway sits an intricately engraved glass door which punctuates the house's pale blue siding. Impossible is the only word I can think of to describe it. Not quite human in architecture or design, they must have built it here for a reason.

But why?

We approach a small concrete post and Trocker punches a series of buttons too quick for me to catch on the panel below the intercom.

"Kaius," Trocker says and suddenly I'm being shoved into his arms. He takes me by the shoulder and leans down to meet my ear.

Standing directly behind me, his lips brush across my earlobe as he whispers, "Behave and you may be able to survive this. Perhaps I'll even keep you as mine…"

Sounds of a scuffle. Then Mikey's gruff voice. "Don't you fucking dare, Trocker. She's mine."

The way he calls him by his first name makes me wonder if they know each other. That could help us…or hurt us. Knowing Mikey, he's not exactly the kind to make fast friends…

Trocker doesn't flinch, but turns me around to face Mikey and lines my back with his body. He reaches between my legs and I try not to let it faze me as he rubs *hard* and then brings his fingers up to his mouth and sucks them *loud.*

"That's not allowed," Mikey snarls. "You can't take the blood of someone who's already bonded."

Trocker laughs and so quietly, I don't know if Mikey can even hear him, he says, "What does it matter when you're already dead?"

He turns towards the house again and steps up to a small intercom built into a massive wrought-iron gate.

"It's Trocker," he says into the black speaker box, "We located the source of the scent. The human girl travels with a companion."

Words float through the intercom in a voice that I can identify only as male. The words themselves are all alien, even if Trocker responds in English, maybe for my benefit.

"Yes, he is Heztoichen."

Light, malicious laughter crackles on the other end of the line and makes me shiver. Then in English, the voice says, "Well, of course. Invite them in for dinner."

Chapter Seven

Mikey and I stand next to each other in the doorway of an enormous dining room. I'm weaponless and confused more than I'm afraid for the moment and when I share a glance at Mikey, I can sense that he feels the same.

"Straighten up. Look decent for the Notare," Trocker says, kneeing me in the back.

The force of the blow throws me forward, but he moves quickly enough to catch me before I face-plant.

"There you are," he coos, helping me onto my feet.

I pull away from him quickly, or a I would have if he weren't standing so, so close. He leans in close to me and inhales deeply over and over. He brushes the hair from my eyes and slowly unbuttons my coat. Removing it, he drapes my jacket casually over his arm.

"I believe I'm beginning to grow fond of you, human."

Mikey releases a low growl that gives me flashbacks. Kane's made that sound before. It's not a human sound, either, but something alien. Animal.

Trocker shoots Mikey a slick glare as he takes one step to the left. They're toe-to-toe now. "You don't need to worry for much longer, Mikael," Trocker says with a grin. "And when you're gone, I'll take good care of her."

Ice slides down my shoulders and settles in my fists. I'm not so worried about Trocker getting me alone, but about the implication for Mikey. That's twice now the goons in black have talked about his death like it was already written.

Trocker laughs. "You were never worth very much to begin with, were you, Mikael?" Mikey's jaw clenches. He tenses. Blood rushes into his face. "You don't deserve a female who smells like this. Not even a human one. What did you do to her to convince her to travel with you? Or did you force her?"

"He didn't," I say, anger sitting like a stone in my throat. The skin tightens all over my body. I roll my shoulders back.

I may hate Kane's little brother, but I still don't think he deserves to be spoken to like this. To be made so small when he's already powerless.

"He didn't force me," I say, face heating. "And I liked traveling with him, I just know I shouldn't've. We should have never been…traveling together."

I lick my lips as Trocker glares at me, expression twisted in confusion. He opens his mouth to say something, but another male speaks first.

"Trocker," says the voice at my back.

Trocker straightens, steps back and bows towards the hallway behind us. Mikey and I catch each other's gaze as we turn to face the balding, middle-aged alien hobbling up a flight of stairs towards us. Dressed in clothes that betray his age — even if the wrinkles hadn't done it for him — he looks about seventy in human years, with sallow skin and small, slanted eyes.

His modest, corduroy slacks and oversized, beige button-up clash with the decadence of the world around us — dark wood, flashy carpets, sculptures and paintings hanging on the walls in gold frames.

As he shuffles towards me, the male grins and I immediately feel my body tense and pivot, shifting into a fighting stance. But the male just smiles to show a mouth full of greying teeth and cups my palm in both of his. His delicate skin is cracked like dry leather, and I don't miss the way he shakes.

"Hello," he says, voice kind and warm where I didn't expect it to be. It's confusing, because even though he's the villain out of a nightmare, my gut is telling me to trust him.

"How do you do? I am very pleased to have human guests in my home, particularly of such importance. Sistana Abel, the Notare Kane's queen. You are more vibrant in person than even what the reports suggest."

My voice catches and I glance at Mikey, but with his eyebrows raised and lips hanging open dumbly, he looks just as shocked as I feel. Even Trocker looks surprised by the information, his pale face flushing and his eyes heating as he looks at me again in this new light.

"How do you…" I pause and clear my throat. "How do you know who I am?"

"I am privileged enough to have access to a great deal of information, my dear Sistana."

"And who are you?" I blurt out.

I brush my crusty curls behind my ears and smooth down the front of my white thermal. It's covered in soil and flecks of blood.

"It has been too long since I have been called by my given name," he says with a grin and when he smiles again, even more broadly than before, I can see that his grey teeth are surrounded by bright red gums. "Please, call me Crestor."

"Holy fuck." I glance at Mikey at the same time Crestor does. Mikey's face is ashen as he says, "Crestor, you're still alive?"

When the alien called Crestor does nothing but smile and lace his long, skeletal fingers together, Mikey lurches back and swings his fists at Trocker, nailing him hard in the throat.

Two other guards that had been loitering nearby surge forward while Trocker finds his feet. Ramil surges for Mikey, who kicks him in the stomach.

He lurches towards the dining room and over his shoulder shouts, "Abel, run!"

I don't stop to ask questions, but take off, sprinting past Crestor, who makes no move to stop me. I make it to the end of the hall and hang a hard left, but Trocker is on my ass like a fire on a fuse.

He tackles me against the wall, using his whole body to flatten mine to the silk wallpaper. He's breathing hard in my ear and I get the impression that he isn't tired. He's hungry.

He moans, "Notare Kane's Sistana…a human?" He sounds half-outraged, half-incredulous. "A human with blood that smells so sweet."

He combs his fingers back through my hair, almost lovingly, and the pressure of his hand is just as hard as the wall in front of me. With an ounce more pressure, he could crush my skull.

I kick my elbow into his ribs. He grunts and, wrenching my hands behind my back, drags me down the hall and pitches me into the dining room. I crash into the side of the round table, gasping for air.

Mikey's still fighting in the hallway, and I know already that it's a doomed affair, so I glance down the length of the long table at porcelain place settings, the crystal glasses, the sterling silverware. Dear heavens, this table looks like it's been set for thirty people! Thirty ghosts…Just so long as I'm not among them.

The serrated steak knives are sharp and I grab one when Trocker grabs the back of my arm. Swiveling faster than he expects me to, I manage to catch Trocker across the shoulder, drawing black blood. He staggers back, shocked more than hurt, but I use that opening. I toss the knife up, taking it in a backwards grip and slash down again, this time aiming right for Trocker's heart.

He falls to the ground on his knees and I grab him by the hair and wrench his head back, back, back until he can't breathe. Time for the kill.

Trocker looks up at me, shocked, and as I stare down at him. Does he knew I'm going to cut off his head and take it to Kane as a trophy? Maybe we can mount it to the wall over our bed.

Then Crestor says glibly, "Your Grace." Wait — is he talking to me? I look up and see that Mikey's on his knees with a knife to his throat in a mirror image of Trocker. A parody of it.

"For the sake of your friend's — or should I say your brother-in-law's — health, I suggest you release my guard. I am, after all, quite fond of him, as I suspect you are of your king's brother." He passes his gaunt hand across his receding hairline slowly. It quivers, like his lips, though he looks neither excited nor afraid. Something is wrong. I've never seen one of the alien look so old or frail or get the shakes.

Cursing, I throw the steak knife onto the table, shattering a crystal champagne flute. As Trocker stands up to his full height, I gather my fists in front of me and wait for retribution.

"Trocker," Crestor says, and Trocker freezes, one foot off the ground. He glances over his shoulder once and snarls before turning away from me.

"There." Crestor clasps his hands together. "Now that's all settled, let's take a seat. Dinner shall be served promptly."

I'm guided to a place at the far end of the seemingly limitless expanse of slick black wood. Crestor takes the seat to my right at the head of the table while Mikey's shoved into the seat across from me.

"You give the human the place of honor at your table?" He sneers and I hate him just a little more for it after coming to his rescue earlier.

I glare at him across the table, but he doesn't look at me.

"Better the human than the criminal." Crestor's face flashes and for a moment he's not the same alien he was. He's masked violence. "And from this moment forth, you will address my guest by Sistana or Your Grace. I do not tolerate willful tongues at my table."

Mikey's lips tighten to a thin white line and he rips his shoulder from beneath one of the guard's hands. Crestor's eyes haven't left Mikey and I feel my stomach pitch when he calls Trocker over.

I grip the smooth edge of the wooden table so tightly my fingers turn white around the nails. Low words are exchanged between the two before Trocker stalks out of the room.

He returns moments later with seven human escorts in tow, even though there are only three of us. Then he stands at the wall behind me so that I can no longer see him. But I can feel him. He's everywhere. Staring holes through the back of my neck. Searching low, lower, lower…

The humans pour dense red wine into our crystal cups. Nearly black, it looks less like wine and more like tar, and when Mikey reaches for the cup without hesitation, I balk.

"Mikey," I hiss. Mikey meets my gaze and his hand hesitates over the crystal. I shake my head once, stiffly. "Don't…"

"If I have to be here, I might as well." He lifts the cup to his mouth and drains half in a gulp.

Rage. Disbelief. I don't know which one is stronger. Maybe they both are.

Crestor laughs a little and shakes his head at me indulgently. "My dearest Sistana, do not trouble yourself."

He tucks his white linen napkin carefully into the collar of his shirt and reaches for his own glass. It's a darker red than Mikey's and mine and it *stinks.* Definitely not wine. But it's too dark to be blood. I don't know *what* it is, just that I'm not going anywhere near anything he serves me.

"Thus is the way with all sentient beings. Heztoichen or human, we all have our weakness." His eyes glitter. I don't know what he means.

Just that it's bad.

"Crestor," I say, trying a smile. I swallow hard and clear my throat and unfold my napkin, tucking it into my shirt in the way he just did.

"Thank you very much for inviting us in. It's been a long journey on the road."

Crestor claps his hands in his lap and grins to reveal almost all of his teeth. I was wrong before. They're not grey. They're black and spotted.

"Sistana, I must confess, it is a rare pleasure for me to dine with such beguiling company."

He angles his chair towards me and takes a deep draught from his glass, and it's as if he's entirely forgotten about my haggard appearance, my drunk brother-in-law and the fact that I was about to cut the head off one of his guards.

"Can I offer you another beverage? I see that wine is not to your taste."

He snaps his fingers once and a human attendant comes to my side and whisks it away. There's no eye contact and no recognition at all between us. I can't get his attention. He's like a ghost. *This house is full of them.*

"Water would be fine."

Crestor nods once, though there's something mischievous about him. Trust? Had I felt that once? I don't know what I feel now.

"A bottle for the Sistana. Be sure that it is uncorked."

"Thank you, Crestor."

"Notare Crestor," Trocker blurts out at my back. "Apologies for the intrusion, Notare."

Crestor nods towards Trocker behind me, then lifts a hand to quiet him. "The Sistana has no need to refer to me by my former title. Her rank supersedes mine. Crestor is just fine, Sistana."

Surprise forces me to ask, "You're a former Notare?"

"I am, but as you can see my Tare has long since faded." He gestures to his chest, which I can't see anyway underneath his coat, but I believe him if he says he doesn't shine.

"I was Notare before Kane. He replaced me after my light died. I always viewed him as a son."

"Alright," I say, feeling hopeful. "If you're like a father to him, then maybe you can help us…"

Mikey bangs on the table hard enough to topple another champagne flute and send it crashing to the floor. "Don't you ask him for anything. *Anything.*"

Crestor's dry lips purse and he raises his voice. "If you do not learn to control your tongue, Mikael, then I will see fit to remove it."

He looks up and smiles, shifting in and out of expressions seamlessly, like shedding skins. The snake.

"Ah, look. Here you are now. A bottle of water for the Sistana, and more wine for her lowly servant."

His eyes slide sideways to find Mikey and I get a very bad feeling in the pit of my stomach.

The human servant ghost-robots bring out a corked bottle of water. They make a great show of uncorking it in front of me. They bring food out too. Soup. It's green and smells salty and delicious. My fingers twitch towards my utensils, but at great pains, I manage to restrain myself.

"Your Grace?"

I glance at Crestor. His hands are folded politely in his lap and his eyes are gentle, never prying. He's a big, giant question mark.

"Yes?"

"You are free to request other food if this is not to your liking. However, if I may be so bold as to suggest that your fears are unfounded, I would do so. The food has not been tampered with. As a gesture of good faith, would you like me to have Trocker as well as one of the human servants test your food for you?" He reaches out and touches his alligator skin hands to mine.

I force myself to stay put and speak evenly and say, "Yes, I would like that. Thank you."

Trocker looms over me with a spoon and takes a sip of my soup. One of the human waiters — a tall, gangly boy with bad skin — does the same. When neither drops down dead, I weigh my odds and take a bite myself.

Mikey asks for another glass of wine and as he drinks it, he watches me eat. Only after he finishes his third glass, does he eat too. Like a savage, he gobbles down everything.

"So, you know Kane well?" I say.

"Why, of course." Crestor nods as he picks at his own dish. It's different from ours. I don't know why. No soup, he just went straight for mains, and his plate is full of a black slab of meat that looks absolutely revolting.

"He sends me regular reports from the Diera, as a courtesy. It is very difficult to take on the responsibilities of being Notare as a child. I think I helped ease his transition."

I nod, though can't quite picture Kane as a child, and let the servants clear my plate. A second course of fragrant meat and potatoes soon follows.

Mikey barks my name the moment I lift my fork. His eyes are bloodshot and his cheeks are flushed. The hand he uses to hold his wine is clenched around the crystal so fiercely that a fine crack shimmers up the side of the glass to meet his palm. Deep red wine seeps through it and stains the knuckles of his hand. He shakes his head once more and says my name.

Crestor laughs and sets down his own fork and knife when I do. He rocks back in his chair. "Oh, Mikael, it seems that you fear the rumors about me."

"Rumors?" Mikey says and I don't miss the way he slurs. He's only a couple glasses in though, and I've seen him drink two bottles and still articulate clearly. Something's wrong. Fuck. *Fuuuuuuck.*

Mikey's cheeks flush as he rounds on Crestor. He jabs his pointer finger at him, and it would appear more threatening if he weren't using his other hand to anchor himself to the table.

"*Rumors* imply that they're conjecture. That they might be wrong. You've been tried and convicted of your crimes. The only reason you're still breathing is because you were Notare and Kane has a soft spot for you.

"If it weren't for Kane, the Council would have had your head three hundred years ago — the second your light died and you became irrelevant. A blemish in the history books.

"Parents don't tell their kids about you when they sing songs of hero Notares like my brother. They tell their kids about you to terrify them. You're the monster little Heztoichen children have nightmares about."

Crestor's lips have tensed to the point that I can no longer see them. He snaps with his left hand and with his right, dabs at the bloody spots at the corners of his mouth with white linen. I've got my own napkin crushed in my fist.

"Human," Crestor says to the one that approaches him, "Please fetch Mikael another bottle of wine. Nothing from the bottom shelf. We don't serve good wine to criminals."

"Well, isn't that the sheep calling the pot black?" Mikey laughs, butchering the expression in a way that might have made me laugh had I not been so riveted to the scene and it's impending outcome. Like those machines, the big ones with the blades at the top. You hold the rope and when you let it go…slice goes the neck and thud goes the head when it rolls away from the body.

Whose head will roll? If I had to guess, it'd be Mikey.

And soon.

Crestor raises the glass in his hand. "Silence, Mikael, or I will have you removed from the table before desert. Ramil," Crestor calls and the one with the braid steps forward. He's got the knife in his hand he was using before to keep Mikey contained. He tosses it up now and with no ceremony at all, he catches it by the sheath and swipes the hilt across the side of Mikey's head.

I flinch, grateful only when I hear Mikey grumbling out curses and trying to staunch the flow of blood running from above his left ear.

"Apologies, Sistana, both for the scene your kin has caused here, and that you had to travel in such undignified company for so long. After all that you have endured,

Your Grace, I certainly hope that you find what it is you seek."

"You know that Kane is missing?"

He smiles. "Kane is not the only one from whom I receive reports."

"Then you know where he's been taken." I drop my fork and it clatters loudly as it lands.

"As do you, I'm sure." He glances down at my chest. "Blood bonded to the Notare as you are, it must be a terrible burden to feel his suffering."

"You know…you know what she's doing to him?" Rage. Disbelief. This time, I know which one screams louder.

"I am well aware that Notare Elise has taken him. What she intends to do with him is a mystery."

"Guess," I bellow.

He watches me critically, sizing me up as calculates something I can't see. I don't dare breathe. I just seethe, pouring my anger out through my gaze. And I don't blink.

He cuts his meat up into small slices, severing the connection between us. He smiles as he chews and as he swallows, says, "Perhaps I have some idea."

He slips the serrated edge of his knife through his meat. It looks tough, and black liquid seeps across his plate, dyeing the potatoes there grey.

He says, "If I were Notare Elise, with ambition equal to her own, it would seem to me that the best way to secure my power would be to eliminate my competition."

"But what does it matter? Her light is dying."

Crestor smiles at me secretly. "And how could you possibly know that?"

I balk. "Because I saw her when she took Kane away. She has him and I want him back."

Crestor nods considerately, like we're discussing our favorite hobbies, and not matters of life and death —

mostly death. "Unfortunately for you, she needs him if she is to succeed in her experiment. So far the blood of the royal families has not produced the results she had hoped for."

He pulls meat off the tines of his fork with his teeth. He chews, swallows, chews, swallows in a way I find absolutely disgusting.

I look away while my stomach gurgles and the pain in my lower back intensifies. "What results were those?"

"I should have thought it obvious. Using the royal families' blood, she attempts to create her own light."

"You can't fake Tare. It's not possible. Smarter Heztoichen have tried before her," Mikey shouts, though his speech is so badly slurred at this point I can hardly make sense of it.

Looking up at him for the first time in minutes, I see that his eyes are droopy slits. His head lolls on his neck and his hands are relaxed around his utensils.

My pounding heart breaks.

We're not going to make it.

No — we're not *both* going to make it.

And when I find Kane, what would he say?

"On the contrary, Mikael," Crestor says, ignoring Mikey in his sorry state. "Notare Elise's greatest secret is that her light has been dying for nearly two hundred years. Her scientists have discovered a means by which the Notare can keep her light alive by synthesizing royal blood and injecting it into her veins. It is not true Tare by any means, but the shadow of life is enough to keep her above suspicion."

"How do you know all this and why don't you seem to care? Kane was like a son to you and you know that she's using him." I reach across the table and grab Crestor's frail hand. "Help us get him back."

Crestor's eyes dodge mine for the first time all day. His knife clatters against the edge of his plate noisily so he sets it down and, slipping his other palm free of mine, wipes off his hands on his black-stained napkin.

"Apologies, Sistana, this is not a comfortable subject for me." He meets my gaze and I shiver. There's a bleakness in those lying, dying depths. And it's so lonely. "Notare Kane and his family not the first of Elise's subjects. She has been practicing her art of blood transfusion for a long time. Centuries. Six or seven of them, by my count, and long before her light ever began to dim.

"My sister was one of her first victims and unlike Mikael, my sister Lara did not survive the trials Notare Elise put her through."

"So…what?" I blurt. "What happened? Why couldn't you take her down then?"

"If I could have, I certainly would have. But I could prove none of it. I never even found her remains."

Crestor inhales once, sharply, and when his eyes flutter to meet mine the touch of sadness I thought I'd seen in them is gone as if it had never been.

He says softly, "Notare Elise is quite adept at covering her tracks, as you will soon discover. If she has your blood bonded mate, I am sorry for you, for you will not be able to recover him."

Rage. Just rage.

I throw my fork across the table, shattering a dozen glasses simultaneously. "You just gave up, then? Why don't you fight back?"

"Can't leave…" comes the groan from across the table.

"What?"

"Silence, Mikael."

Mikey slumps forward, bracing his arms on the table, one elbow landing directly in the center of his plate. "He can't leave!"

Crestor watches Mikey icily, then throws his napkin onto his plate. "I believe we will have to skip desert. Apologies, Sistana, but alcohol seems to have severed the connection between Mikael's brain and his mouth."

"What does he mean you can't leave? I didn't think that Notare were even allowed in Population."

"I am a former Notare, remember."

Ramil and Kaius grab Mikey's arms and wrestle him from his chair. "That's not the reason," Mikael moans, throwing his elbows back and forth in a failing attempt to get free. His legs drag lamely beneath him.

Crestor drinks more from his glass while I fight the urge to go after Mikey. I wouldn't get far. I have to be smart. Smarter than Mikey, at least, and definitely smarter than Crestor.

"I have been placed under house arrest by the Council. When the decision was made, Kane spoke for me and allowed me to keep this residence along with whatever equipment and support staff I might need. I lead a very comfortable life on a cause of your husband, my queen."

The slight bow to his head suggests an end to the conversation, but I can't not ask, "What's your crime?"

"That is not civilized dinner conversation, my…"

"Cannibal," Mikey slurs from the doorway. He's got a grip on the wall that the guards don't immediately break. When they do, it's too late, because I can still hear Mikey when he says, "Crestor the cannibal…"

Crestor hisses, drawing his head back into his shoulders and clutching the arms of his chair, making him look like some kind of giant, carnivorous bird. The two guards on Mikey's arms drag his limp body out of the dining room while my gaze returns to Crestor's plate.

I don't realize I'm standing until I hear the chair behind me hit the floor with a thwack.

"Where are you taking him?" I say, breathing harder now. In the back of my mind, I already know the answer. What I meant to ask was *how much time do I have?*

Crestor rises from the table and servants flutter around us both. They pick up my chair, replace his napkin, rearrange the plates, glasses and cutlery. "My Lady, you have no need to fear. I would not dare harm my Notare's Sistana. Your food and drink are fine, untampered with and untouched and no humans were harmed in the making of this meal.

"The meat is a particularly succulent piece of Heztoichen. A young woman by the name of Marlina, I believe. She had a daughter who I ate last month. An exquisite rarity, procured by Elise and delivered to my estate.

"She sends me these little gifts from time to time as a torment to remind me of all that she took from me. I am not a perfect male." He shakes his head and when he grins he looks totally insane. "I find it hard not to indulge. There is so little to inspire me these days."

"Not interested in eating people with names." I gulp, putting my chair between us. "Not even aliens."

Crestor just smiles and nods. "I understand, of course, and if you'd like, I'd be happy to prepare you with some cheese and fruits so that you may be on your way. It will be a difficult journey, I imagine, if you still intend to enter the Saltlands."

"I do. You know I do."

"I know."

"But you also know I'm not going without Mikey."

"Ah, but Sistana, you must."

I glance at the doorway, but Mikey's already gone. I can hear the thud of boots on the stairs. Likely the ones that belonged to the dead guy from the kitchens. Those damned kitchens.

Why did we have to stop there? Why did Mikey have to find his bottles? Would we have been able to avoid this if he were sober? Would he have heard Trocker and the others approach? Would he have been able to keep himself from tonguing me down there when I didn't give him permission to?

I don't know.

And I'll never know.

"Crestor, please. It's Kane we're talking about here. Your son, remember?"

"Kane may be my son, but Mikey is no relation of mine," he sneers. "The child is barbaric and rude bordering on cruel. I could smell your blood on him and unless you truly are undeserving of Kane's attentions, then I will assume that he forced you. That crime alone is punishable by death."

Crestor gives me a knowing look then. I can either admit that Mikey attacked me and get him killed, or I can admit that I liked it and likely get me killed. I don't know what the punishment would be for that.

Crestor nods again. "No, I do not believe you would be so easily swayed by the affections of this male when you have the adoration of one far, far superior."

Crestor starts to move past me, but I intercept him and grab his arm. "I love Kane," I implore. "And Kane loves his brother. I can't abandon him."

"My darling," Crestor sighs and his dry fingers sweep my hairline. "You do not have a choice."

He snaps and Trocker reappears, grabs me and starts to force me out of the dining room. I grab chairs and linens and anything I can to try to keep myself there, in Crestor's earshot. I've only got seconds left to reason with him.

But he's resumed his seat I shout all kinds of things, but he just saws into his meat and just before Trocker carries me out of the room and down the stairs, Crestor says one last thing.

"Sistana Abel, when Kane spoke for me, it was his intention that I continue living as *punishment* for my crimes. In the wake of my sister's death, I engaged in these *proclivities* that I'd long denied myself for the sake of my family and its reputation." He gestures at his plate and meets my gaze with a smile.

"But I have no family. No reason not to indulge. And while the Council was merciful and wanted me executed, your Notare Kane wanted me exiled so that I could live the remainder of my years in loneliness and bitterness and torment.

"He is a cruel male, your mate. Cruel, but just."

I suck in a breath, feeling my whole body shudder on the exhale while I thrash against Trocker's arms. "So you're going to kill Mikey to get back at him?"

"I was always going to kill Mikey simply for the taste."

"You can't do this. I *command* you," I say, in one last attempt to get through to him. "I'm the Sistana now. *Your* Sistana. I outrank you, you said so yourself."

He smiles just a little with one edge of his mouth and when he looks at me, he manages to look impressed. "Very good, Sistana. Very good. And you are correct. An order from you is not one I dare disobey. So, when you retrieve Notare Kane, I will gladly welcome my punishment."

He cocks his head and Trocker forces me down the staircase and towards the front door. He throws it open, and a cool wind batters back the warmth of the world behind me. He grabs me by the nape of the neck, fingers digging into my pressure points as he drags me outside.

It's still light out, though I can tell that the day is dwindling somewhere above the grey. He shouts an order to another black-clad alien walking the perimeter and the gate swings open before us.

He pushes me so hard that I fall onto my hands and knees. My jacket lands on the ground beside me. Angry, I curl my fingers into the gravel. It's wet, and that's the first I notice of the rain. Somewhere up above the grey, I can hear a mighty growl. It's been years since I've heard thunder.

Trocker looks tormented as he shuts the gate between us. I charge at it, not expecting to be able to make it inside, so it's no surprise when I don't. Through the bars, Trocker punches the heel of his hand against my sternum.

A splinter of pain lights there and fades as I gasp for breath and drop back down onto the gravel. By the time I've got my breath back in order, Trocker's already crossed the driveway and is standing at the front door.

I watch him watch me in the orange glow of the open doorway. His eyes meet mine and they are darkened by the shadows of his eyebrows.

From this distance, he looks like a skeleton. Black suction cup eyes, hollow cheeks, pale skin yearning for sunlight.

He sucks his teeth, and mouths a string of words between us that I can't make out before shutting Mikey in, and me out.

Chapter Eight

Sticking to the trees, I circle the house three times, marking the entrances, exits and low-lying windows as I move. The thin mist dampens the sounds of the world around me — sounds that are already difficult to make out with one eardrum blown.

A few times I think I catch the sound of screams drifting along the breeze, but it might just be my imagination. *God, please let it be my imagination…*

Crestor's house is built like a fortress. The fence surrounding it is twice my height and each post is sharpened to a point, sure to shred anything that tries to climb over it. There's no porch, no awning, no terrace, and on the first floor, there are no windows. Aside from the front door, there's no way in.

No way except for the one: a cellar door.

The rain is white and everything else is black — the sky, the castle, the earth, the fence, the basement's camouflaged entrance.

It's one of those cellar doors that's built flat to the ground just a few feet away from the house. Just slightly raised, I can see enough of it if I squint just right and from what I can see from the other side of the fence, even though the wood is dark and looks like it could be old, the lock is silver and shiny and looks new. Recently replaced.

As I crouch under the cover of a prickle bush while two guards scan the woods surrounding me, I debate this for the millionth time.

Mikey is a drunk slob who's slowing me down. I could go for Kane and together, we could come back for Mikey with an armada. Kane could take Crestor apart single-handedly and rescue his brother. *But in how many pieces? How much of Mikey would be left?*

I close my eyes and grit my teeth and clench my fists into the soft soil below me. There are bugs on my fingers. The kinds with the armadillo shells that roll up into a little ball when they get scared. That's what I feel like doing.

I'm not going to make it. The guards are on my trial. They can smell me, even with the rain, of that I'm sure.

Rage. This time it's followed by frustration and that frustration is followed by an idea…

My blood is making them crazy. *Crazy*. So maybe I should let it.

Cautiously, in as few moves as possible, I slip back into the trees. They help block some of the rain, though by this point it hardly matters. My clothes are soaked and muddy and I'm cold again. I dream about the bath that Kane and I shared and wonder…hope…we'll get back to that place.

Yanking my wet pants down to the knees, I pull out the bloody towel and rip it into a dozen strips. Keeping just beyond the cover of the trees, I mark a perimeter around the house, dropping pieces of fabric at arbitrary intervals as I run.

I notice the effect almost immediately and pause long enough to smile and wipe the last of the blood on my hands off onto the nearest tree trunk.

Routes ruined, the guards start pacing now. They're shouting between each other angrily, scanning the woods but without focus. In the rain-dampened distance I hear Trocker screaming orders in alien, followed by the unmistakable sound of Crestor's gates opening.

They're coming. *Perfect.*

I dive underneath a couple thick bushes, my adrenaline spiking and my heart clattering in my ribs. It seems to take forever for one of the Others to appear and there's *two* of them.

A dozen paces away, one shouts at the other, hands him a hunting knife and points to the forest before charging off to the left. The one with the knife turns towards the trees and starts stalking forward slowly… towards me.

He's got a gun on him, but it's lowered at his side. With the rain as thick as it is, dulling his senses, it's like he's walking blind — at least as blind as I am.

Five feet from where I'm hiding, he doesn't hear my pulse or my light breath and with the bushes swallowing me up, to him I'm likely nothing more than a dark smear against a larger darkness.

His right foot crinkles over damp leaves inches from my nose as he moves deeper into the forest. I wait until he passes before springing out of the bush and latching onto his back. He grabs the gun, but I want the knife. I pry it easily from his hand and with way too little resistance, I manage to stab him in the neck.

Remembering what Kane did to Drago, I take the wasteful minutes needed to saw the Other's head off. I can hear the cavalry coming — voices not too far off — and I know I need to move fast.

Throwing his gun across my back, I hack him to pieces where he lies, removing just his arms but keeping his legs. He'd be too heavy to carry otherwise and I've got to make it to the fence.

I haul his body through the mud, which is slick and aids my progress. I slip half a dozen times before reaching the fence's thick black bars. I cling to them with one mud-stained hand. The rain is coming down harder now and when I look to my right, I can see someone running towards me from the forest.

Shit.

I lift the gun, wishing it came with an instruction manual because I've never been any good with firearms — only gangs have guns. By the time the male appears and I recognize him as Kaius, I finally manage to get the safety off.

I pull the trigger and the force of the blow throws me back into the fence. My head hits the metal and the impact knocks the breath clean out of me. Kaius falls, clutching his abs, and I let him writhe in agony. I don't have time to deal with the dying. The living are my concern now.

I slip my shoulder beneath the decapitated corpse and lift it as high as I can. Then I throw. I slip, get a mouthful of iron bar and curse while my mouth fills with blood. My lower lip burns, splitting down the center as I barely keep my teeth.

The once-distant shouting is louder now — right on top of me — though when I look around I don't see anything but mist and rain and grey. I don't know how much time I've actually got, what with my panic making everything feel both faster and slower all at once.

I haul the corpse up out of the mud again and grunt as I throw it up onto the fence. This time it catches and folds at the waist. One of the fence spines pierces him all the way through and black blood rains over me from the new wound in his torso.

Don't care.

I yank hard on his legs. They hang at my hairline and dirt from his boots showers my face. He's anchored there pretty good and, not wishing to waste anymore time, I brace my feet against the fence, grab his legs and climb.

I grapple and claw my way up the length of his body until I reach the spikes at the top. His corpse is a solid buffer between me and being impaled. I wonder just how I'm going to get *back* over the fence as I swing my legs over the other side and drop down onto the gravel. *Eh. I'll deal with it later.*

Mud squishes under my feet and I run towards the cellar. My head hurts, my lungs burn, my mouth tingles and I know that all I've got on my side is time. Rain and time. Rain and time and absolutely no exit strategy.

I come up to the cellar door and point my gun at it. I fire without waiting. The gun has a mind of its own and steers me wildly to the left before taking me off my feet. Tac-tac-tac-tac-tac-tac. Bullet casings rain.

Shouting behind me is loud enough to touch and I turn, finger on the trigger. I shoot the guard sprinting towards me in the head and the one behind him in the stomach. My heart is pounding as I wait to be besieged.

I take in a breath, and then a second, then a third. No one's there. Just the dead and an overactive imagination.

I turn back to the cellar door and fire off another dozen rounds. Eventually, it's not the latch that breaks but the wood surrounding it. I slip my fingers into the woodchips and wrench open the door. I keep my weapon elevated, unsure of what to expect.

"Hello?" I shout into darkness, beyond which nothing stirs. My voice doesn't echo. The rain gobbles it up. "Mikey? Mikey, get your ass up here!"

"Mikey can't hear you, Sistana."

I flinch and swing my gun around. Trocker grins. His gun hangs across his chest, but he doesn't have it raised. I hadn't heard him approach and wonder for a moment why I'm still alive. Then it occurs to me in the way his eyes drift to my pants, that it isn't my life he wants.

"Give me a reason I shouldn't shoot you, Trocker."

Because I can think of one. If I fire, the recoil will send me plummeting into that darkness, and I have no desire to go down there with no clear path back up.

Blood and rain drip from my eyelashes into my eyes, turning the world to rose long enough for Trocker to take a step towards me. I counter by placing my finger to the trigger.

His grin spreads wider. He says, "I can't." And then he dives for me, moving too fast to follow.

I fire and miss, and it's his hands on me that keep me from falling into the cellar hole at my back. He grabs my leg and starts to drag me over the ground, when all at once, a white blur soars out of the cellar and breaks the contact between us.

My eyes widen as I stare after the *thing* sprinting across the gravel. It looks lost. Naked and lost. And it looks…like a person. Like an alien. But it's missing both hands at the wrists.

Bullets fly, taking the escaped alien off of its feet. The sound of approaching guards stirs me to action and I grab for the gun and swing it up, but Trocker blocks with his forearm and the pressure of his arm cutting upward is enough to unbalance me.

I try to stand, but I stagger and lose my grip on the gun and on the soft soil beneath my feet. My heel catches on the opening to the cellar and Trocker is staring at me with horror as I fall forever, then the ground and I collide with unforgiving force.

I can hear movement around me now that I couldn't from up above. Scratching, clawing, shuffling. The world is grey, illuminated only by the pale ring of light hanging like a halo some fifteen feet up. The ground beneath me is black, hard and cold to the touch.

"Mikey?" I whisper.

Then bodies come at me all at once, from every direction. Scrambling over the cool, earthen ground and struggling to regain my breath, I draw the knife from the cargo pocket in my pant leg.

A hand wraps around my ankle the moment I stand and pulls my feet out from under me. I hit the ground hard and when I blink down the length of my legs at the body clinging to my ankles, I don't understand what I'm seeing.

It's an alien, or at least…it used to be. Now, it's got arms and hands but it doesn't have eyes or ears or feet. My heart hammers in my chest and I glance around, realizing for the first time that these aliens are *all* missing parts.

I shove the thing off me, ripping my feet out from under him, only to be approached by a female with arms severed at the shoulders. She steps on my knee and stands on the blind man's back and only then is she able to jump high enough to reach the exit, legs kicking uselessly as her torso hits the dirt above.

More bodies begin scrambling towards the light, shrieking as if they haven't seen any for years.

Maybe they haven't.

Some cower from it and as they move around me like river water around rocks. Heart beating like a goddamn snare drum, I search the throngs for Mikey.

"Mikey! Where the hell are you!" I scream.

A woman with cracked, ashy skin charges towards me from the depths of the darkness. She has only one leg and is using a long, wooden stick as a crutch. She jabs it at me and I spin out of her way only to be pulled to the ground by a heavy arm.

I stab when it doesn't release me and catch only a glimpse of the Other's deformed face. He's got no tongue and is missing his left shoulder. He bares his teeth and I slash at his cheek when he jolts towards me, but he doesn't seem to feel the pain.

He comes at me again as a tower of bodies begin to form, the weaker taking the bottom positions of the pyramid while the others pour out of the darkness and into the world. Into Population.

Blood spray slashes across the opening and I hear Heztoichen words flung between the living. The male attacks me again, this time shouting the same word over and over again. I kick for his face, but a body slips between us, stepping directly on my stomach. It lurches up into my throat at the same time that the guy holding onto my leg bites down.

Roaring up into a seat, I shove the body off of me and stab downward blindly. I hit his shoulder first before aiming a second time for his neck. I stab him again and again, but he doesn't let go of me, and there are bodies now stepping on and over both of us. I'm being trampled to death and this dying guy won't let me go, even as he exhales his last breath with what sounds like relief.

Feet are pressing on my chest and ribs and hands and arms. I keep hold of the knife through sheer will power alone, but I'm not sure how I'm going to be able to get up. Not when I'm the bottom layer.

"Kane," I shout, tears of frustration making it hard to think clearly and rationally about a way out. "Kane…"

A sudden surge of energy blooms in the center of my chest right before a voice shouts very near to me, "Not likely."

It's familiar, though rougher. Still drunk. A heavy boot crushes the skull of the man on my leg and two bloody hands reach through the disembodied limbs to grab the front of my jacket and rip me out of the rubble.

Mikey grabs me to his chest and starts to climb. He steps on backs and arms and legs, some of which break apart beneath him. He steps and pushes and punches and claws and I cling to him with my eyes closed. I can't watch. It's unbearable what Crestor did to these things.

Nobody deserved to die like this. Not even aliens. My mortal enemies.

I'm grateful when Mikey jumps all at once and somehow manages to clear the opening. He lands on the soft soil on his stomach and has to kick his legs free of the hands that have grabbed onto him.

Screams light up from below while more screams light up the grey.

A bullet whizzes past my ear and Mikey curses. Rolling out of Mikey's arms, I look up to see a black-clad guard rushing towards us. The knife I'm still somehow holding nails him in the throat and he hits the ground without ever firing.

Mikey finishes him off by twisting his head off his neck. He swipes the machine gun the guard had been holding, loops the strap over his head and looks back to make sure I'm following. I am, despite the staggering pain in my leg.

My skin is all messed up and mauled, but I can't worry about it now. I don't have a plan or the time to come up with one.

In the time it takes me to wrench my blade free of the headless guard's neck, Crestor's unfinished meals pass like a current between Mikey and me as they shriek their way to freedom. Mikey shouts my name as they inundate us, but they seem to be less concerned now with my free flowing blood than they are with the guards storming towards us.

The guards and the victims clash at the open gates to Crestor's house and I keep my bloodied blade poised at the ready. Mikey fires first. Tac-tac-tac-tac-tac-tac-tac. A whole host of guards hit the ground, and distantly, I wonder what happened to Trocker because he isn't among them.

Resounding gunfire follows us across that muddy arena. I feel the wind rush off of the bullets as I'm narrowly missed. Mikey cries out and collapses against the trunk of a tree just as we follow the bodies out of the gate and make it to the trees.

"You've been hit."

I'm panting now and try to reach for the fresh wound on his shoulder but he shrugs me off and surges to the right. I grab the back of Mikey's pants, noticing for the first time that he has a painful-looking gash across his left pectoral. His right eye is swollen entirely shut and his left is a burning blood red. He's still high and hasn't come down yet.

"Where are you going?" I shout, pulling him to the left. "I canvassed earlier and there's a garage just over here. I think I might be able to hotwire a car and we can try to punch our way out of here and hope to high hell that they don't chase us, guns blazing."

As I say that, I glance over my shoulder. The dozen guards still alive on the gravel driveway are working to finish off most of the dismembered aliens, but those aliens have something the guards don't — numbers.

Numbers and desperation.

They're fighting back.

They outnumber the guards three to one as they fight for their survival. Or their revenge.

I still can't believe the state of them, or that Crestor was able to get away with this. Not just Crestor, either. But Elise, the guards — even the human slaves working the property. How could they have stood by and let this happen? They *knew.* They knew and did nothing.

They deserve to die. All of them.

"I'm going back for my pack," Mikey says, jerking my attention back around.

"What?"

"My pack. I'm going back for it. Kane's sword…"

I nod automatically, until his words actually register. I grab the back of his pants since his shirt's still missing, and jerk him back to me.

"No, Mikey." I shake my head. "I understand it's sentimental, but we need to focus on Kane first. If it's on the way we can stop…"

"Stop fucking telling me what to do. I'm going back for the pack." His one good eye is wild as it looks at me. And then it clicks when he licks his lips.

"How many bottles were left?"

"Four," he answers automatically and in that one word, I learn everything I need to know.

I step away from him, limping on my left and mangled leg. "I went back for you…" I can't believe it. "Why did I go back for you?" I can't think. I don't think I've ever been so angry, and yet…the rage doesn't come in the way I expect it to.

I feel *sad.*

It spreads through me like ink through water. Tears come to my lower lids as I back another step away from him towards the garage, and then another.

"I need them," he grates, voice still a slur.

I shake my head and try to hold onto something. My sanity, above all else. "Your brother needs you, Mikey."

"It's not going to take that long…"

"It's time he doesn't have. And I need you! What about me?"

"What about you?"

"We're surrounded by enemies and I can't run!" I gesture feverishly at my wounded leg. Mikey's gaze passes to it and widens, but not enough. "You're just going to leave me behind? I didn't leave you behind."

Mikey's gaze hardens, sharpening on my face for the second or two it takes him to say, "Maybe you should have."

"You want to be trapped again? You want to end up like them?"

I point to the driveway where the fight is still going on. Far fewer guards stand against the rest of the horde. This is a true battle now to the end, and Crestor, I guarantee, won't live to see morning.

Mikey winces, but takes a step away from me. He looks into the woods and is lost. "I'll get the sword and the packs and catch up."

"You'll get the bottles."

"Those too."

"I hope you drown in them."

"I'll find you." His eyes flick back to look at me but they are unseeing. His body language says it all. He's itchy. Withdrawals from being drunk for the past seventy-two hours.

"I'll find you," he repeats, but he's already angled towards the woods as if he just can't wait to get out of there, and away from me.

"Don't bother." I take a step back and leaves and branches crunch softly beneath my feet.

His eyes flare as some soft semblance of understanding passes through them but like a candle snuffed, it's gone. He opens his mouth as if to say more but I don't wait to hear it. I turn away from him and sprint for the garage.

The chaos has overwhelmed the guards and I don't have any trouble making it inside the squat structure. It's metal and tin and a close gathering of trees blocks it partially from view, but wasn't enough to obscure it from me as I made my rounds earlier.

Inside out of the rain, I grab all the keys from the rack hanging on the near wall and slide into the front seat of a massive red truck. My arms are shaking with a residual rage and I fail three times to stuff the correct key into the ignition.

The truck roars when I start it, choking three times as I back out of the carport and onto the driveway. I haven't driven a car in four years and it isn't an automatic. I thank whatever sick gods lord over Population that my parents taught me to use a stick. My mom always said that it's better to learn how to drive on a manual in case you're ever abducted or need to make a quick escape. I wonder if she hadn't been a sorceress, and predicted this.

The huge vehicle climbs down a narrow dirt road that spits me out onto the highway, that dreaded abyss. On the road, there's no sign of guards or Crestor's victims. Just trees on all sides, and occasionally a pile of metal.

I turn onto the highway and find myself fighting back angry tears again. I want to cry. I want to scream. Instead, I force myself to remember the last time I was driven down a lonely highway road. It hadn't been lonely then, though.

I'd been with Kane and nothing had touched us. I'd slept. He'd told me about his family. He'd taken care of me, dressed me, carried me, put me to bed when I was unconscious. I'd been blanketed by his invincibility.

I clutch the steering wheel, imagining that I'm invincible now…

A leaden weight slams into the side of the truck and I scream and veer wildly onto the shoulder. Mud and rain splatters across the windshield, smeared by the wipers into a paste too thick to see through. Swish swish, swish swish, swish swish.

There's an ominous crunching across the roof followed by a crack. The roof craters. I flinch and there's a pounding above me followed by the distinct sound of laughter.

"Sistana," Trocker roars, "Don't you dare run from me!"

His hand punches in through the roof of the truck like a brick through paper. I slam on the gas. The truck goes airborne over a fallen tree branch blocking the road and my teeth clack together painfully when we slam back down.

I try swerving left and right, but Trocker's winning. He starts to claw his way down through the hole he's created, coming into the truck.

"Don't try to run, my queen," he shouts, spittle flying from his mouth to wet my cheek.

I try to head butt him but he reaches down, falling now, and grabs the steering wheel over my hands. The car spins, but I shove the gas harder while I pull my hands off the wheel and search frantically for my knife in the passenger's seat.

All I feel is urgency as we hydroplane around the next curve and skid along the guard rail. The horrible screech must affect Trocker more than me — hey, who knew being half deaf would be good for something? — because he lets go of the wheel long enough for me to take control.

I slam the wheel right, correcting so that we're back in the center of the road. The abruptness with which the car moves throws him to the side and his arm, which is half-in-half-out of the cab at this point snags on the jagged metal opening.

The sharp roofing tears into his flesh at the elbow, and I scream as half his arm rips free when I jerk the car back to the left. All the way down to the bone.

"You bitch!" Trocker roars, and suddenly he's gone.

He pulls back through the opening and I have to hope that I've managed to shake him…a hope that's crushed when he reappears in front of the windshield. His boots pound down onto the hood of the car and for a moment we lock eyes.

Then he grabs hold of the top of the car, using the opening he created to anchor himself there. He jumps, hangs suspended in the air, then his boots slam forward through the windshield.

Glass cuts through the world and I close my eyes, straighten my elbows and pray that I don't crash. I feel the shards against my face as a large mass of cracked glass shreds the backs of my knuckles. The windshield folds down on itself like a frozen wave, and when I rip my hands back I tear away skin.

As I fight to keep my foot on the pedal and the steering wheel straight, Trocker glides into the passenger's seat like water and the blood on his arms acts as a lubricant between us so my fists deflect off of his arms. I can't get a good punch in, or a good grip on him.

"Fuck you," I shout, slamming the heel of my hand upwards and into his nose, successfully breaking it. The act hardly phases him at all. He lunges towards me and sinks his large, square teeth into the flesh of my right arm.

I scream, hands grappling over the dash as I seek out a weapon. Finding a massive shard of glass, I grab it as hard as I can — until my palms and fingers bleed — and stab it into his back twice, quickly.

He roars away from me and laughs, bloody spittle flying from his lips. "You think I don't like the fight in you?" He sucks his lower lip into his mouth and it's wet with my blood. His eyes roll back into his skull.

"I love it, *Sistana,*" he sneers.

He throws his head back and laughs, blonde hair dyed bright pink now with blood from my arm. In the brief lull, I notice the gleam of my knife down by the gas pedal. I try not to react towards it, but he still follows my gaze. He cocks his chin towards my feet and grins. Blood cases each of his teeth. It's mine and Kane's too, and Trocker has no right to it.

"Go ahead," he says. "Take it. You are at a disadvantage, regardless. We can even pull over if you'd like."

I snatch the knife from the ground and clasp it in my right hand, switching to a backwards grip while my other hand holds the steering wheel steady. I don't decelerate. I don't pull over.

"Bring it on, asshole."

We grapple in the front seat of the cab wildly until I gain the upper hand. He's reckless. More and more crazed with each drop of my blood he spills. I've got tears in my clothing and blood streaming from multiple wounds in my arms at this point.

My jacket hangs around my shoulders in tatters, and with each strike, he continues to rip into it, devolving from Other to animal, his most primal functions taking control.

Every time he comes at me, I slash his face, chest, shoulders, arms and hands. His black tee shirt gapes in the center to reveal his strong stomach covered in dozens of shallow grooves.

Bracing his arms against the far side of the cab, he exhales deeply. "You can't keep this up forever." He smiles in spite of the gashes covering his forehead, neck and cheeks, "Didn't anyone ever tell you to keep your eyes on the road?"

He comes at me and I just manage to brace my right arm against his bulging, veined neck, successfully keeping him off. But as my eyes pan out to the road, this becomes a pebble-sized problem, buried beneath the mattress of a much larger problem.

Spikes.

I don't know what they're called, but I've seen them before. They were more common in the beginning when people had cars that other people wanted. Since cars were abandoned, so were these.

Until now.

Across the road, rusted metal spikes unfurl, like a roll of red carpet. I slam my foot onto the brake, but there's no avoiding them. The chain spikes catch the front tires and as the back end of the truck fishtails violently, the momentum is too much. We go flying.

Trocker's teeth slam into my bicep, breaking my arm through to the bone. I don't think he even meant to do it, funnily enough, but we're both thrown up and into the roof of the cab, the jagged opening scraping every bit of my jacket and head it can.

The sheet of folded windshield hits me square in the chest. The airbags explode, punching me in the face, but shred themselves open against shards of glass. A gust of curls float around me and I smell concrete after a cool spring rain.

The truck hits the ground.

Total obliteration.

Chapter Nine

Images hit me, tossed haphazardly against the insides of my eyelids. Paint splashed against a wall. A black hole in reverse.

Blood rushes to my head, making it pound, and for a moment I hear nothing but that thick sloshing sound. I relish that nothingness, because in the next instant agony takes me into its arms.

I cough and pain ripples up my sternum. My eyelids peel apart and gobs of blood dripping onto the roof of the truck from my suspended hands. Suspended? How? I didn't put my seatbelt on…but the glass windshield is wedged across my lap. I'm upside down.

The pounding in my head gets louder and more forceful. Somewhere nearby I hear a scrape, scrape, scraping sound that matches the tattoo of my pulse.

A body drags itself through the collapsed passenger-side window, coming in? Leaving? I can't tell. I'm totally disoriented. Smears of blood decorate white flesh and I think then of the fawn.

It hadn't been my first kill, but it had been the one that haunted me the most. It and I, starving in the forest together. My hand outstretched, it hadn't seen the knife. A swift singing across its throat and blood splashed across my hands. Its eyes had turned up to me in unveiled terror, and then all at once, peace.

It looked at me and was grateful, and in that instant, I envied it.

Scrape, scrape, *scrape.* A face turns up to me and I look back at it without recognition for the first moment. Then I register the hunger in his eyes. My hand fumbles for the glass locked around my hips, but it doesn't obey the commands I give it. The glass I used to stab Trocker cut too deep and now the muscles are mostly severed. Crap.

"Hello there, princess," he gasps.

His body has taken a beating from the crash and his tone betrays both desire and pain. But that isn't the sound that frightens me the most. There's another sound, just beneath his voice, which carries like the rush of a fierce wind or a sea at storm. And that low, dangerous chant carries with it promises of thunder. Of war.

Clapping. Low, malicious laughter. My heart pounds brutally as I start to scramble.

I smell smoke and fire and can hear the tires screaming as they spin even faster now without the concrete beneath them. The gas pedal has jammed. My bloody fingers slip over the windshield, pushing at it.

Trocker, the helpful ass hole that he is, sees my dilemma, grabs the windshield and wrenches it back. I drop into his outstretched hands.

Pain lights in my neck as I land at an awkward angle. Trocker shouts in excitement and then again in anger when I kick him in the face and drag myself out of the shattered driver's side window, glass cutting into my stomach.

Behind me, his fingers slip over my bloodied legs. His nails catch my skin, but I don't care at all about him.

Outside, the air smells like gasoline and smoke. I stand, left knee buckling as I take my first step. There's a gentle buzz floating through my head and my neck hurts like hell, but I don't feel any of my other injuries. Not with my heart pounding like it is. Hard and frighteningly fast.

I feel the strangest surge throughout my whole body as if there's another pulse there, pounding alongside my own. *Kane?* But for the first time since he left me a day ago — or has it been an eternity? — I really hope he isn't there and that he hasn't come back. *Look away, baby. Don't watch from here.*

Because this won't end well for me.

I'm going to die like all things die on the road. Painfully.

Because these guys don't know that I won't give up. I'll die fighting. Or I guess I should say that I'll fight until it kills me.

They won't take me alive.

They have us surrounded, looking like something straight out of a nightmare. In fact, I think I've had this nightmare before. It was the same one I had every day after Matt and Aiden were killed and Becks, Ashlyn and I had to fight the rest of the world alone.

Three women against horrors untold.

The men surrounding me now aren't scavengers, alien,s or even a twisted colony like the Hive. These sixty or so men are pure predators who've taken advantage of disorder and chaos and thrived. The worst of their kind. *My kind.* I hear Trocker fumbling around in the cab of the truck and realize that I need him if either of us are going to survive.

"Trocker," I rasp. "Get out of the fucking truck and I'll give you what you want."

My eyes flit from man-to-man while smoke from the truck wafts lazily on the breeze. The men are dressed in dark leather and wood, black jean and metal. Skulls sit stacked atop most heads — decoration or trophies? — and I can tell by the larger size and high-set cheekbones that some of the skulls belong to the Others, though most are human. I do a second sweep.

Half of the guys hold weapons visibly, though I guess more than that are armed. A few guns, lots of knives, about a dozen machetes, one scythe. My odds are dwindling. *Look away, baby. Don't watch me die.*

One guy at the edge of the ring is holding a torch, but I'm distracted by the man standing just behind him. On top of his shaved head he wears two smooth skulls stacked one on top of the other. Both are huge, both are alien.

He stares harder than his peers and without smiling and, caught in the haze of the torchlight, I catch the gleam of his quiet, troubling eyes that are far too light for his brown skin. His skin is ash brown, lighter than mine — but those eyes.

They're arresting, those eyes. They're the eyes of someone who died a long time ago.

Hollow through and through.

Trocker claims my attention when he rolls, grunting, out of the truck and lands on his back in front of the cab. He staggers drunkenly to his feet and, seeing our new friends, roars, "She's mine." When he speaks, he sounds just as drunk as Mikey did.

He shoves out his arm, hand extended in a claw, while the wounded one hangs limply from the stump of his shoulder. The men don't seem impressed and move forward until they're standing shoulder-to-shoulder.

Trocker snarls around at all of them while I edge to the right, propelled by the sweet scent of gasoline. My injured hand clenches around itself and I will it to work for me just for a few more minutes.

One of the scrawnier men peels apart from the crowd. His torso is bare, but he still wears his many scars proudly. He's got a human head stacked on top of his own and a baseball bat studded in outward-facing nails slung carelessly over his shoulder.

"Every man has the right to a fair fight to decide if he should live, die, or join us. Since we're generous men, we even allow them to choose their opponent. Unfortunately, I don't see any men here."

Light laughter picks up as the man looks over his shoulder towards another. This one is standing just outside of the circle — a spectator to the sport that will ensue. The massacre. And as the smoke clears between us, my breath jerks in my lungs.

Kane?

My heart beats faster. He's Kane, but not.

With black hair and tan skin, he could've been Kane's doppelgänger. He has the same broad shoulders and imposing frame Kane does. The same blood red lips. The same superman curl, even.

The differences lie in the gestures, the aura. This male carries confidence, like Kane does, but it's bleak and damning and desperate and makes me want to curl up on the ground in the fetal position and hide from the world. It makes me want to give up and give in. It makes me want to beg.

He's staring at Trocker with an intensity that makes me feel bad for the alien who was just trying to kill me. *This doesn't end well.* But I get the feeling that it might end worse for Trocker than for me.

I'll take it.

The Kane lookalike nods once and the scrawny guy raises his bat high. "So come on, then, gentlemen," he shouts, stealing impish glances around at his fellow monsters, "What are you waiting for?"

That rumbling chant begins again as every single man standing around us moves forward in sync and I realize that I can't wait any longer for Trocker to do something.

I make a break for the man carrying the torch and I reach him before anyone else reaches me. I use my full bodyweight to knock the guy to the ground where we grapple over the wooden handle.

I kick him in the groin and as he buckles, I snatch up the torch, run back to the truck and toss it into the wetness that smells like gas.

It hits the ground, sizzling in earnest. Bright orange fire licks at the concrete, tearing towards the truck's gas tank. Men start shouting and backing away from me as the fire grows and swells. A flare of sparks shoots up into the sky — I can feel its heat — but as quickly as it appears, cold fills its place.

The man with the alien skulls and empty eyes rushes forward while the others run back, takes off his jacket and throws his jacket and throws it over the encroaching flames, turning them to ash.

In just a tattered vest made of black jean, he looks right at me, and I fall into the void of one man's lonely eyes as several other men drag me off the road and into the woods.

We don't go far, and there's no camp where they drop me. There's just a dirt clearing studded by a single, strong tree that the men are working to ring in stones and big sticks.

The two men at each of my arms drop me in the center of the ring and tie Trocker up to the tree upside down. They coil rope around his feet and it takes eight or nine of them to successfully loop the rope over the largest tree bough and hoist him up, up, up. He kills two of their guys in the process, but they don't seem to care. The ones still alive just loot the corpses of the ones that are dead and use the bodies to form the perimeter of this circle. This arena.

This crucible.

While Trocker thrashes, his blonde and stained hair trailing over the soft, squishy ground, several of the men step forward into the ring. I brace myself to get strung up or attacked, but they don't touch me.

Instead, they pull daggers from their pockets and throw them down into the soft earth a few paces away from where I'm kneeling.

"Is that it? No more takers?" one of them shouts as he throws down his knife. He laughs then, kicking up dirt so that it showers over me.

"Wait for the others," an older man rasps — one of the oldest in the group, though he can't be more than forty. "I'm sure Jack will want a say."

Silence descends while the guys all wait restlessly at the edge of the circle. I don't try to run. At least not yet. I wouldn't make it far. *I'm not* going *to make it far.* I cringe at the thought and grit my teeth.

Now that I've stopped moving, my adrenaline is coming down and I'm beginning to feel my injuries with clarity. My whole body has been worked over with talons and teeth. Looking down, I see that my period blood has seeped through the crotch of my pants and I grin down at it, shaking my head slowly. The problems of my morning are irrelevant at this stage, aren't they?

"Where's the bucket?" The Kane who isn't Kane at all says, appearing at the circle's edge.

A few men peel apart from the others and drag a large plastic bucket underneath Trocker's head. One of them slits Trocker's throat, the act so fast and so impartial it shocks me in a way I thought nothing could anymore.

Are these things here even human? Or are they less human than the aliens are? They're less human than Kane is, that's for sure.

He's only ten feet away and though I should be used to the smell of their blood, I'm not. It smells like eggs and shit and it's black as it weeps over Trocker's face, like tears cried in reverse.

The droplets wind through his hair before spattering against the bottom of the pot beneath him, sounding like rain. I watch as Trocker chokes on his own blood, dying for a few moments until he's resurrected. Each time he blinks back to life, the same man with that skinny, slender blade reopens his wound, and each time he dies he meets my gaze.

I wince as bile pitches in my stomach and crawls up the back of my throat because he doesn't look like the fawn. There's no peace here. There's only rage and pain.

Another dagger hits the packed earth to my left and I look up at Hollow Eyes. He stands near to me now and is watching me with his head cocked slightly to the right.

Two of the other men who threw their daggers down before come to retrieve their weapons. At this, the Kane lookalike laughs, "So afraid of little Diego, are you?"

He steps into the circle and pulls a blade from his own belt. "Maurice. Come here," he says.

The man who I stole the torch from blubbers something unintelligible and drops to his knees. He pulls a gun out of his back pocket and raises it to his temple. He looks up at the Kane-not-Kane being and fires without hesitating.

I jump, my stomach pitching, my heart pounding. Cold sweat covers every inch of me. What is *wrong* with these people? What is wrong here?

Hollow Eyes watches the dead man drop forward onto his stomach without flinching. Two others near him do the same they did to the others. They steal the weapons off his person, then shove his body out of the arena.

"This girl bested Maurice already in a contest for that torch. It's only thanks to Diego here, that we didn't lose half our numbers."

Kane-not-Kane comes up to Hollow Eyes and places his hand on the back of his neck. He massages him in a way a father might a kid. Or maybe it's *weirder* than that. Maybe it's the way lovers might hold one another. I remember Kane in the woods holding onto the back of my neck like that.

Diego doesn't move though, doesn't lean into the touch. His eyelids don't flutter. He doesn't react at all except for the slight tick in the corner of his jaw. *Wrong.* There's something altogether vile happening here and now and between these monsters.

"You all can take back your daggers now. There will be no contest for this one. I think she's earned her right to a fight. Maybe she'll be a good replacement for Maurice, depending on how she holds up."

Kane-not-Kane moves away from Diego and goes to Trocker. He crouches down next to the bucket and dips his fingers inside. As he stands, he licks them clean and smiles. His eyes flick to me.

"So. Are you ready to fight?"

I nod. "What do I get if I win?"

He laughs and when he does, several of the other men in his group laugh with him. "Your life."

"You've got the advantage. You've got their blood in your system. I should get something else if I win."

He grins at me in a way that shows all his teeth and he suddenly looks nothing like Kane at all. He looks like a vulture. "You have their blood in your system, too. Or did you think I wouldn't notice the way your wounds are healing all on their own?"

He glances down at my hands and arms, the cut on my leg. He's right. The skin in all these places is nearly meshed together. Still red and enflamed and covered with crusted blood, but I have very few open wounds left at this stage. And I should. I shouldn't be walking. Hell, I probably shouldn't be breathing.

But I am. And I'm not going to stop anytime soon.

I don't answer but fake Kane still laughs. He steps forward towards Diego's dagger still embedded in the soil. Though the others came to collect theirs, his was the last one left. He still hasn't moved and when Kane comes towards me, he flinches, like he'll do something.

"Move, Diego. This one is mine. You'll have another chance to fight to get your dick wet soon enough." He kicks Diego's knife free of the dirt.

Diego doesn't retaliate. His expression remains flat as he bends down and wraps his fingers around his dagger's ornately engraved hilt. He stalks to the ring of men, standing stiffly at the inner wall, watching in a way that I find distracting — and I can't afford to be distracted. Not as Fake Kane watches me with his head cocked to one side, bright jade eyes darkening.

The expression is familiar. Appraising. Interested. I see him working things out in his head like a puzzle he can't quite solve. And then all at once he smiles and shrugs out of his coat.

As his faded leather jacket hits the ground with a soft thud, he says, "I can't let you fight one of my men. That'd be unfair, what with their blood in your system and all," he says, tone mocking, "I'll let you fight me, though and if you can beat me." He whistles and it's a sharp, eerie sound. "If you beat me, I'll let you walk out of here in one piece.

I'll give you a car and a gun. You can even take your blood bank with you."

That's a good deal. Too good a deal.

But I can take him. I'm sure of it.

"Deal," I tell him and he beams.

"You know, I almost hope you survive this."

Fake Kane moves across the circle, putting a not-yet-dead Trocker at his back while I amble up onto my feet. There's not much hope for a weapon here, but I still take note of the rocks demarcating the outer ring of this battlefield and the few thick sticks lying within it.

The men standing on the other side of those rocks don't say a word, but I can see items being exchanged between hands. It's not hard to guess what they're doing. They're betting. To see if I'll win? Or to see how long I'll last?

"I admire your gusto, little lady," Fake Kane says. He stretches out his arms. "What's your name?"

I don't want to tell him, but something is aroused in me by the sight of his nearly familiar face. "Abel." My fingers curl around my healing palm.

"Nice to meet you, Abel. I'm Jack."

"I always liked that name."

He smiles in a way that fills me with heat and adrenaline. My heart pounds like a fist on the other side of my sternum and for just a second, the flicker of a second beat blazes through me. *Kane, it's only one-on-one,* I'd tell him if I could. *I might just survive this.*

Jack takes a step in my direction and drawls, "Well, aren't you a sweetheart?" His voice holds a distinctly southern lilt, which frightens me. It tells me that this gang has traveled far — that *he* has — and that he's survived everything Population has thrown at him.

"Not really. Now are you going to attack or should I?"

He barks out a laugh and runs his hands back through his oil-slick hair. "Which do you prefer?"

"You first," I say with a pause.

He bats his thick eyelashes at me and nods. "Alright then. But remember what you asked for."

He comes at me like a goddamn hurricane, moving with a violent grace I can't match. No human moves like this, and for a second I wonder if he wasn't lying before. I'd think he was an alien if there wasn't something so human about him. So awful.

He punches without restraint and though the first strike I manage to duck, the second nails me in the cheek and everything under my skin breaks.

I don't give into the pain but whirl around and nail him in the gut with my heel. He flies back and I advance on him, but when I kick at him a second time, he grabs my ankle and hurls me through the air.

I hit the ground hard, along the outskirts of the circle. My head hit a rock and everything fades in and out for a second while my lungs fight for air.

I grab the bloody stone that wounded me and when he comes up behind me and grabs me by the hair, I spin and crush his nose with it, then bound back up — stagger drunkenly onto my feet — and into the center of the circle.

As we approach one another, he laughs and keeps laughing as he reaches up and feels his completely broken nose. Blood pours down his face and it's both red and black at the same time, swirled all together.

"Brilliant, Abel! That's wonderful." He rubs his hands together and turns to face me fully. He bangs on his chest. "Again!" he roars, "Again!"

We fight for hours. For days. Until I'm slowing down and he's still in top shape. I still have the rock in my hand

and when I swipe it for his cheek again, he grabs my wrist and breaks it.

I scream as he kicks in my knee and he curses as I punch him with my good hand in the dick. He knees me in the cheek and I fall back.

It's getting harder to move. Harder to fight. Harder not to give up. Rule number one. The only rule. *Not even when you're dying, Abel,* I remind myself.

What about when I'm dead?

No. Not even when I'm dead.

I feel the ground around me for a stick and when he comes and grabs the front of my shirt, I stab. I catch him in the eye, but he shoves my hand out of the way while blood drips down his cheek and grins. He lowers himself onto my body, straddling my waist and as he pins both my hands together with one of his, he pushes my hair back out of my face and speaks to me very gently.

"You did good, girl."

And then he draws his arm back and punches me again and again and again.

Shadows and light. There's no pain at all though. Just the pressure of a heartbeat that doesn't belong to me because mine might have stopped beating a few minutes ago.

I can feel its urgency, and its desire to communicate, but I can't hear the words. All I can see is Kane in the bathtub, my foot trapped in his. I hold onto that image and that memory and I live in it for a while, until the darkness parts and I become aware in ways that I wish I didn't have to be.

Now, I'm aware of me.

"Come on, sweet cheeks." Fingers grab my face and tilt my head up. I feel some small semblance of life return to me as air jerks back into my lungs in one abrupt punch.

Jack laughs. "And the angel lives! God really does see you out of the corner of his eye, doesn't he?"

The blood in my mouth is sulfuric, and I know it's the only reason I'm still breathing. Struggling to blink my eyes open, I see dry ground but am unable to reach for it. My wrists are being held in place by ruthless hands, so that my arms are spread wide.

My bare knees are pressed to the soft and icy soil and, against that chill, I recognize that I'm naked and Jack's hands are covering my rib cage and lower back. I shudder, teeth chattering as a panic washes over me, an occultation to block out everything else.

"Don't worry, sweetheart. I don't want what's between your legs." I'd ask him what he does want then, but my tongue is swollen in my slack mouth and I can't feel my lips.

"I want you to watch and see what happens to Others out here when they come into my world." He strokes my hair lovingly. "They think they're so much stronger than I am, but they don't know and you don't know, either. I'm king of Population, sweetie."

He slaps my bare ass, stands and begins shouting orders to his men. My head lolls on my neck and blood pours out of my mouth onto my chest.

"Now I want you two to hold her there and make sure she's got the right kind of view for this."

They lean me back a little so my face tilts up and my eyes tilt open. "The rest of you can start passing the bucket around. A cup for every man except Diego. You know how he never liked drinking with us," he speaks in mock hurt like the whole world is just some big joke to him.

"And you. I want you to keep those pretty blue eyes open, darling. You know, it's those eyes that really do it. You look like you could be Diego's sister, don't you?"

He's absolutely right. And maybe that's why Diego speaks to me on some primal level. He looks like Aiden, resurrected, if Aiden had fallen into the clutches of this madman and lost all the humanity he ever had.

Sadness pulls through me while the pulsing of a heart that isn't mine surges up into my throat with force, willing me to do something that I just don't think I can anymore.

It wants me to live.

"Abel, I know you lost the fight, but I like your spirit, so I'll make you another deal. If you manage to keep your little emotions under control while I kill your alien friend over here, then I'll kill you quick after.

"If you don't then, it'll be slow. Okay?" He says cheerily.

I'd nod if I could, but I can't so I don't.

Smoke chokes my throat and I cough while behind me Jack says, "That counts as a reaction, sweetie. I'll give you this one, but not anymore than that."

I try to hold the jerking of my lungs as suddenly heat bursts against my chest. I open my eyes and see sparks in violent shades of orange, catching the smaller sticks and twigs stacked beneath Trocker's head. Thick, putrid smoke billows as a cloud between us and I have to stop taking in air altogether in order not to cough or choke on the smell.

Trocker was out, but now he's awake again and the hole in his throat sealed itself closed, which is a shame. That would have been a better way for things to end for him.

He starts to thrash, but the fire's already caught his hair and is chewing its way towards his face. I can't watch but the second I look away heat flashes between my shoulder blades. I've never felt anything like it. An incendiary spark, followed by a deep, bone kind of ache.

The sound of the whip striking air is the only indication I have of what just took place. "Don't look away now, honey. You hear?"

I struggle to breathe. My eyes sting. Trocker's eyes are melting in his skull. They're watching me.

I can't do this.

The smell.

The way his melted eyes are puffing up and exploding. The way his skin is charing in sections and falling off in chunks, then mending itself anew only to repeat the process.

It's too much.

My stomach is in my throat and I vomit all over myself while Trocker drips to the ground like candle wax. The lash comes for me again and again and when it doesn't come a third time, I realize that Jack is a special kind of person. He wields hope as a weapon. He's successfully weaponized human emotion. I know in that moment that if he offered me to join his gang or continue on the path I'm on, I'd jump the tracks, throw myself at his feet and beg to enlist.

I can't do this.

And then Trocker's head falls from its perch and bounces across the soft ground, coming to rest at my knees. My throat constricts again. More vomit rushes up into my mouth and I don't swallow it. I physically can't.

I close my eyes and I ready myself for this to end.

The whip comes down and I don't feel it anymore. I just hear the fluttery sound it makes every time it's drawn back.

And as my eyes close, I recognize that I didn't give up on the rule book. I fought as hard as I could. But in a fight, not everybody can win.

Sometimes when you fight, you lose.

Chapter Ten

This can't possibly be heaven.

It tastes like burnt rubber and smells like fire. My body is still being held up, but I'm being jerked all around now as the ones holding me step and shuffle from side to side.

People are shouting and they sound a little bit panicked. Crackling fire. Heat. Boots hitting the ground. Thunder.

There's pained gurgles from nearby and I'm falling forward. My chest hits the ground at the same time another body does and when I blink my eyes open I can see one of the gang members lying inches away from my face, his black eyes bright and dead and open.

He's got a cut across his throat and a moment later, there's another thud and another body falls, an arm hitting my back and making everything erupt in me. The pain is so surreal, I pass out.

It doesn't last.

It never lasts.

The heart in my chest isn't mine, but it's exploding with power and the hands on my body aren't mine, but they're hard and lifting me upright.

A jacket comes over my wounds and then arms circle my body. I'm being carried.

Kane?

But when I blink, I'm caught by Diego's hollow eyes looking down at me. He doesn't speak, but I can feel him running. He's carrying me somewhere and I don't know where, but anywhere is fine so long as it's away from Jack.

The thought of him brings tears to my eyes. They wet my cheeks. I've never known suffering like that. Suffering built on the stilts of escape, like there's some way I could have changed my own fate. But I failed Jack. I failed him, so he did what he had to do…the only thing he promised me.

The sounds of screaming become more distant, and when my head swivels on my neck, I see trees.

"What the fuck are you doing!" A voice shouts from somewhere close. "That's Jack's!"

That. No, I'm not a person anymore am I? The things that make a human human, I no longer possess. I'm just waiting, really. Stuck here in limbo, that blood-embellished purgatory, hoping that when I next blink, I'll open my eyes and see Becks.

No. I think, but the thought isn't mine at all. It's coming from somewhere else.

Diego doesn't answer and he doesn't stop. He keeps walking forward, towards the trees, until the man shouts again. Then he stops.

He looks down at my face as he sets me down in the tall grasses. They're scratchy and hot in places I need them to be soft and cool. I cry out, tears coming harder now, and when he pulls away, I reach for him.

I take his hand and hold onto it. It's the only lifeline I've got.

But he untangles his fingers from my fingers and takes a couple steps away from me. I can still see him as he fights. He moves almost as fast as Jack as he he blocks his attacker's first strike with his wrist. With that same arm, stabs into the side of the man's neck. Diego kicks the man in the gut and the corpse flies over the tall grass, disappearing beneath it.

A soft thud pulls my gaze to the right and I look to see a dagger shooting up out of the ground. The hilt is intricately carved sterling silver, poorly polished, studded with three jade beads. I wonder what this means, and wish I could ask, but Diego just turns and walks away from me, shoulders back, face proud, eyes haunted and haunting.

He's going to die.

He's going to die for *me*.

Emotion jerks in my chest, making me wonder if I remind him of a forgotten sister that the world took and, if not, why else he's doing this. He killed his own for me already three times tonight. Maybe more. And now he's giving me his knife. Somehow, my arm manages to move just enough to curl around it.

I bring it to my chest and close my eyes. For a moment, I fade from this world into one of utter darkness. I fade and come back, then fade again. The finale is near, and I would have given myself up to it completely had I not felt a sudden fire burning where my heart was supposed to be and a distant voice whispering my name. *Abel…Abel…*

"Abel!" My eyes flutter open. Dense tufts of smoke billow up into the world. So much smoke. So much fire. I can hear huge trees burning and breaking in the distance. Above me, the tall grasses sway.

"Abel, where are you? I can smell you, but I can't find you. Say something for fuck's sake!"

The thrashing is closer now. I can't draw its attention anymore than I'm doing. I don't actually want to. I don't want to see Mikey now. I just want to sleep…

"Abel."

It's the way he says my name that makes my eyes open just long enough to see him. His face blots out the sky above me. His beard is burned in parts now and I'd smile if I could. I still have no idea what Kane's brother looks like underneath all that hair, and I've been traveling with him for over a week.

Until he abandoned me.

"Abel." There it is again. Hoarse and cracked, it makes me wonder what he sees. What do I look like now? Like a Mister Potatohead with all the parts in the wrong places? Probably.

His hands are reaching for me, but he doesn't touch me. He doesn't dare.

"Oh God, oh God, oh God. Jesus fucking Christ! Fuck, Abel. Abel, please…please…"

His panic jacks up my heart rate and my lungs contract until I can't get any more air. Oh no. Is this it? Or is this just wishful thinking? The blaze in my chest pulls my focus away from death. How annoying.

"Come on, Abel. I've got to get you out of here," he croaks. There are tears on his face. "You don't…are you… you're going to make it," he says, dropping to his knees.

He pushes the grass out of his way with his arms. He's still missing his shirt, but I can see that he has no new wounds on him, and those he received earlier are mostly healed. He's wearing his backpack and he's got Kane's blade tucked into his belt loops. It's stained in red.

He reaches around my body but I scream bloody freaking murder at the pain. "What…what is it?"

I just writhe. I don't have enough clarity to answer. I cringe away from his hands when he reaches for my body again. He hesitates, then lifts up just a little on one shoulder. He peels Diego's jacket away from me and the sight of his face when he sees…

Two little droplets of water streak in parallel down his either cheek.

"I did this." He breathes heavily, as if he's in a flat-out run.

"I did this." His gaze pins mine.

"I did this."

And then. "Abel, stay with me."

As he tips me into his grip with as much care as he can, I focus on the sight of the trees and the grey above them. I remember the bathtub and stay there.

Mikey's panting is jarring and heavy. His beard drips blood and his cheeks are flushed, probably because of the booze. I hope he enjoyed it.

"Abel, say something." Mikey lurches and I hear splashing just before he tells me that something is going to be cold. "This might hurt."

That makes me laugh, or would have if I could talk.

"Hold on, Abel. And hold your breath." He lowers my whole body rapidly and ice cold water hits my back, then every other inch of me. I gasp, against Mikey's instruction, and suck in a breath of near-frozen water. The shock of it forces my conscious mind to retreat.

I burrow into myself, fighting past the pain to revisit the beating pulse thrumming through me. The bathtub. I sigh as Kane smiles at me, beckoning me into his light and his heat.

Chapter Eleven

Time passes. I'm not sure how much. Hours? Days? I'm cold. Then warm. Then freezing. Is this what death feels like? The motion beneath me suggests I'm in a car, though at another point I wake to find myself in some spacious building with white walls and floors made of cracked tile. It's in this building that Mikey locks me in a room while outside I hear the familiar sounds of fighting, of dying. Mikey roars, and as the door flies open, he fills its width. With blood slashed across his chest, he's got a head in one fist. He tosses it aside as he comes to me and takes my hand while my head rolls to the side. I see a sign in navy, hanging askew. The sign reads: Harborview.

"Abel, no!" He's shouting again, "Don't you fucking dare."

That incessant heartbeat within me is pounding triple time, but it's all that I feel, even as Mikey stuffs needles into my elbows. I pass out. I wake. I feel heat. I feel fever. I feel nothing. Movement. Silence. Calm. Crashing. Warmth. Hands touching my hairline, tracing the patterns my damp curls make. I'm sweating all over.

“I’m sorry,” he says, and though I’m not asleep, I pretend that I am. A silence wraps around me and is absolute. I give up and dive in.

I’m swimming somewhere in the darkness, towards an unknown surface. There’s a shadow obscuring most of my thoughts, like a thin veil pulled over my consciousness. The harder I fight against it, the more tangled I become in the threads.

A voice calls my name. A voice that my whole body, and not just my mind, remembers. It’s accompanied by a growing warmth in my middle that pulses in time with a slow, patient heart. Not my heart to be sure, but another tempo. Its rhythm is fierce and wills me awake, and as I wake, it fades into nothing. Like it hadn’t been there at all.

My eyelids are sticky, as if cemented shut. Muted light filters through curtains against the far wall, silhouetting Mikey in darkness.

He kneels before me, head bowed, wearing only beat up, army green cargo pants. He’s knuckle down on the hardwood, breathing loud.

“I offer you myhr,” he says, presumably to me because there’s no one else there.

I’m on my stomach and with a grunt, I register the objects within reach of my right hand. A gun, a baton, a rock, Diego’s silver dagger.

The bandages around my right palm make it hard to move, as do the drugs coursing through my system. I don’t feel. The whole world seems light years away.

There’s a fire in the hearth to my left that keeps me warm, but otherwise I’m naked, covered in flannel up to the waist. The material beneath me is surprisingly soft, though I can’t tell what color it is. Actually, I can’t see anything out of my right eye at all and when I try to blink, a strange numbness blankets me.

The right side of my face, including my eye, is entirely swollen shut while the left is only mostly swollen. I don't have much depth perception, and when I reach out towards Mikey, I'm surprised to find that he's close enough to touch.

I start to cry. I don't know where it comes from, but it comes.

Mikey moans like he's hurt. He says, "Please, Abel. Choose your weapon. You have to give me myhr. You have to take it. It'll make us both feel better."

I don't know what he means and moan down into the flannel sheets.

"Abel, please."

"You left me," I whisper.

I don't acknowledge that we might *both* be dead now if he hadn't. All I know is that I feel hurt in ways that has nothing to do with my swollen face or my back, which is one exposed wound. I'm not healing like I was. That thought frightens me since blood bonds can only be broken through death and I'm still breathing.

Mikey takes the gun, presses it to my fingers and holds my hand up to his chest. "Shoot."

I do.

My arm shakes as the bullet fires from the tip of the gun, missing Mikey altogether and puncturing the drywall a dozen feet behind him. He doesn't so much as flinch, just repositions my hands around his and moves the gun back to his chest.

"Again," he says, but I've already clicked back the hammer. I hit him in the right shoulder, though I'd been aiming for his heart.

The force of the blow makes my whole body quiver and slices of a tender pain brush across my back. I drop the gun while Mikey straightens, showing no signs of pain. The only action he takes is to scoop a handful of white powder from the bowl to his left and smear it over the wound.

"Thank you," he whispers. "Now please, go back to sleep."

"Where are we?"

Mikey hesitates before answering. "Seattle."

"How far from Kane?" My mouth is gooey with saliva. I can taste fever on my tongue.

"Don't worry about that now…"

"How far?"

Mikey sets the bowl of white powder aside and collapses back onto his ass. Crossing his ankles, he drapes his elbows over his knees.

"Just over a mile," he sighs.

"We need to go. Get to him. We need to…"

I make an effort to slide my palms beneath my shoulders and push the ground away, but I can't flatten my right hand and my left is trapped in a makeshift splint made of wood and gauze, elastic bandages and adhesive tape.

Mikey shifts towards me and draws a set of blankets up over my legs. It's only then that I realize he's doctored all of my wounds and draped towels around my hips.

"You can't move."

"I have to." I lash out with my right hand and, unable to control its trajectory, I knock over the bowl of white powder. Mikey hisses and quickly lifts my hand away from it.

He cleans the mess and speaks in low, gentle tones. "You shouldn't touch that. It's salt." He laughs through his nostrils, though his face is still drawn. "You know why the word for Seattle is the same in English as it is in Heztoichen?"

The question is rhetorical and I don't respond. I just watch Mikey pull a black duffel bag to his side and shuffle through it until he finds the syringe he was looking for.

"It's a word in our language with meaning. It means salt. Ironic, actually, considering that salt is one of the few things that slows our healing abilities. The only thing that creates scars. Figures she'd have set up her torture chambers here in Seattle. The salt land."

I twitch when he changes the dressings on my back as small flares of pain light up across my skin. He presses a needle to my elbow and pushes the plunger, sending a clear liquid running through my veins.

"Don't let me sleep too long. We need to get Kane," I whisper, "I can feel him again."

"I know. You said so last night. When I was about to give you my blood. I should have," he whispers, combing his fingers back through my hair in a way that's loving and welcome.

"But I was selfish and didn't think I'd be able to find Kane without you. I still don't. Please, forgive me."

I close my eyes, feigning a sleep that only comes for me a few minutes later.

Chapter Twelve

I'm standing, though I'm not sure how. The clothes irritate my wounds even though Mikey layered bandages over my skin so thick, my back hunches beneath my coat like a gargoyle's. It smells like mold and lint when I don it and I want to know where Mikey found it, but not enough to want to speak to him. He barely meets my gaze as he tells me that he wants me to rest for another night, and when I look up, he looks down quickly.

"Let's go," I say in a strangled pitch that's hardly recognizable. Even to me.

Mikey opens his mouth but doesn't defy my request. Instead he takes a peek out of the half-boarded-up windows, careful not to flutter the blinds. Just before he pulls a shirt over his head, he crushes more salt into the bullet wound and slaps a bandage over his shoulder. I want to ask him if that's really necessary, but when I next blink, the world is blurred.

He asks me if I'm alright. Blinking, I nod, and when I next open my eyes he's pulling a tattered flannel around his shoulders and the entire world disintegrates around me. My feet slip out from under me and Mikey catches me as I fall.

He curses. "Are you okay?" My face is pressed against his shoulder and I can't lift my neck. He's so warm and I'm so tired. "Abel, please rest."

"Mikey," I moan as the black and blue world returns to living color.

"Yes?"

"Put me down."

Setting me on my feet, he seems as averse to touching me as I am to being touched. We don't speak as we pack up our stuff and move out of the darkness of the apartment and into the grey.

The complex is only two stories. Modern with exposed brick walls and stainless steel appliances, it was probably full of successful young professionals before the Fall.

I take the stairs slowly and carry nothing. Mikey has the sword tucked into his belt and an overfull pack strapped across his back, and when he jumps down to the ground floor landing, glass bottles clink delicately against one another.

He winces and opens his mouth, as if to explain, but I don't comment. I don't care. I don't know why I ever cared in the first place.

The glass in the apartment building door is shattered, so I step through the opening carefully out onto the sidewalk. Strangely, I feel heat, like the sun is shining, and when I look up I have to squint. They grey is thinning, or at least, thinner than it had been.

"What is it? What's wrong?" Mikey's face is severe as he reaches towards me.

I flinch back. "What?"

"You're crying."

"I am?" I touch my cheeks with my bandaged right hand, and on my fingertips, wetness gleams. "Oh. I don't know. Maybe the drugs."

Mikey nods, curling his fingers around his outstretched palm before lowering it. "Are you sure?"

"Yeah. It's nothing." I wipe my face with the makeshift splint on my hand, fabricated from two pieces of wood, cotton and gauze. I take a step forward, stumbling off of the stoop and catch Mikey's sleeve. He tries to encourage me to take a seat, but I say, "Why isn't Kane's blood working anymore?"

Mikey cringes as he speaks. "You lost too much of it."

I nod, glad that that's the answer and that it's not something else. "Keep going."

We walk down a hill, the street marked Pine. I don't expect to survive long enough to reach downtown — we've got no cover, are in the center of a huge city, and the only weapons we have on us are a dagger and a sword.

In low tones, Mikey explains that he had to pass a border guard in order to get into the city. Notare Elise had the whole place blocked off. According to Mikey, the only reason we were able to get in was because a huge motorcade was exiting, leaving behind gaps in security.

Carrying me, he was somehow able to slip in undetected, and shortly thereafter, find the hospital. There, Mikey surprised a small group of Heztoichen guards, killing them and stealing the medical supplies they'd been guarding. With every step Mikey takes, the vials of painkillers and antibiotic rattle in his pack against other, larger glass bottles.

I move so slowly it takes us almost an hour to cover two miles. According to the internal map branded into my mind from before, it's nearly a straight shot. Thank the lord.

We move down Pine, pass a squat, red brick building and signs for an old bookstore called Elliott Bay. Parking meters jut up in vibrant shades of green, and one broken-down sedan has a sticker on the back window that reads, Equality.

A movie theater decorated with crumpled posters looms up on the left. *Carol, Willy Wonka and the Chocolate Factory, Macbeth, The Princess Bride.* I don't recognize any of the titles.

The downtown looms up before us, and the light sky glitters against so much glass. It's beautiful here. The most beautiful city I've ever seen. Water glistens beyond the edge of the metropolis, overtaking it in some places, and from where I stand, I can see a market half-submerged, commerce, shops, a lonely, decrepit Ferris wheel.

The wind smells of salt and sea, and I wish Kane was there to share it with me, instead of his brother. Mikey watches me a lot as we walk and never complains about the pace. He offers me his hand whenever he can, offers to carry me when I stumble. I reject all his attempts.

The guilt he exudes moves with us as we walk, like a third person in our party. It's almost unbearable. A few times I think about speaking, but I don't. I can't think of one good thing to say to him.

A theater comes up on our left, the stumps of shattered light bulbs spelling out the word, *Paramount.* It's just after this that I tell Mikey we're close.

"I can feel Kane. He's only a couple blocks from here, to the left. Inside a white concrete building."

A stitch in my side forces me to stop under the awning of a place called *Pacific P...* Don't know what the rest of the word might have been, as it's too faded now, but when I peer through the murky glass walls, three stories of battered boutiques face inwards as if caught in the eye of a cyclone and frozen there.

"On the eleventh floor."

"You can tell what floor he's on?"

Mikey leans against the glass, watching me with that critical look I've gotten so used to.

I nod, searching through the haze of the drugs for Mikey's face. "Yeah, I can tell what floor he's on. I can feel how big the room is around him. I know that he's alone and that he's hurting but he's hanging on for us."

"For you."

"For us," I correct. "He loves you."

"He did," Mikey concedes after a moment. His gaze passes up and down my oversized attire and he shudders. "But I don't deserve it."

I don't debate him on this.

Mikey mumbles under his breath, and when I ask him to repeat himself, he says, "Can you move?"

We've been loitering here for a while and we're too exposed. The sky has also started to darken.

"I'm fine," I lie. I'm running solely on willpower.

"I can hear bodies nearby," he says, shifting from foot-to-foot. "We should find cover."

I nod and follow Mikey down the road, past a golden plaque that reads Westlake Center. We cross the street beneath the abandoned tramline and enter a Bartell's drugstore.

We move to the far end of the store and I grimace as I slump to the ground against the empty racks. "Leave me," I whisper, clutching my knees so hard my fingertips turn white. The agony is back again and I can't think past it. Everything burns.

"I'm not leaving you anywhere." Mikey presses his palm to my jaw and forces pills down my throat. I suck them down dry since we don't have any water.

"We're almost there. You're not giving up on Kane now."

Mikey reaches for my face and uses his thumb to smear the tears across my bruised cheeks. "Are you with me?"

I shake my head. "Are you going to leave me again?"

He winces and sucks air in through his teeth. "I should never have left you. I'm a rat bastard."

"Yes, you are," I moan pitifully.

Mikey's mouth jerks up into a smile and he ruffles my hair. Even that hurts. "Good. Now that we're on the same page."

Crouching before me on one knee, Mikey starts rummaging through his pack. As he works, he lifts a finger to his lips and gestures for me to look around the edge of the aisle. He points towards the glass wall towards the street outside where two alien guards are wearing all white.

Surprised by the sight of them, I glance back at Mikey and mouth, *How many?*

He holds up four fingers, then points outside towards the guards there.

Four to one aren't great odds — and I'm not including myself in this. I cringe, but Mikey leans in close and whispers low, directly into my ear. "Don't worry. Take this."

From his pack, he produces two more bottles of liquor. I tense until he withdraws two rags and a lighter. He hands them over and it's only then that I break, grinning despite my better instincts.

Mikey shuffles a few inches forward, lifts his hand and grazes my cheek with the tips of his fingers. I would have pulled back if he hadn't lowered his hand first.

He mouths, *I'm sorry,* then he shoves the bottles, the rags and the lighters into the pockets of the man's coat I'm wearing.

The drug store abuts the building where Elise is holding Kane, but there's no direct route to the entrance.

We'll still have to exit the drug store and pass the white-clad stormtroopers in order to reach the front door.

On Mikey's mimed orders, I move out from behind the aisle and moan a couple of times. It doesn't take long to draw the guards' attention. They burst into the drugstore and, distracted by the open wounds all over me, Mikey cuts them both down easily.

He pillages their bodies for weapons, passing me a gun whose weight I can barely support. I drag it behind me as Mikey leads the way into the next building. There, my heart lurches and stutters and heat sweeps my limbs. *We're close.*

Signs reading *Medical Dental Center* hang everywhere as we wade through a marble foyer into a stairwell. I'm panting by the time we hit the third floor. My head swims. Though my body is numb thanks to Mikey's drugs, my legs are heavy. Slumping against one concrete wall, I tell Mikey to go on without me.

"Fuck, Abel. Stop saying that." His jaw clenches and I get the feeling he'd like to shoot me with the gun in his arms.

"Go," he orders, pointing at the staircase. As I move tediously to the next landing, I notice that the dust layered thickly over the concrete has been very recently disturbed. My lungs burn, heat that I can't make sense of blossoming between my breasts — is it Kane's heart or mine that's about to explode?

I'm still mulling over the odds of surviving another flight of stairs when I notice that Mikey is no longer behind me, urging me up the stairs with the butt of his gun.

"Mikey…"

"Shh," he rasps from a few steps below. He cocks his head to the side and his eyes grow wide all at once. "Run." Footsteps echo up the stairwell and I get the impression that it's not one set of feet against the concrete, but dozens.

"Abel, move!"

I throw myself up the stairs and the world rushes by even though I know that I'm moving slow. Way too slow. The drone of feet on concrete blurs and burns until all at once it's disrupted by the sound of bullets firing. I close my hand over my one good ear, hobbled by the magnitude of the sound, and when I turn I see that the guards are already on us.

A horde, they run three abreast, packed into the stairwell like cattle. Mikey fires back and the second row tramples the first when they fall.

They keep coming and Mikey continues firing and, with trembling fingers, I draw the first Molotov cocktail from my inside coat pocket. It takes me three tries to light the rag, only just managing to strike flame when the fourth row of guards kneels over the bodies of the third, and take aim.

I throw the bottle at the same time that three shots hit Mikey in the torso, knocking him backwards. His head hits my feet on the stairs at the same time that the entire stairwell fills with warmth.

Roaring, Mikey throws his body over mine, shielding me, as fire chases up to the tenth floor. He tosses his weapon to the side and half-shoves, half-carries me while bodies plummet over the railing, wreathed in flame.

"Mikey," I shout.

Mikey curses as he looks up at the six guards busting through door marked twelve. They charge us and I try to aim for them, but the gun in my arms is too big and the recoil knocks me back. I miss.

A responding shot punches me in the right shoulder and I gasp as it spins me around. My head cracks as it hits the wall. Mikey swings his body in front of mine as I collapse on the steps. He takes my machine gun away from me and fires again and again and again.

He shouts my name, and it's probably the drugs, but I don't feel pain as he drags me onto my feet by the collar of my coat. He kicks open the metal door with a huge number eleven painted on its front while bullets and fire and screams continue to echo up the stairs.

More are coming.

Soot on his face, blood on his hands, Mikey shoves me hard. "You go and find Kane. I'll stay here and hold them off," he says as I slam into a white wall. My shoulder streaks blood across it. Palm-shaped imprints come off black under my hands.

"What about Elise?" I groan, trying to stay present and focused.

Mikey shakes his head once and pushes the blond hair from his eyes as he turns to face the door. "She's not here. I can't hear her at all and I would be able to hear her."

"How can you be sure?"

He nods at me once, looking more confident than I ever remember him looking before. His eyebrows knit together over his nose and he juts his strong, beard-covered jaw to the left.

"I wouldn't send you into a death trap. This floor is empty. Now go." He kicks open the door to the stairwell and unleashes a round. Screams explode. Bullets explode. Bodies fall. I don't need to hear more.

I can feel Kane burning in my chest like a beacon and I know which way to go. Down the hallway to the right, I take the second left and pass through the broken door. My heart is pounding. It has been all along. So close to him now, I never thought I'd get to this point. I feel like I'm in a video game. Pain making everything so hard to follow.

My hand stills over the cool stainless steel handle of a door. It gives easily beneath my weight and I step into the room with a new terror making me tremble.

It's hope.

"Kane?" My fingers fumble with the light switch on the inner wall. I take a step into the room and the sneakers I'm wearing echo against the tiles beneath me. The room is cold and smells like bleach and blood.

"Kane," I say again, this time with more conviction. Finding a panel of lights, I flip them all and harsh fluorescents flicker in and out of life before beaming bright and strong.

"Kane!"

I rush forward. The room is littered with metal tables and medical equipment so that it looks one-part hospital, one-part science lab, two-parts torture chamber.

Wearing only the same pair of pants I last saw him in, Kane hangs upright in the center of the room. He's strapped to a gurney by metal cuffs at his ankles, neck and wrists. A large metal strap holds him down at the waist while clear tubes puncture his skin in a dozen different places. They don't feed anything into him, but feed out into a single drain on the floor.

His once-olive face is as pale as the walls surrounding us, but he still carries the light. The Tare that Elise so desperately covets continues to pulse in intermittent waves, in time with his precarious heartbeat. I stagger towards him, enraged and afraid.

"Kane?" I stagger into a metal table and trip into a pile of tools, all covered in blood. I shove them aside and they clatter noisily to the floor.

"Kane, wake the fuck up!" I say, falling against his body. I brace myself on his stomach and try to hold myself upright.

I reach for the cuff around his waist, but I know already I'm not getting through this without a key. Not unless he's strong enough to help me.

He stirs. "Mikey?" His voice is a relief and I bow my head, exhaling breath onto his stomach. His skin is unnaturally cool — only as warm as the room around us — but I still hold onto his hips with ferocity and am reassured.

"No, it's me," I sigh, laying my hand over his heart. "It's Abel."

"Abel," he groans, head rolling to the side. "I smelled you, but I hoped it wasn't." His hair drips down around his cheeks. His face is covered in unwashed stubble. "You shouldn't be here."

"You think anything could have kept me away?" His thick black lashes part and he looks at me and whatever color there was drains from his cheeks.

"Abel," he barks. "What happened to you?"

I'm still all swollen and I clutch the gurney he's mounted to in order to keep myself vertical. I shake my head and smile shakily up at him. "You know me." I swallow. "Making new friends."

Kane doesn't smile back. Gloss comes to his eyes that make my knees even jellier than they had been. "Don't do that," I whisper. "We just…we need to get out of here."

He blinks down at me slowly, and beneath the blood, I inahle the scent of his skin. Sweat. Cedar. Spice. He smells like his house or rather, his house smells like him. But whichever came first, I find myself back there, safe now that we're together.

"You always did have a…knack for making friends," he says and pain shifts over his features when he tries to move.

I bark out a laugh and when I look up at him, I'm crying, which is okay, because he's crying to. "Our bond is so weak," he whispers. "Why isn't my blood healing you?"

I shake my head and ignore the question, focusing rather on the problem at hand. All the many, many problems. I can't seem to escape them.

"Kane, I'm not strong enough to free you. You need to free yourself." I shove my sleeve down and hold my unbandaged wrist up to his mouth. "Drink from me."

"You need it." His eyes flutter closed.

I feel a sudden fluttering in my chest where his heartbeat should be pumping strong. The whole time I was dying, he was dying too. He only fought before for me. Now it's my turn.

Gunshots crackle in the hall. "We don't have much time."

I grab Diego's knife from my jacket pocket and bring it down across my wrist without hesitating. "You've got to get us out of here. Please," I beg him when he reels back, closing his eyes at the sight of my blood. "Kane, I need you to save my life."

He opens his mouth, like he'll argue, but I use the opening to shove my wrist in past his teeth. "Drink," I command him, and his eyes slink shut. He moans. And then he drinks.

The response is instantaneous. He pulls in a rush of blood that makes my whole body light in euphoria. I manage to feel horny — *horny* — even though I'm standing all bloody in Elise's house of horrors.

"Abel," he moans and I stagger closer to him, pressing myself to his warmth.

I grab the top of his pants, fingers sliding between his skin and the fabric. "Kane…"

He groans and his chest pulses stronger. Color floods his face and torso and I can feel him pull himself up, holding his own body straighter.

A shiver shudders through me and I feel dizzy with lust and maybe, possibly, also bloodloss and pain medication. I touch his abs until soon, my knees don't really hold up the rest of me. Everything turns a little grey.

"I felt you," I hear him say, though it sounds like it's from a distance.

Metal is suddenly bending and tearing and I hear a pop and a snap that sounds like a gong. My arm is shaking with the effort it takes to hold it up to his mouth, but when it starts to slip, I feel his hands. They hold me at the elbow and wrist as his mouth opens and bites down even more firmly. He drinks.

Stormily, he says, "I felt you receive pleasure and I hated it. What happened, Abel? Abel?"

As his grip on my arm releases, I realize it's the only thing that was holding me up. I hit the bloody tiles beneath me and feel suddenly, wretchedly cold.

"Abel!"

There's a crash before a second voice fires into the space. I know this one too, but it takes me a moment to place it. "Kane? Kane holy fuck, you're alive. Where's Abel?"

"Mikey! Get her."

Scrabbling and scraping as metal is thrown aside. Then Mikey's inhuman roar, "No!"

The sound of his voice reverberating off of the ceiling and walls shocks me to consciousness, like the sharp jolt of a defibrillator. I lurch awake and see Mikey sliding to his knees at my side. He rolls me onto my back and punches his hands through his hair.

"What did you do!" He grabs my wrist and tries to bandage it with the shirt he's wearing.

In the background, I can hear metal bending and breaking. I can hear Kane fighting against his restraints and winning.

"Out of my way."

Kane drops down at Mikey's side and opens his wrist, but the blood that drips onto my face tastes like pennies. Almost entirely human.

Mikey shoves his brother aside and pulls back his own sleeve. "I'm going to have to give her my blood." Mikey lifts his own wrist to his lips, but Kane lashes out so quickly and so brutally, he reminds me of Jack for a moment.

Mikey's face is streaked with red where Kane hit him. His eye is swelling and the bones surrounding it are crumpled. But Mikey doesn't protest.

He just looks at his brother and bares his teeth. "She's dying, Kane. I won't let that happen."

Kane's eyes narrow. He grabs Mikey by the throat. "If you touch my mate again, I will leave you here strapped to that gurney so that Elise can finish what she started."

Mikey grapples with Kane's hands while his face turns from cream to crimson to violet. Kane shoves him back and Mikey spits onto the ground. He looks at me, but doesn't try to offer me his blood a second time.

"If she dies," he coughs into the floor, "it's on *you.*"

"Stop talking and get me that centrifuge," Kane snarls, gesturing towards something I can't see with his chin while his hands continue to hold me.

"The what?"

"Those vials!" Kane slams his fist into the floor so hard that loose tiles shatter around my motionless form. "Bring them to me."

Mikey staggers up and returns a moment later with a fistful of empty, clear tubes. "What good are these? They're empty. She's dying, Kane!"

Kane rips the vials from Mikey's fingers with his left hand. His right is trapped around my wrist, stemming the flow of blood. I'm pleasantly lightheaded and prepared to die as Kane tosses aside three of the vials before flipping the lids to the remaining two.

He angles them to my lips, one at a time, and I feel drops of blood hit my tongue. Two from the first vial, three from the second. The blood is tangier than Kane's and significantly more sulfuric.

"Kane, are you fucking kidding me?" Mikey looks poised to kill something, someone, everyone. "She's going to die! A drop of your blood isn't going to save her life…"

"It isn't my blood," Kane says, sweeping his hand over my forehead. I breathe a little more deeply after that and hold Kane's gaze without fading like I thought I might.

Mikey stands at the sound of shouting just outside of the room. "You gave Abel *her* blood?" His voice is a low, quiet threat.

"Better hers than yours, brother."

Mikey rips his sword from his belt and lunges for his brother at the same time that shots crackle in the hall. I jolt, but Kane doesn't react at all. He just looks up at his brother and says something to him in Otherspeak that makes Mikey's shoulders slump. He drops his sword.

"Kane," I croak, drawing both his and his brother's attention back to me.

I cling to his arms and try to pull myself up into a seat. "Can she walk?" Kane asks Mikey. Then, "Barricade the door."

"Barricade the door?" Mikey shouts, but I notice he still starts towards the door and starts barricading it, as instructed. "How are we going to get out of here?"

"Up. Elise has a helicopter on the roof and there's an entrance that leads directly to it from this one. She did not want others to chance by me for any reason."

Smart cookie.

"Fuck me." Mikey races away from the entrance while bodies slam against the other side of the door. Stacked metal tables are the only thing separating us from the reinforcements.

"I found it. Now, come on, Kane, go. I'll get Abel. No, Kane. Don't touch her. Don't…" His voice catches when a scream tickles the back of my throat.

Kane, who just tried to lift me, lowers me back to the floor.

His jaw sets. His eyes read fire and bloodshed. "Where is she injured and how badly?"

"Badly. Let me…" Mikey stoops down to my side, but Kane grabs him by the throat again.

"Why aren't you injured if she is?" He seethes.

Mikey is spared from having to answer by the sound of the barricade caving. Kane shoves him off and scoops me up and I scream through the pain as Kane starts to run.

Mikey fires at the aliens forcing themselves through the opening. The Other collapses, but a second is close on her heels. "Mikey," I manage to say.

He turns to me and I gesture to my jacket pocket with my chin. He grins at me. "That's my girl," he says and I feel Kane's arms tense around me. He doesn't say anything as Mikey frees the molotov cocktails from my pocket.

Kane heads to the back door, bursting through it onto a set of white painted stairs. We reach the top landing just as an explosion goes off below.

The door bangs open and Mikey's thundering up. He meets us on the roof where wind buffets us around and a helicopter sits quietly waiting, that little accidental savior.

"Hallefuckinglujah," Mikey grunts, throwing open the door and helping Kane lower me inside.

They buckle me into a seat in the back and Mikey makes sure to put me on my stomach, drawing searing stares from Kane. They draw the door shut with a thwack and then climb into the cockpit.

"Kane, please tell me you know how to fucking fly one of these things."

"Sort of." I can hear shots refracting against the outside of the helicopter as it lurches awkwardly into the air. But then they fade, and we straighten out and when I open my eyes again, Mikey's flying and Kane's staring at me over the back of his chair.

He says something, but it's too loud to make out.

I smile at him around the blood-taste in my mouth.

He smiles back at me and before I know what's happened, he's unbuckled his seatbelt and is kneeling on the metal ground in front of me. He's kissing me hard and our fingers are locked together and as feelings of safety wash over me, I sleep.

Sometime later, I blink and see Kane asleep on the floor right underneath me.

I gasp, panicked, but Mikey shouts something I can't make out from the front. I look up and he's giving me a thumb's up over his shoulder. When we make eye contact, he points to the right and I look up to see a set of earphones.

I put them on and Mikey does too and when he talks, I can hear him clearly.

"He's okay," he tells me, returning his gaze to the windshield. There are bright lights coming from somewhere that make my eyes hurt. I blink many times against them, but nothing works.

"Abel, you should see this. Can you sit up?"

No. The answer is definitely no. I just laugh into the headphones. Mikey flicks some buttons and undoes his seatbelt. He reaches over Kane's body, but the second he touches me, Kane lurches away and grabs his arm like a zombie with its first taste of human flesh.

"I told you what would happen if you touched her again, didn't I, brother?" I can hear his snarl, even over the wind.

Mikey's face turns bright red and he nods, then pulls back his hands. "I just want her to see this. Show her outside."

Kane struggles up into a seat and then carries me into the cockpit where he sets me on his lap. The pain in my back is surreal and I have a hard time keeping my eyes open, but Mikey was right.

The pain is worth it.

"Sunlight."

I whisper the word with reverence as I look out at the world in front of me.

Clouds line our feet and above them, there's just blue. Pure pale blue and light. It's yellow and bright and turns the grey clouds below us white, making them look like snow.

Kane is very, very gentle with me, but I cling to him hard now as my eyes shut and the emotion monster waves at me from its contented position nestled in the very center of my soul. In each of my bones.

I weep.

I cry like a baby and as I try to staunch the tears, I remind myself that Population doesn't allow for tears.

But we're not in Population anymore.

I try to stay awake for as long as I can, but between Kane's warmth and the jarring pain in my back, it's not possible.

Kane feeds me more pain pills and as their effect loosens my tongue, I smile and say, "We did it. I can't believe we did it."

Kane isn't wearing the headphones, so I don't hear his answer, if there is one. Instead, he pets my hair lovingly while Mikey smirks into the speakers, "*You* did. And you know what else?"

"Hm?"

"We didn't even have to fight any tolta."

"Or maltrons," I whisper.

Mikey laughs then, quite abruptly, and the sound is enough to thaw the ice that sits in my core, covering my flesh which has just begun to prickle. I'm starting to be able to feel again. And I feel terrible.

I cringe into Kane's chest and cower there while the sunlight warms me, inside and out.

I wake with a jolt, disoriented and disappointed that there's no sunlight anymore. My body pitches, but there's a belt across my waist holding me down and next thing I know the helicopter doors are flying open.

I see Sandra first, black hair streaming in the wind the helicopter creates. Maggie and Calvin next, followed by Gabe, several others I can't name, and then finally, Ashlyn. Tears come to my eyes as Sandra shouts orders and Ashlyn, ignoring them, climbs into the back of the helicopter.

Crying, she wraps her slender arms around my head, burying her face in my neck. "I never thought I'd see you again." Her voice cracks as she speaks. "You told me to run and then I did, but you were gone."

She's crying hard now and I rub the tears from her cheeks with my thumb, or at least that's what I imagine I do. I can't move my hands.

"Baby, I'd always come back for you," I say, voice shallow. It hurts to speak.

Her hair smells like lavender soap and is soft against my neck. Someone has recently cut it. Her clothes are clean too. She looks like a kid is supposed to look and I feel nothing but gratitude.

She pulls away from me, rubbing her ruby eyes with the backs of her wrists. "Why are you…what's wrong?" Her cheeks burn a brighter red as she looks me over.

"Sandra," she shrieks, "help me!" She doesn't sound eleven anymore. She speaks with authority. "We need to get a…a thingie," she gasps.

"We need two stretchers immediately. Calvin," Sandra says, completing the sentence for her as she moves to Ashlyn's side.

"On it."

"Only one," comes Kane's low growl. "I'm fine."

"You're not," Maggie argues.

"He's definitely not. He was completely drained…"

Horrified gasps light up the space.

Hands are on me and some of them are Ashlyn's. Others are Kane's.

But soon, I'm being hauled onto a stretcher away from him while Lady, Lanis and Maggie block his path. "Let the good doctor do her work…" I hear Maggie say before I'm rushed around a corner.

Back to my old room. Inside, I recognize the wallpaper.

Sandra shoos away the chaos so that it's just me, her, and Ashlyn. She begins directing Ashlyn in terse orders that I hardly understand. Ashlyn has no trouble, and soon I'm stripped down to my last layer. With the blood and sweat covering most of me, even warm air makes my skin prickle.

Ashlyn takes a pair of stainless steel scissors to my shirt, but Sandra stays her hand. Quietly, she says, "Mikael tells us that Abel has been hurt very badly. Do you want to stay?"

"I want to stay."

Her eyes flare when she peels back my shirt. They roll me onto my stomach and the bandages go next. I'm grateful I don't have to see Ashlyn's reaction, but I can't block out the sound of her sniffling. Sandra shoves a needle into my arm then and sends Ashlyn to find Maggie.

Alone now, Sandra squats down so that I can see her face. "I have never met a fighter I admired more." Her lips quirk and her gaze rakes over my back. I wonder how it looks. "You fight until the last breath, and then continue breathing."

She sighs and runs a hand back through her thick, jet-black hair. It's so long it reaches her lower back, even in a pony tail. I remember the first time I met her, I commented on it. She told me that she never cut it because she's Indian and her family was Sikh. Though most of the younger generations have never heard of such a thing as religion, she still adheres to the traditions of her ancestors in honor of their memory.

I blink and hope that can serve as a thanks. Speaking is suddenly impossible as a brilliant warmth consumes me. She fixes IV bags up to a pole and, as Ashlyn and Maggie enter, adds a bag of blood to the drip. *Human* blood. I can tell by the color of it.

Ashlyn's been crying. I can tell by the swelling of her face when she returns, but she doesn't cry now. Methodically, she removes the bandages around my arms and legs.

Maggie there too, and when she arrives at my side, she gently lays her hand on my arm.

"Kane." I cough, but the word's still intelligible enough.

Maggie nods indulgently, laugh lines crinkling around her eyes and lips. "You can stop worrying so much about others, my dear. You just focus on yourself for once. We have him well taken care of. Kane will be just fine."

"Thank…thank you," I say.

Sandra and Maggie exchange a few words rapidly as I begin to fade from this place.

"Sleep now," Maggie whispers, "You're safe."

Chapter Thirteen

There's light streaming in through the window when I wake. Muted light, but I can tell that it's day. Everything is quiet and I know that I'm home.

Home.

I never thought I'd be able to say that word again.

I sigh. Someone else sighs in response. I open my eyes. Ashlyn is in the bed with me. I can see her knees, but not much else.

"Sorry. Did I wake you?" She says and I sigh again, whole body tingling.

"I'm not convinced I'm not still dreaming," I croak.

"If this was a dream, it wouldn't be very good."

I exhale laughter into the pillows. They smell like honeysuckle and vanilla and are as soft as ever beneath my bare body. I'm naked again, except that I'm wearing underwear this time that actually fits me and I can feel a fabric pad lining my panties rather than bits of bloodied towels shoved in there all akimbo.

"Don't look pretty, do I?"

Ashlyn doesn't say anything for some time, but I see the bloody gauze pads she throws into the wastepaper basket. "You're hurt real bad."

"What's the prognosis, doc?"

"Good,"Ashlyn answers, "Well, it would be better if Kane could give you his blood, but Sandra said he's not ready."

"Of course he isn't." I pause. "How is he?"

Another wad of gauze floats over the edge of the bed. She reaches to the side table then and pulls off a bottle of antibiotic ointment. "Sandra says he still has two more days until he restores his red blood cell count to normal. The puncture wounds in his arms won't fully heal until then either. He might even get some scars."

"Christ," I murmur.

Ashlyn pauses, then adds, "He would heal faster if he took human blood, but he won't."

"He won't?"

"No."

I clench my right fingers around my wounded palm, able to move them more freely than I last could. I can feel the hard ridges of stitching against my hand and imagine that from above, I probably look like a jigsaw puzzle.

"Has Kane seen me yet?"

"No. He's been trying but Maggie said no. She said if he saw you he'd try to give you blood and it wouldn't do any good and he'd only lose more of his own blood in the process."

Ashlyn rubs my back with her little fingers in small, circular motions. They're soothing and I close my eyes, surrendering to the sensation. It's the most comfortable I've felt in days, and again I'm rocked by the fact that Mikey and I emerged from that cave only days ago — a couple weeks, at best.

"They posted Mikey outside to make sure he doesn't come in."

"Mikey's outside?" And I'm confused by the hope I hear in my voice, because I'm supposed to hate him.

"Yeah. But he's not allowed to see you."

"Sandra says?"

"Kane says."

"Fuck."

Ashlyn giggles at that. "Potty mouth." For a moment, I entirely forgot she was eleven.

Smiling against the sheets, I ask, "How did you get so close to Sandra?"

Ashlyn doesn't answer at first. Instead, she edges off of the bed and stands. For the first time, I'm able to get a complete picture. She looks bigger than I remember, more meaty. Fuller than the flesh and bone she was when I pulled her out of that cage.

"I'm supposed to change the bandages on the bullet hole in your shoulder. You got lucky. The bullet went in and out. At least, that's what Sandra says."

I raise a single eyebrow at her and she pouts, "I got into a fight." She holds out her right hand and I can see nearly healed scrapes shimmering across the backs of her knuckles.

"You're lying." I gawk.

She stamps her foot and rolls her eyes. "Okay, fine. I got into three fights."

"*Three* fights? Are you crazy? What were you thinking? If I could, I would slap you upside the head. What were you doing fighting?"

She pulls on the bottom of her shirt, stretching it out. It looks slightly too small for her and I'm surprised. In the past months, she's grown so much. "When me and the other girls got back, we met the other kids. They haven't been out in Population."

Her voice drops and she stares at me, willing me to understand. I do. She doesn't need to say more.

I nod.

"One of the guys tried to touch Judith. I stopped him. She doesn't like when boys touch her. They just don't understand," she repeats, looking away as if ashamed, or as if recalling a memory I wished I could incinerate.

She comes close enough to touch and I take her hurt hand in my left one. My fingers don't move like they should beneath the splint, but it's enough to be able to touch her.

"But I do." I give her a light squeeze. "I'm sorry for what happened to you."

She shakes her head. "You came for us. All the girls think you're a superhero." She smiles then. "Me too."

I smile back. "I think superheroes usually heal faster than this."

Ashlyn shrugs. "Maybe." But her smile fades. "At least you're still alive."

She looks at me then and I know she's thinking of Becks. "Oh shit, Ashlyn, I'm so sorry," I sputter, remembering that Ashlyn has no idea because the last time she saw her mother, they were both alive.

She shakes her head and I can tell she's fighting to keep it together. Her voice trembles as she says, "How did she die?"

"She died fighting for you."

"Actually," Ashlyn says, eyes steely in their determination. "How did she die?"

Her voice is severe and I can't deny it. I tell her the truth that no eleven-year-old should have to hear as I recount to her the final stand Becks and I made for her.

"She didn't feel pain," I lie, and as I do, vow that it's the only lie I'll ever tell her. "Her last thoughts were of you. She'd be so proud to see you now."

Ashlyn sniffles and wipes her cheeks fiercely, but she isn't quick enough to catch the tears that fall. I take her hand in mine and grip it firmly. Too quickly, she calms.

"You can cry, Ashlyn."

"You don't cry." She shakes her head.

I tense. "It's normal to cry."

"You aren't normal?"

I smile at her, albeit weakly. "Have I ever been?"

Sniffling, she laughs ever so slightly and rubs her nose with the back of her hand. I imagine that if it were light — or if I had Kane's vision — I'd see it was bright pink and slightly swollen.

"No, I guess not. And now you're the queen."

That takes me aback. "How do you know about that?"

"Everybody's talking about it. Maggie is freaking out, trying to prepare everything already. She's already got a guest list that's like a mile long, but Kane says she can't send anything out until after he deals with Elise."

"Do you know what he means to do with Elise?"

Ashlyn shrugs and shivers, returning to the task at hand. "I don't know. I'm only eleven," she teases.

"I forget all the time." I smile at her and hope that in the darkness she can see it.

"All I know is that somebody called the Lavhe is supposed to come in a few weeks."

"A few weeks?"

Ashlyn must catch the skepticism in my tone because she says, "Yeah, I don't know. You'll have to ask Kane." She chews on her bottom lip. "Kane told me you killed Memnoch."

"I did."

"Good."

I want to know what happened to her, too, but I don't want to know, if that makes sense. I'm a coward with a ruthless imagination, so I tell her a truth, one that won't change the past but that is something we can both cling to,

"Nobody's going to hurt you again, not while I'm still alive," I say.

"I know," she sighs. "I love you, Abel."

My heart beats hard, just once. "I love you too."

She leans down and kisses my cheek and as her hands flutter over the gauze wraps, my gaze drifts back to the cuts on her hands. I'm no Becks. What she's dealt with is too hard for me to help her through. I hope she'll talk to Maggie about it, or someone more able to.

But for now, I say, "So now you work with Sandra? I still don't get the link."

Ashlyn shrugs. "After I punched Martin, she asked me if I'd help her out instead of going to Maggie's class."

"You like it?"

"Yeah." Ashlyn grins. "I do. Sandra says I'm good at it."

I exhale and make a mental note to thank Sandra next time I see her. "I'm so proud of you."

"I'm proud of you, too."

Ashlyn changes all my bandages and just as she applies the last piece of medical tape, she stiffens. Whatever she hears, I don't, as my busted ear is facing up, good ear pressed to the mattress.

"What is it?"

She grabs a scalpel lying on the bedside table and I tense. "Ashlyn, is everything…"

It's only then that I hear the voices. "…in my own house…let me…you fucking…" A roar and then a huge weight slams into my bedroom door.

Kane bursts through it shouting, "I want to see her."

Mikey is beneath him when they hit the hardwood, splinters of wood showering the Oriental runner that leads to the bed.

"Kane?" I say, distracting Kane long enough for Mikey to shove his shoulder under Kane's, flip him onto his stomach and wrench his arms behind his back. Kane strains his neck to look up at me and Ashlyn throws a sheet over my body before he catches sight of the carnage.

Kane speaks into the floor. "I want to see her." But Mikey has him safely pinned. Kane roars and throws his full weight back, lifting his brother off of the carpet and slamming him into the dresser. Mikey wraps his thick arm around Kane's throat, but it's Ashlyn, of all people, who quiets him. She quiets them both.

"You're scaring her," she shouts, voice shrill in an eleven-year-old's pitch. "She's not supposed to have her heart rate elevated and you're messing everything up!"

Kane's eyes hit mine, and though the muscles in his neck strain, he lets Mikey wrestle him out of the room. The door slams and it takes time for the commotion in the hall to subside. The moment it does, Calvin raps his knuckles on the back of my door before stepping through it.

"Christ." I cough. "What happened to you?"

Calvin edges into the room, rubbing his jaw. "Kane's in a particularly…explosive mood." He's got a welt on his jaw and a shallow scrape above his left eye.

"And Mikey's the worst person to be watching him. I wish Tasha was back." He ruffles Ashlyn's hair as he moves past her. "Mind if I sit for a while?"

Ashlyn blushes and tucks her hair behind her ears. "I guess so." And when she stares at him as she exits the room, I know just what to make fun of her for later: Ashlyn's got a crush.

I laugh as Calvin pulls up a chair beside the bed.

He asks me what's wrong but I change the subject. "Where's Tasha?"

"Ironically, she's at the Lahve's estate in the Diera. She's persuaded him to investigate the disappearance of her Notare and his Sistana, and last I heard, they were working on convening all of the Council *in person* by next week."

"How?"

"Apparently there's a couple working planes still, and the one coming up from South America will get here by boat." He shrugs. "Just glad to see you alive and well, *Sistana*." He smirks.

I glare.

Calvin laughs and bows to me deeply before plopping into a chair. "I do believe congratulations are in order, by the way."

"Not funny."

"You really didn't know?"

"No idea."

He laughs. "That's rich. You deserve it though."

I don't know what to say to that and shiver.

"You need more blankets?" He says, noticing.

I shake my head. "No, I'm okay. Just a little itchy. Nice haircut though, by the way."

"What do you think?" He cocks his head and pretends to flip long locks.

I laugh and cough simultaneously. "It's a good look for you. Makes you look older than twelve, for once."

Calvin bites his bottom lip and leans forward onto his elbows. "If you weren't looking so corpsey right now, I'd go a few rounds with you."

"You know you'd never win."

"I know," he concedes, rubbing his nose. "But you make losing fun."

Laughing lightly, we lapse into a pleasant sort of silence before both speaking at once. "So I just wanted to say thank you…" "Look, Abel, I'm sorry…"

I laugh through my nose. Calvin's cheeks brighten with soft pink swirls.

"You first," he says.

I clear my throat. "I just wanted to thank you for what you did with those girls."

"Are you kidding me?" His jaw drops. "I didn't think you'd even want to see me after that."

"What? Why? You did amazing. You got them all back here, didn't you? Alive, at that."

Calvin concedes, then stutters, "B-but you. I left you. I should have sent the girls ahead and gone back."

I sigh against the sheets and sink even deeper into the bed. I'm surprised I haven't melted in with the fabric. "If you had left them alone I'd *never* have forgiven you."

Calvin shakes his head and breathes air through the side of his mouth. "Well, for a married couple, you and Kane certainly seem to have different priorities. He nearly crucified me when I came back without you. I had bruises for almost a week."

He's in a short-sleeved tee shirt and I see that the freckles on his arms match the ones on his rubicund cheeks. "I think the only person Kane hates more than me right now is his own brother. Crazy after all the guy did to get him back."

I shift uncomfortably, wincing when I stretch the new sutures winding across my back.

"The whole thing was pretty crazy," I say dryly.

"What happened?"

I shake my head. To reveal anything would be to condemn him. "What happens in Population, dies in Population."

Calvin's face falls. "That bad, huh?" His gaze sweep the gauze covering my back from neck to pelvis. "But why would…What did Mikey have to do with it?"

I close my eyes. "I really don't want to talk about it."

"Sorry," he whispers.

I shake my head again. "It's alright."

"I'll let you sleep, Abel," he says, rising to his feet.

"You sick of me already?"

He shakes his head, looking quite serious for once. "You need to get some rest. Sandra says you're not looking so good."

"Damn that woman. She seems to be spreading lies all over the place." I'm trying to make a joke, but I don't laugh and neither does Calvin.

Instead, he stares down at the sheet covering me and traces its shortest edge with his pointer finger. "Can I take a look?"

"Only if you do me a favor."

"Anything."

"There should be a mirror on the vanity." He nods. "Bring it over. I want to see for myself." I regret having asked the moment Calvin pulls the gauze away in one big sheet and engineers a couple mirrors so that I can see, too.

It looks like a map of downtown Seattle, lines forming in a checkerboard pattern, a few thicker stitches slashing sideways across it as they vainly work to hold the little skin there is together.

"You can put the mirror down now," I whisper.

"What in the world happened?" Calvin says a few painful seconds later.

"Mikey didn't tell you any of it?"

He shakes his head. "Mikael hasn't said much of anything except that he doesn't like being called Mikey."

"Of course not. Big stubborn oaf."

"He says you're the only one."

"The only one what?"

"That can call him that. Mikey."

"Oh." I quickly change the subject. "Do you have water?"

Calvin jumps to his feet, exits the room, and returns from the hallway carrying a cup, a pitcher, and a straw. He helps me drink, because in neither hand can I hold a cup without it falling. And when I'm finished with half the pitcher, he presses a small pill to my lips. It's only after I swallow that I bother to ask what it is.

"When I was out there, Sandra told me to give it to you. Morphine tablet. Apparently you're running them out of the good stuff." He flicks the IV line.

My head flops down onto the pillow beneath it and I close my eyes. It's hard to keep them open.

Calvin touches my right wrist, gives it a little squeeze. "I'm really glad you're back."

"Me too," I breathe.

"I'll leave you alone. Get some rest."

"I'm supposed to be bedridden for the next couple days. Will you come back?"

"Yes, ma'am. Or should I say, Your Highness."

"Don't you fucking start."

Calvin gives me a short salute from the open doorway. "Whatever you say, My Lady." I mean to make another jab as he steps out into the hall, but I'm asleep before I even hear the door shut.

I wake what would have felt like minutes later had the world not been shrouded in total darkness. My eyes open and my senses are alert and on the defensive, because I know I'm not alone.

"Who's there?"

A light flicks on and for a moment I don't quite make sense of the world in front of me. There's a sheet hanging a foot away from my bed that spans the full length of the room, dividing it. The light is on the other side. It's soft and orange, and illuminates a silhouette against the dark fabric.

"I didn't mean to frighten you." Kane's deep voice hits me like a bucket of ice water. It's shocking in its submersion. "I'm sorry."

"Kane," I exhale, "I missed you."

Kane doesn't answer right away and I start to breathe faster, harder.

"Kane?"

"I missed you too," he says brutally. "So badly everything fucking hurts. And these pesky humans that I afford so much power succeeded in keeping me from you for hours."

"It's only so you don't worry," I whisper. "At least that's what they tell me."

"They say many things," he breathes and he sounds exhausted. If he is, I feel him. Seriously. "They say I would not like what I would see if I looked at you." He pauses long enough to take another breath, this one even deeper. "Are they…correct?"

"It's just a few scratches."

"Are you lying to me?"

"Yes."

Kane snarls, the sound ripping from the back of his throat and making me flinch. "Don't do it again."

"I'm sorry," I whisper. "It is bad. You know the worst part was that the guy that did it — Jack — he looked just like you. And the guy that saved me — Diego — he looked just like my brother."

Kane doesn't speak again for some time, but I can hear him subtly shuffling, shifting, like he's trying to get comfortable, but can't.

"I want to see you," he says.

"I want to see you, too." I answer. "Please take the curtain down."

As if he'd been waiting for me to ask, Kane rips the curtain free of its staples and wrenches his chair closer by three feet. I gasp when he appears at the edge of the bed, face lowered so that we're eye-level and separated by an arm's length.

I don't miss the way he hisses, or the way his hand shakes. There are deep, plum bags beneath his eyes and though he's clean-shaven and his hair has been cut, it's sticking up all over the place. His body glows between us and a gold shimmer refracts off of his emerald eyes, filling them with intensity and with light.

His lips part and they look warm and supple, blood red as they had been, before Elise. I notice all this and more in the second before he kisses me.

He crushes his mouth to mine, like he's trying to pull the last breath from my lungs. His tongue invades me, meeting mine and tangling. Heat shoots through my body and my toes curl. I try to lift up, but he holds me where I am, breaking our kiss but only so he can kiss the edge of my jaw and trace the outline of my ear with his tongue.

"Mmm," I moan. "Kane…" I reach for him and grab whatever I find — I meet beard. It's trimmed now, shorter than it was and just a shadow lining his jaw and hollow cheeks.

"God, you're beautiful," I whisper in the space between us.

Kane sucks in a breath. He seems to be struggling with something. Finally, he bows his head and settles back in his seat. Looking back up at me, he traces his fingers gently across my swollen cheek.

"I told you once before, Abel, that I am a selfish male. When I felt your pleasure while Elise was busy draining the blood from my body, I have never known such rage…"

"I'm so sorry," I start, but Kane shushes me. He places a single finger on my lower lip, then slides it into my mouth past my teeth. I bite down, sucking on it, while the pleasure tethering us together swells in me.

He shifts where he sits, but doesn't bother to hide his erection. In just those damn silk pants again, it's obvious. And I want him. If I could take him like this, I would.

"When I felt your pleasure a second time, I was so angry that I…" He chokes and struggles to speak. "I wanted to see you punished for it. It was all I could think. I knew I was wrong and so I pulled away, severing the connection we share." He looks me over, and slowly shakes his head. "But I never could have imagined you in pain like this."

I bite my swollen lips together, unsure of what to say. I'm not good at this stuff. All I can feel is a mounting panic as he pulls away.

"No. Please. Kane I…you're not…are you done with me? You can punish me, if you want…"

I close my eyes, knowing I can take it and that it would be worth it not to lose *this*, but Kane only laughs humorlessly in a way that makes the hairs stand up on the back of my neck.

"You are a fool."

"I know."

"Mikael told me how he stole my sword from you, *hit* you, and forced himself on you. He also told me that you single-handedly rescued him and countless other Heztoichen from Crestor's clutches. And he credits you entirely with my rescue."

His voice trails off before picking back up with poorly restrained violence. "He loves you."

Kane growls and I hear a piece of metal clink as it hits the ground. I wonder what he's bent, or broken.

"Mikael has never made any effort to protect anyone other than himself, and yet now, every word out of his treacherous mouth is to protect you. He's protecting you from me and what he thinks will be my fury."

"No, that isn't…"

"Do you love him?"

"What?"

"Do you love him?" he repeats.

"What? No! Oh my gosh, of course not! I love *you.*"

"Did he rape you?"

"Kane," I choke. "*No.*"

"Did you invite him to pleasure you, then?"

"No! I would never…" I'm too flustered to marshal my answer and immediately after, I realize my mistake.

"Then what difference does it make?" Kane roars.

He surges onto his feet, grabs the standing floor lamp and throws it across the room where it shatters against a painting. I can still see in the light of his chest, but only in that. I'm a little scared now by the way he paces, and scared to interrupt him when he's like this. I've never seen him like this.

"My brother took permissions with you that were not given. And I know already of your history with assault. You gave me this information in *confidence.* I know that you have never had a male worship you as I did and I was so ruthlessly jealous when I realized you were receiving pleasure that I wished you *ill.* I wished you pain when I *knew* that you were inexperienced. When it is possible that you do not even understand the concept of permission. Do you even know how to rebuff a male's advances?"

"I…" No. I don't. "Fight? Probably fight…"

Kane crosses the room, grabs the dresser and tosses it like it weighs nothing. I squirm, squeal and close my eyes. My heart is pounding as I hear his footsteps come closer.

When he touches my hair, his hands shake with a quiet rage betrayed by his gravelly pitch. "I left you in a position where you could only think to fight and it was with my own goddamn kin."

And then he quiets and his tone grows dangerously soft. "I will kill him for this."

"No, Kane. Please don't. I know that what he did was wrong. That what *we* did was wrong. I asked him for help when I got my period — I never had a period before and I was scared…"

"You got your period for the first time and my brother assaulted you?"

More things shatter. Wood this time. When I blink my eyes open, I see what got got. There goes his chair…

The bed dips beside me and I see him sliding beneath the covers. He lowers himself down so that we're eye-to-eye. He doesn't look like him, though. He looks like Jack. Too much like Jack. I close my eyes against the image. Against the rage. Against the memory.

I try three times to formulate coherent words but only manage a strained grunt, a swallowed mumble. My face floods with heat and I begin to feel sick to my stomach.

"Kane," I murmur when he still doesn't say anything. "I don't mean that what he did was right, or that what we did together was intentionally wrong. It just all happened so fast. He'd been in prison for years and hadn't had blood in months. I never had a man down there but you…"

Kane closes his eyes, face appearing stoic and still in a way that frightens me far more than his fury. "And now you're making excuses for him too."

"They're not excuses. They're just reasons not to tighten the noose. If I can forgive him, then you can forgive him, too. Just…so long as…you can forgive me."

Kane keeps his eyes closed and exhales deeply, then inhales in equal pulls.

Tears prick the backs of my eyes as I whisper, "I felt like I betrayed you when it was happening. I never felt anything like that before. I didn't know…don't know about this stuff. But I understand if you don't want me to be your Sistana anymore. I don't know how to break a blood bond, but I will if you want me to."

A tear trickles down my cheek. Kane flinches. "Is that what you want?" He opens his eyes and they heat as they track the tear all the way down to the sheets.

"God, no," I blurt out. "I love you." My stomach hollows. I can't swallow or breathe or blink. "I love you so damn much."

Kane looks at me in the quiet dark before scanning the rest of my body. I'm grateful for the blankets separating us. I don't want him to see the rest…

"Please, Kane," I whisper, watching as his large fingers trace the shape of my left hand down to the wrist until it disappears beneath gauze and plaster. "Say something."

He back teeth clench and his warm, rough hand tightens around my palm. My fingers twitch in discomfort and he releases me. He flips onto his back and massages his eyelids.

"I have been in love with you from the moment you challenged me for the key that opened Mikael's crypt — perhaps even before that. Seeing Memnoch and his minions go after you in that alleyway, I assumed it would be a quick death for you humans. But when you emerged, still breathing, and dragged me off into that disgusting store to *save my life*, I knew I'd met my match."

A smile appears then at the corner of Kane's mouth. "And then later, when you finally found me in Elise's torture chamber and pressed your wrist to my lips, I knew I was wrong to hate you. I knew with absolute certainty that I didn't. That I was weak. That I was jealous," he exhales, like a great weight is lifted.

He breathes out again, "I was jealous. Jealous to the point that I nearly killed you." Kane's fists clench, as does his jaw. He looks directly at me and his green eyes glow. "I wanted your blood in me so no one else could have it. All of it. And when Mikael offered you his blood to save your life, I denied you that."

He exhales, and his breath smells like peppermint. Just like he tastes. "So when you ask if I still want you, you fail to realize that it is I who should be asking that of *you.* You were taken advantage of by *my* brother, and I almost killed you."

Licking my lips, I try to speak. My heartbeat is firm and even and, if I concentrate just hard enough, I can feel his, firm and even, fluttering in my rib cage alongside it.

"There is nothing to forgive," I say. "I still want you."

"And I, you." He smiles at me, though it's a starved thing. Full of hope, yet still seeking salvation. "The blood bond will only break between us with my death."

"Or mine. Which is probably more likely at this point."

Kane doesn't laugh at my joke. He just shakes his head. "Not even then, Abel. You are mine for the rest of my life and I am only yours. I'd like to ask you a question I should have asked you weeks ago. Before the ball."

"I…okay," I grunt, struggling to clear my throat.

He reaches beneath the blankets, presumably into his pocket, and withdraws two long, delicate strands made of rose gold. Small sigils hang from the end of each, and when he tilts them to the light of his chest, I see that they are two intricately woven knots that have no ending.

"Would you honor me by becoming my Sistana?" Color rises to tint to his hollow cheeks and I grin outright. He's *nervous.* I didn't think such a thing was possible.

"Yes," I say, bellowing out a shaky laugh. "Of course I'll be your Sistana."

He exhales as if I might have given some other answer, and I laugh again, even if it makes my back ache and causes me to wince.

I cough. "I sort of thought I already was."

"There's a ceremony and mountains of paperwork — more so because I'm one of the Notare and you're a human. It'll be a huge affair. A ball. The Chancellor will need to be present, and wherever the Chancellor goes, hordes of sycophants follow. You'll be required to dance for hours."

Laughing, I try not to let signs of pain play out along my face, but I can feel the stitching acutely and every time I become aware of it, I'm revisited by the pain of the whip.

"Sounds like fun," I say.

Kane laughs quietly under his breath and drapes the heavier of the two chains around his neck. The finer one he reaches over me to lay on my bedside table, next to emptying jars of antiseptic and unused gauze pads.

"For when you're on your feet again. It was my mother's. The symbol is that of the blood bond, though each pair varies so as to be unique." Kane shakes his head quickly and chews on his bottom lip, looking suddenly concerned.

"Though if there is some token, or some way I might appeal to your human traditions, please tell me what you need. Anything within my reach is yours."

I smile. "I don't have any traditions." Pausing, my nerves flare unexpectedly. I lick my lips. "Kiss me?"

Kane hesitates, looking my face over, and for a moment I think he just might deny my request. But then he edges forward, moving more slowly than I otherwise would have thought possible, and very tenderly brushes the hair from my cheek. His lips meet mine and my whole body stirs. All I feel is pleasure and a numbing intensity.

He pulls back too soon and I whisper between his lips. "Do you forgive me?"

He closes his eyes, then opens them, and around the back of my head I feel his fingers curl into the hairs at the nape of my neck. "I can't go through that pain again, Abel. I won't."

"Nothing like that will ever happen again."

"And I vow that no one again shall ever put you in that position. From this moment forward, we shall not part."

I smile, feeling a tension leave my body like a bird taking flight. "I'm okay with that."

He kisses me again, more deeply this time, but it's still not enough. I want more. More and forever. Kane draws back with a slight hiss and tucks my hair behind my ear. His entire face is flushed.

"Have I hurt you?"

"No," I exhale.

He clears his throat and everything about him softens. "Your face is swollen. You have a cut here." His finger moves from beneath my eye halfway down my cheek. "And here."

I don't feel the pain, but I still shudder. "That's the least of it."

Kane curses. "I don't understand how this could have happened. Why was my brother not more severely injured?"

My mouth parts but I blank entirely on what to say. "He didn't… He didn't tell you what happened?" Calvin I understand, but Kane? How does this fall to me, now?

"I learned only that you were separated and that he found you like this. That, in the time you were apart, you were discovered by a gang which *tortured* you."

My heart beats harder at the memory, which I actively work to repress. It's easier with Kane watching me as he is. Around Kane I've always felt safe, even back at the beginning when I thought he was my worst enemy, and not the future love of my life.

I choose my next words carefully. "We got separated after I broke him out of Crestor's place. It was chaos with the survivors fighting the guards. I got chased by an alien called Trocker. We fought in the car, and then the gang caused us to have an accident. Our car crashed. I tried to escape, but they got us in the end."

I exhale, "They burned Trocker alive and told me that I had to watch. That they'd whip me unless I could keep my reactions in check."

"And you did not."

I shake my head. "No. I threw up." I couldn't stop throwing up.

My stomach gurgles audibly at the memory and Kane closes his eyes again and clasps the back of my neck. He rolls onto his side to face me and leans in again and kisses me more deeply this time. Pulling back, he just holds us close like this.

"I'm sorry I didn't kill him when I had the chance," Kane whispers. "If I had done what the Council suggested, then Crestor would not have slowed you down. You would not have been separated. Mikael could have protected you."

Crestor wasn't the problem with Mikey. But I don't tell him that.

"Why was Mikael not with you in the car when this Trocker hunted you and you were taken by the gang?"

"Good thing he wasn't. He'd have probably gotten drained and burned along with Trocker."

"You did not answer my question."

And I don't want to. I shake my head. "We just got separated."

"Abel…"

"What good is the truth," I whisper, "when all it can cause is pain?"

Kane doesn't respond, but his face takes on a distinctly murderous glint. "What did Mikael do?"

"Nothing."

"Mikael told me that he offered you myhr. Myhr is only offered between loved ones as an act of redemption for an egregious wrong. I thought he offered it to you for taking your sweetest blood against your will, but you're telling me that that wasn't even the worst of it? That he did something more to wrong you?"

I hesitate. I don't know what to say. "Mikey should be telling you this."

"*Mikey* should stay far away from me if he values his life. I want to hear from you what happened. Why did he offer you myhr, Abel?"

I close my eyes, clenching them tight. I feel so weepy and weak these days. Maybe I deserve them — these tears. Maybe here, out of Population, I'm safe.

"He left me." The words come before I can stop them.

Kane doesn't speak. I don't want to open my eyes to see how he reacts to this. "Why?" His voice is stone and hoarse.

"He wanted to go back for our…packs. I didn't want to."

"Do not tell me, Abel, that this has something to do with alcohol or drugs."

I don't answer. He told me not to.

Kane flips back the sheets and stalks towards the door. I see him reach it and he's holding the doorknob in a shaking fist. He's fighting to calm down. I can hear it in his labored breath.

"I'd like to see."

"What?"

"I'd like to see your back."

My fingers curl into the sheets. I try to sit up, but don't make it very far. Fresh pains light up all over my body. "I don't think that's a good idea. Sandra said that the cuts will leave scars, even with your blood, because the wounds have already started to heal."

Kane looks so tenuously stitched together, all it would take is a single pull. "I know. I hate that my blood isn't strong enough to heal you now. I'm not as old as Elise. A few drops of her blood kept you from dying. If I'd had a few drops more, you wouldn't be here, in pain."

"Sandra and Ashlyn are keeping me pretty hopped up on morphine." I smile. Kane doesn't. Instead, he turns and takes a brutal step towards me.

"Don't," I say. "You'll be angry." Angrier than he already is. "And maybe you'll decide to take back that necklace. Not sure I'll actually look the part of a queen after this." My voice is light, though it fails to mask a very real concern.

I get the impression that Kane senses it because all at once he comes towards me and presses his forehead to mine. He kisses it. Then kisses my nose, my lips, each of my cheeks.

"You have never been more beautiful than you are now. You're *alive*. You're with me." His hand clenches around the back of my head. "But I need a distraction right now. Give me a reason not to hunt down my brother and kill him in cold blood."

"Don't say stuff like that. He's your brother."

"Let me see, Abel. I will need to see, eventually."

I nod just once, too tangled in the sound of his voice and the tenderness of his touch. I don't stop him when he takes the soft edge of the medical tape and peels it back.

Cold air sweeps against my wounds and I struggle to look over my shoulder at his face. It's expressionless, and that frightens me.

"Pretty, ain't it?" My toes twitch as I wait for him to react.

For a long moment, Kane doesn't speak. When he does, his voice is hoarse. "Where is the man that did this to you?"

I shrug. "I don't know. Mikey didn't come across him, so he's probably still out there somewhere."

Another protracted silence. "How did you survive this?"

"Your blood is my best guess."

"You had so little of it. This should have killed you."

"When I was dying, I could feel you in my chest."

Kane replaces the bandages with care and draws the covers over me. He slides back into bed and brings himself as close to me as he can, but doesn't touch me. His hand hovers near me, but doesn't light down.

"I could feel you slipping away from me and had never felt more powerless. I couldn't move. I failed you."

"You did nothing of the sort."

Kane gulps audibly, though he keeps his eyes closed. "I let you down when I told you I never would."

"You didn't."

"How can I say it will never happen again when I could not prevent it this once?"

"Kane. Look at me and hear the words I'm telling you."

He opens his eyes and this time, I touch his face with my bandaged palm. His skin is so smooth. He doesn't look quite human like this…but he still looks so wounded.

"You don't get to play hero all the time. Sometimes, I get to be the hero, too."

"Never again," he growls, narrowing his eyes. "Next time, you'll leave me behind."

"Never." I shake my head, and close my eyes. "Never."

He leans in towards me and brushes my lips with his and wrapped together in him, I sleep as I never have before: unafraid of the darkness.

Because in Kane's light, there never is.

Chapter Fourteen

The next day, more visitors come and go. Gabe, Maggie, Calvin, Sandra, Ashlyn, Judith, Rebecca and a couple of the other girls. They clamor around me until a particular point midday when they all disappear at once.

I hear a banging that sounds very much like thunder and tell Ashlyn to go out and investigate. She's halfway to the door when it opens.

Tasha enters with purpose. Her tan silk shirt flutters in the wind her body creates. It's the first time I've ever seen her in pants, and like everything else she wears, it's a good look for her. She looks like she just got off a horse.

"Pardon me, Sistana, for not having come to see you sooner. I arrived this morning and have been struggling to navigate the murky waters between Kane and Mikael. As you can see, I didn't even have time to compose myself."

She swats at the flyaways that have escaped from her soft bun, perched so precariously on the top of her head. Her cheeks are flushed, as if she's been caught in a full out sprint, though I can't imagine her running for or from anything.

"Good to see you too, Tasha." I laugh. In her presence, I just can't help it.

Tasha straightens. "Well, yes. It is a pleasure." When I roll my eyes, she smiles a little more fully. "I *am* glad you're alright."

"Alright is relative, I'd say," I groan, twisting to the side in a fruitless attempt to get more comfortable.

I've been on my stomach like this for a week now? I glance at the necklace Kane left there the night before. Lord, has it really only been two days?

"Truly, Sistana, what you have done is incredible. You saved Kane in the time it took for me to even open an investigation with the Lahve. He is so damn slow."

I laugh. "Wow. Why don't you tell me how you really feel?"

She gives me an annoyed look before her gaze pans out to the sheet draped over me. Without asking for permission, she takes hold of the sheet, pulls it down, then reaches for the gauze and peels it back.

"Hey!" Ashlyn chides. "I just taped all that back."

"Wow. Thanks, Tasha," I mutter, getting the chills.

Tasha gasps and she whispers a series of alien words that, together, might have been either a curse or a plea.

I grunt, "Now is that any way to treat your damn queen?"

Tasha blinks at me several times, but doesn't replace the covers. She bows and looks down at her feet. "I'm sorry, Your Grace."

"Seriously, Tasha. If you don't cut the name-calling out I'm going to sic Ashlyn on you."

Tasha takes a seat on the edge of the bed and looks at Ashlyn fondly. "It's good to see you again, little warrior."

Ashlyn's cheeks turn pink. "You too."

"Is it safe to move Her Highness?"

I'm shocked by the question — first because Ashlyn is being spoken to with such a degree of respect, and second, because it's Tasha. I never thought Tasha liked humans very much.

Ashlyn wrinkles her nose and crosses her arms over another too-small tee, orange this time. "Why?"

"Good question, Ashlyn," I grunt, letting my head fall back against the mattress below. I'm tired of trying to see stuff. "Tasha, as much as I love you, I don't think I'm up for a leisurely stroll."

Tasha clears her throat daintily into her fist. "Unfortunately, you don't have much choice in the matter. Mikael has gone and made a mess." She pauses. "Another mess."

Her fingers flit over my wounds and she asks Ashlyn to bandage me. Single-handedly, she lifts me into a seated position, and I don't try to help her. All the energy I have goes into listening.

"The myhr Mikael offered Kane took place this morning, at Kane's behest. He wanted it to take place before he gave you his blood, lest you should attempt to watch."

"Bastard," I grumble. "Did you see it?" I wince as Ashlyn smoothes another piece of tape over my shoulder.

Tasha nods. "I did. My presence was required."

"What for? We didn't need a witness when Mikey gave me myhr."

Groaning, I stretch out my legs. The hinges need oil. My right knee pops half a dozen times before I manage to straighten it.

Tasha stands and paces abruptly to the door. Opening it, she stares out into the hall. "Witnesses are not required for myhr. I insisted on being present for other reasons."

"What were those?"

"To ensure Mikael's survival. Technically, a myhr can result in death. The accused cannot fight back and any weapon may be used. That's why to offer myhr is such a sacrifice."

She returns to me when I reach my toes for the ground and try to stand. With a hand on my shoulder, she keeps me seated.

"Don't get up. Sandra should be arriving shortly with a wheelchair."

"Thank freaking God," I mutter under my breath.

Ignoring me, Tasha moves to a stack of clothes I hadn't noticed piled on top of the dresser. Well, the thing that used to be the dresser. It's missing a couple drawers, but Calvin did manage to get the thing into some kind of a square-ish shape. I told Kane I probably could use a replacement, but he just said that I didn't need it, or anything in this room anymore, reminding me that my room was now his.

"In the meantime, try this on, Sistana."

She picks a floor-length peach-colored gown from the top of the pile and pulls it over my head while I protest.

"Christ, Tasha, I look like an idiot. I'm a cripple with a half-swollen face and I haven't showered in a week. This dress is not…"

"Is not up for discussion, Your Grace."

She smiles at me in a clenched sort of way and stabs her fingers into my curls. As she pulls them away from my face, I wince and curse. Ashlyn admonishes her, but she doesn't listen and comes at me with a bag of makeup.

We argue for a few seconds before I drop the bomb. The big one.

"Tasha, I *order* you to put that shit away."

Her lips twist up, but I'm pleasantly surprised that this new tactic works. I grin, she stomps her foot, and Sandra enters.

Just before they help me into the wheelchair, Tasha lowers the chain over my neck that Kane gave me. "Thank you," I tell her.

"It suits you beautifully, Abel," she says. "Kane's mother, Arianna, would have been so pleased to see you wear it." She's got tears in her eyes that bring tears to mine.

I punch her in the arm. "Stop that."

"Apologies." She sniffs, then fans her cheeks.

I laugh and turn towards Sandra, hoping to keep the emotion monster from yanking my restraint away. "Let's get this show on the road."

As Sandra rolls me down the hall, Tasha leads the way, looking more annoyed than usual. Maybe annoyed isn't the right word either. *Anxious*. She looks increasingly more anxious…

"So why exactly did I have to get out of bed and put on this ridiculous outfit?"

"I beg your pardon?" Tasha shoots me her fiercest glare.

"I mean, why did I have to get out of bed and put on this *gorgeous* outfit?"

It's Sandra, above me who says, "Mikael has requested a Tentalin."

"What's that?" Ashlyn asks, jogging to catch up to my side. We're moving quickly, an urgency I don't understand in Sandra's stride.

"Nothing good, judging by the way Kane almost leveled the house."

"No. It isn't," Tasha says, rounding the next corner. "I'll explain when we arrive in the ballroom." We walk for a few more minutes in silence before the grand ballroom opens up before us.

The room is surprisingly full. Most of this little village's occupants line the room's walls. There are also a few aliens present standing just apart from the rest of the rabble.

"Who are they?" I say to Tasha, not bothering to whisper. I know they can hear me.

"The Lavhe sent guards, upon my request," Tasha answers.

"Good work," I say as Tasha moves to my side.

In the gap her body's created, I get my first glimpse of Mikey kneeling in the center of the huge room where Calvin once taught me to waltz.

He's kneeling in a pool of his own goddamn blood!

"Holy hell! What happened?"

I try to stand, but my legs wobble and I collapse back into the wheelchair at the same time that Kane appears in front of me wearing a white tee shirt covered in blood spatter.

He doesn't speak, though the blood stains on his knuckles do. "Remain seated. You feel feverish." He stretches his hand towards me, but jerks back at the last second in a way that is very atypical.

"What…" I start to say, then redirect. "What weapon did you choose?"

"I didn't."

"And it wasn't a pretty sight," Calvin says approaching our group.

Kane doesn't contradict him and I gawk, waiting for an explanation that doesn't come. I don't really need one, do I? I know why he did what he did.

Pushing through the wall of Kane's body, I reach for Ashlyn's shoulder and use it as a crutch. Hobbling awkwardly to my feet, I plod barefoot over the parquet until Mikey's easily within earshot.

I can still feel Kane right behind me as I walk.

"Christ, man, you look terrible."

His whole face is a mess, with a cut on his mouth, blood streaming from his nose and both of his ears. His arms haven't fared much better and I can only imagine what the rest of him looks like underneath his black tee shirt and shredded jeans.

Mikey grins up at me and blood seeps out from between his teeth. He rises to standing and I see that he favors his right leg.

"Could have been worse," he hacks. "I could look like you."

I chuckle, even as Kane spits out a curse behind me — a threat. I feel strangely self-conscious standing between them in the way that I am, especially with the wide room around us completely silent. Everyone's watching.

Everyone.

"Yeah," I say as quietly as I can. "You could have died."

"But he didn't kill me."

"I should have," Kane snarls at my back, and though I want to reprimand him, I distinctly remember shooting Mikey a few days ago. Apparently he inspires similar emotions in everyone.

I turn to face Kane and see Tasha standing at his side. She's whispering in his ear, talking him off the ledge. I know that. I can see it in the fury in his face, the swelling and tightening of his shoulders. It seems to be working, until Mikey says at my back, "Abel, you have to take it off."

Kane roars and Tasha's heels slide towards me over the floor as she uses her whole body to block him. Two of the other aliens peel apart from their comerades and approach Tasha, and help her restrain their Notare.

"You selfish bastard," he shouts.

"Kane, no," Tasha grunts while the Others — a male and a female, both dressed in gear that makes me think military — push Kane back towards the door.

Tasha rounds on Mikael, even as she takes me by the shoulder and guides me away from him. "Mikael, control yourself."

As Kane reluctantly yields, he paces away from Mikey and me, moving into the center of the room. He laces his fingers over his crown and takes jerky, shallow breaths. I don't know if I've ever seen him so angry.

I turn and watch the room's occupants watch me. I've never felt more exposed as they follow me wordlessly with their eyes but don't speak. The entire room seems to be waiting for something.

"Your Grace, please have a seat." Tasha smoothes down her hair, then gestures for Sandra to bring the wheelchair.

I take a seat and let Sandra push me to a point near Calvin at the entrance while Kane and Mikey move into the center of the hall and square up against one another. "There's gonna be a fight? But I thought they did myhr?"

Tasha clenches her teeth. "They did, but Mikael has demanded a Tentalin be held today."

Maggie comes to stand beside me and lays her hand on my shoulder, and I get the very distinct impression that something terrible is about to happen. Sandra takes the place to my left and Ashlyn sits cross-legged at my feet.

"A Tentalin," Tasha explains while Kane and Mikey each drop to one knee in mirrored acts of genuflection, "is an ancient tribunal whose outcomes are to be respected by all parties involved." She licks her lips, and swallows hard.

"You are called forward as a witness to this Tentalin, which has been called in your honor."

"In my honor?" I mouth, searching her face for answers.

Tasha only nods. "Mikael has challenged Notare Kane in a Tentalin for the right to your…*bond*." Her voice breaks. "Should the Notare prevail, preparations for your joining will continue as planned. Should Mikael prove the victor, then he will have the right to blood bond with you."

"No!" I shout, rising up out of my chair, only to drop back down again when it wobbles.

Tasha's face turns bright red and she holds up a hand. "You dishonor them *both* by declining."

My mouth hangs open as vocabulary eludes me. Mikey's gone too fucking far. Does he expect to win? What does he hope to get out of it if he does? He feels guilty — I get that — but he doesn't even like me. Is this about Kane and his deep, deep envy? Or is this about my sweetest blood and his addiction to it, like his addiction to everything?

"Sistana," Tasha says. I snap back to attention. "You must honor the results of the Tentalin." There's fire in her eyes as she mouths a series of words, expecting me to repeat them.

"Fuck. Fine," I say.

She reddens even further and nods just once. "I am sorry, but you will need to remove the knot until after the Tentalin concludes. You may put it back on again should Kane prove the victor."

She doesn't meet my gaze as she steps up behind me, lifts the strand over my head and tucks it away. I'm not a sentimental girl, but when I touch my chest, I still feel loss.

"The Tentalin can begin Mikael, Notare Kane, whenever you are ready."

My stomach pitches as Kane and Mikael come together in the center of the room all at once, moving with all the speed of fire, and its destruction.

The battle seems to last hours and I refuse to watch. I don't care who it shames. I can't watch brother pitted against brother in my name. Even if I've got nothing to do with it.

But I can still hear it. The crack of bone. The slippery smacking sound their bodies make as they slide over blood. Muted thumps and growled grunts. Cries of rage and of pain.

"It's over," Tasha whispers in my ear some indeterminate amount of time later. "You can wear the knot again, Sistana."

I feel the weight of it slide over my neck and I reach down and grip the metal. I hold it, letting it fortify me, before I open my eyes.

Kane is all I can see. Everywhere. There's black blood smeared across his sweaty chest. His pants are ripped. His shirt is gone except for the top half. I try to look around him, but he grips the back of my head and rips open his wrist with his teeth.

"Drink," he says to me, and I don't know this tone and I don't dare deny him.

I press my mouth to his open wound and I drink. I drink and drink until Kane wavers where he stands and Tasha tells him to stop. She hands him a towel and as he takes it from her, she loops his knot over his neck.

"Notare," she says with a small bow.

"Clean up this mess," Kane snarls. "I will be with my *wife* in our quarters. Unless the world is ending, we aren't to be disturbed."

He slips his arms beneath me and even though I can feel my wounds healing themselves whole — the map on my back wiping itself clean, the bullet wound in my shoulder filling itself in, the bite in my leg erasing itself like it never was — and I'm pretty sure I can walk now, I still don't deny him this.

It seems like he needs it.

He carries me from the room, and even though people have started to move back and forth, I still catch one quick glimpse of Mikey in the center of the dance hall — the coliseum — as he's lifted onto a stretcher.

From head to toe, he's covered in blood.

I don't know what's broken or what's whole, because everything looks broken.

Sandra cuts off my line of sight as she hurries towards Mikey. Calvin and another three humans trail slightly behind her, each carrying a bucket and a mop.

Chapter Fifteen

"Kane?"

"No. No talking." He's charging up the stairs like he's late for something and if he weren't tearing apart the dress Tasha put me, I'd be confused as to what was going on.

We make it to the hall his room is in but my legs are around his hips and I can feel his erection through his jeans and am rubbing myself against it.

"I'm still on my period," I tell him, panting.

Kane growls against my throat. "Good."

He lowers my feet to the ground and before I know what's happening, he drops to his knees and slips under the skirt of my dress. He pulls down my panties and the blood stained rag there and covers my core with his mouth.

My eyes roll back and pleasure pricks the top of my tongue, like I'm tasting something sweet and savory all at once. I might have Kane's blood in me, but Kane didn't even have a lot of Kane's blood in him, so I'm still woozy where I stand.

I reach out and catch myself on a painting and clumsily knock it down. It starts to fall over me and I fall and with Kane trapped under my skirt he falls too, and we land together, tangled underneath the painting and maybe we needed it because we both burst out laughing.

I burst into tears too.

Kane crawls up my body over my dress, but under the painting, so we're still hidden in its shadow. He kisses the underside of my jaw and I can feel him fiddling with something below his waist.

I feel his erection press against my wet entrance a second later, but when I expect him to push forward, he hesitates.

"Do I have your permission?" He says, voice catching.

His eyes are worried, even though I'm completely wrapped around him — well, as wrapped around him as I can be with canvas pressing against my arms.

I smile and trace the outline of his face with my middle finger. I brush my thumbs under the bags under his eyes. I scratch his stubble.

"You always have my permission. Forever. Even if I'm asleep."

He barks out laughter at that, but still doesn't come forward. He kisses me sweetly at first, and something *changes* in the kiss. It's no longer so desperate, so feverish, so mad.

His tongue lavishes mine in long strokes and when the weight of his hips sink onto mine and his cock slips past my lower lips, his gaze never leaves mine.

"I adore you," he says and his voice breaks as he enters me, seating himself fully inside.

And it's so full, it's like the very first time. I blink quickly, trying to lift my hips so he'll go faster, but he doesn't break his impossible tempo.

"You're still hurt," he says, as if that explains it.

"I'm healed. I drank from you."

He shakes his head. "I can feel your stitches like individual heartbreaks." His fingers brush over my shoulder and he slows even more.

Our tangled gazes and our tangled legs make me feel like I'm losing my grip on time and space. The painting shadows us like a veil. Like we don't exist in the rest of the world.

"It's just us," he breathes and his breath still smells like peppermint. Mine probably smells like blood. I don't care.

I stretch up and kiss his chin. He holds the side of my face. Our hips push and pull together in a choreographed movement. Tears. They come to my eyes like I'm suddenly releasing everything Population never let me release before.

For my brother.

For my parents.

For Becks.

For everyone who's ever died at my hand to live.

For the four men who I killed in that grocery store.

"I'm not a savage," I say and I don't know why.

Kane slows even more and I'm caught in the brilliance of his smile. "No. You're a perfect creation."

"No, *you* are," I blabber.

Kane refuses to relinquish the vice he's got around my heart. I try, but can't look away from him.

He grinds harder against my clit, knowing what I need and I can feel myself building towards something, but it's different than it was in the kitchens. Not an explosion, and not an arrival, but a release on top of so many other releases. Everything just goes.

It's like he unzips my soul.

I step out and I'm lighter than I was. My eyelids flutter, but I don't let go. Can't let go.

My mouth opens and I struggle to exhale my next breath as Kane grinds so, so slow.

"Oh…"

It comes and pulls me apart at the seams.

I'm only distantly aware that Kane is whispering words in an alien language to me as he straightens and falls forward. His mouth finds my neck, but he doesn't break the skin there as he comes inside me.

His ass clenches under my fingers and I hold onto his abs as he jerks, jolting my whole body forward. His pleasure becomes mine and I don't try to fight it.

I let myself get caught up in the rip tide as our emotions ebb and crest, lap and recede.

It takes a while for the purity of such overwhelming pleasure to release me from its grip. When it does, sweat and blood coat both our bodies and my back is starting to hurt me again. I still don't move right away, but I hold back from reentering the cycle as Kane collapses more of his weight onto me.

He pulls up just enough to be able to look into my eyes. He looks drunk and beautiful at the same time.

"This painting is scratching my ass."

I crack, laughing so hard my whole body shakes. Kane laughs into my neck, brushing little kisses across my sweat-slicked skin.

"There's also a fat baby staring at me," I chuckle.

Kane looks over his shoulder at the cherub painted there and grunts. "Revolting little thing. Does this creature exist on your planet?"

I laugh again and shake my head while he slowly slides out of me. We both groan as his softening cock slips free of my entrance.

"Not that I know of," I sigh, looping my arms around his neck.

"What is it? You just made a face," he says.

"I think I'm probably bleeding all over your floor."

"Good. You can bleed anywhere you need." He slips his hand down my body and his fingers trace over my lower lips in a way that makes my back arch in a natural desire.

He pulls them back and his fingers are covered in faint traces of pink. He sucks them clean and freezes, shakes his head, exhales shakily.

"Have I thanked your gods for creating you, yet?"

"Yes," I say smiling. "I think you already did."

"Well, my Sistana. Let me return with you to our room where I can worship their most magical creation properly."

He kisses me softly, and then he does just what he says he will.

Again and again and again.

Chapter Sixteen

"There. All done." Sandra brushes off her hands and leaves the room and it's only then that the tension Kane carried with him releases, just a little.

It releases a little more when he draws us a bath and sets me in it. He straddles me, like he once did, only this time, he's massaging my back so gently I can hardly feel it.

"Any harder and I could cause you pain," he says when I complain.

"You're not going to hurt me."

He doesn't answer, just keeps rubbing soap into my skin. "You would perhaps change your tone, if you could see what I'm seeing."

I don't have anything to say to that. "How are the scars? Hideous?"

He doesn't answer. I poke his calf.

"Way to make me feel better."

He huffs, "They look painful. I don't like that they look like they're hurting you."

"They don't hurt."

"You asked for my opinion."

"Yeah, I just wish you had a different one."

I reach for his knee and try to tickle the back of it. He doesn't so much as flinch. "Boring," I mutter.

He wraps his arms around me at that and drags me into his chest. "Boring?" He says, chowing at my neck.

I squeal and pretend to fight him off. Really, I just sink deeper into his lap, rubbing the curve of my ass against his erection. "I didn't mean it!"

"You better not have. If you think I'm boring already, what will you think of me in two hundred years?"

"You know humans don't live that long, right?" I say, turning around in his arms so I can straddle him properly.

"With my blood in your system, you never know. You could live as long as I do."

"Well, whatever happens, I want to die in the bath." I love the bath, I decide then.

He freezes. "What?"

"This bath. I want to die in it." I sit back with a splash and kick bubbles in Kane's direction. "Sitting here with you is what I think about every time the pain gets too much. It's my happy place."

Kane's voice gets soft. "Do you want to know mine?"

I nod.

"The first time you came for me and you looked so lost. So surprised. It was the first time I ever truly felt like a king."

I blush and look away from him, but I can't get anywhere, not when he has hold of both my feet. We lapse into a pleasant sort of silence while my mind wanders. I think at some point, I even manage to sleep.

"Let's go to bed," Kane whispers. Once there, he says to me, "What are you thinking?"

"Nothing."

"Tell me." He takes my hand in his and kisses the tips of all my fingers.

"I don't understand. Why would Mikey do that?"

Kane closes his eyes, lips moving over the large scar on my arm from one or both times my wrist was broken. It's a darker brown strip about six inches long, but still manages to look like it's decades old, and not just a few days.

"Mikael has not had much happiness in his life. You make him happy."

"I don't think it has anything to do with me," I say.

Kane doesn't answer.

I elaborate. "I think it's just envy. He doesn't like that you have something he doesn't, because you already have everything he doesn't. He wants to be you."

"Perhaps," Kane says softly, tucking my damp curls behind my ear. "But his envying me does not explain his selflessness towards you."

"Selflessness? Or guilt?" He almost got me killed — a couple times.

"It could be both."

"Whatever it is, I'm glad it's over. No more fighting between the two of you, got it? You're family. I'd kill to have mine back so I'm not going to let you or him or me destroy yours."

"Ours," he whispers. "He is our family. And I will do my best to be on good behavior, unless I am provoked."

"Good lord."

"He is untrustworthy."

I nod, considering. "Maybe. But it doesn't matter now. We're all here and I'm yours and everything's fine. We're safe."

But Kane doesn't agree with me.

"Right, Kane?"

He sighs, "Can we not have a few moments of peace before we reenter the fray?"

"Fray? Oh lord, what do you mean?"

"I mean Elise. She's still out there and now that I have been recovered, I can speak directly to the Lahve and he can kill her."

"Just like that?"

"For her crimes?" Kane nods. "Just like that."

"Where is he now, the Lahve?"

"The Lavhe has gone to Crestor's estate in the hopes of finding and rescuing any of his Heztoichen victims. After he has put Crestor to death, he will come here and together we will discuss what to do about Elise.

"She is still Notare, so the same rules do not apply to her. He can't just have her executed, so she must be captured before she can be imprisoned. It won't be easy and I won't have you involved. My quarrel is with Elise, alone."

I push myself up on his shoulder and stab my finger to the center of his chest. "The hell it is. I'm not sending you back into the salt land after that wackjob nearly killed you. No ways."

"And I won't have you anywhere near her either. The Lavhe and his guard will handle Elise. Likely, we won't even have to leave this house. Or this bed." He flicks my chin, and draws me down for a kiss.

"This Lavhe guy better be all you've cracked him up to be," I say, speaking against his lips.

Kane smiles and I can tell that he's exhausted by the way that he groans. "The Lavhe is the last of an ancient bloodline, a species not entirely like our own. His senses are faster, sharper. He would argue that his higher level of intelligence makes him more capable of impartiality and leads him to have full command of his emotions."

Kane yawns and the last of the tension deflates from his neck and shoulders. "He's over three thousand years old. You will not be disappointed."

Seeing him exhausted makes me exhausted, and we sleep soundly through the next day and night. A blood-soaked honeymoon, I wouldn't trade it for any other life.

Chapter Seventeen

The days leading up to the Chancellor's arrival are filled with a ridiculous amount of Tasha fittings, checkups by Sandra, midnight poker with Calvin, Gabe, and Kane, lightning-round catch-up sessions with Ashlyn, and therapy with Maggie, Sandra, Ashlyn, Judith and the other girls that came from Memnoch's cave.

I don't see Mikey once, or rather, he won't see me. He keeps his door locked, and when I knock, doesn't respond, even though I can hear the distinct sounds of a body moving on the other side of the door.

I move on, taking a tour of the house, stopping by that cherub painting which has been rehung where it was, even if there's an ass-shaped dip in the canvas now.

I find Kane in his den arguing with a big guy called Far, head of the Lavhe's security. Silent and clad all in black, they patrol the house relentlessly. I can feel one following me now, but don't bother acknowledging him.

"Knock, knock," I say aloud as my knuckles rap against the wood.

Both males turn when I enter. Far bows at the waist. "Sistana."

Far's face is almost perfect, with no lines or wrinkles or age marks. His eyes are two small beads of coal, as hard as diamonds, and like diamonds, they glitter as they canvass the room, gaze passing over everything with a hunter's precision. Kane tells me it's because the Lavhe keeps only older Heztoichen for his guards. Far is nearly twice as old as Kane is.

I awkwardly salute. "At ease," I joke. Kane is the only one who laughs between them. "How are things going?"

"Well," Far says, though his face is drawn in a severe expression that contradicts it.

"Yeah?" I wade further into the room, moving to Kane's side when he lifts his arm.

He circles my waist and drags me in to meet his kiss, gripping me with the same ferocity with which I grip him. I slide my fingers through his hair, cupping his neck with my hands until he yields into my kiss, letting it wander.

Wavering on my feet, I allow my full bodyweight to rest against him until he releases a short, brutish laugh between my lips and severs the contact.

Pulling back, he snorts, "Far does have a way with words. We're unable to come to a compromise on the number of guards needed to prepare for the Lavhe's arrival. I found twenty to be a bit excessive."

"Twenty doesn't sound too crazy," I say, trying to regain my footing. Far is staring off into space as if there's something particularly important on the bookshelf lining the wall. I laugh lightly.

Kane lifts a brow. "Twenty in addition to the fifteen already present and the ten that make up the Lavhe's personal escort."

I whistle. "Damn."

Far clears his throat. "I would like to remind Your Graces that these guards will constitute the party sent to retrieve and detain Notare Elise."

"Fifty aliens just to take down one?"

Far doesn't flinch at my nomenclature. "Any fewer would be insufficient and would present a risk to the Lavhe and to Notare Kane."

The lazy way I feel before drops like a blanket at my feet. "Kane, you're *going*?" My pitch rises and breaks as I glare at him, making me sound less condemning than I would have liked. I punch him in the arm. "But you said…"

"I have to."

I move from his side to stand directly in front of him. Placing my hands on each of his shoulders I push his torso back, forcing him to look at me. "Why?"

He grimaces. "You wouldn't understand."

"Help me, then. You said neither of us would have to leave this house and yet you're off talking to Robocop about a battle strategy that you're fully intending to be a part of. So again, let me ask you why you *lied* to me?"

Kane shakes his head, hair sticking out in every direction. "You don't know…"

"You're right." I throw my arms out to the sides. "I don't know, so enlighten me."

"You can't imagine what it was like with her…being tortured…"

"So that's what this is? Settling a score? A vendetta?" I punch my fingers back through my curls and huff, cheeks billowing out like small balloons. "I can't believe you're doing this. You're putting your life at risk because she wounded your pride and you don't even give a thought to *us*. To how I might feel if you…"

"That's *all* I'm thinking about," Kane snarls and I forget how tall he is until he comes at me like this.

He grabs my hips and pulls me under the arc of his body. He holds me tight and his voice shakes with rage as he roars, "*I gave you her blood*."

The words fly from his lips and hit me in the face with the force of a fist even though his touch is soft against my face. He traces the line of the scar there, which drips like a pale brown teardrop down the curve of my cheek.

"So?"

Kane sighs and the tension seems to have deflated from his shoulders. He looks defeated for reasons I don't fully understand. "Her blood is powerful. Far too powerful. I can smell it on your skin. Not even half the blood in my body was enough to overcome the scent of five fucking droplets."

"I still don't understand," I confess. "Why does it matter?"

"It just does." He stands abruptly and for a moment I think he might say more. Instead, he kisses my cheek tersely before moving away from me to the door. "I'm sorry, but I must see this through."

I'm pissed when he leaves me like that, and Far doesn't stick around to offer an explanation. I'm left to try to run through the house in search of him, but instead, I run into the other brother.

"Hey!" I jump. My voice is much louder than I'd meant for it to be. Clearing my throat, I try again. "Hey, Mikey. Wait up."

Mikey's shoulders are bunched by his ears and he hesitates before coming to a stop. I jog over the carpet, hoping to reach him before he changes his mind and runs. It looks like he wants to. He doesn't turn to face me and I don't touch him, though I want to force him to meet my gaze. A warmth hits my cheeks as I move to stand before him, and now that I'm here, I don't know what to say. He's wearing a white tee shirt and black basketball shorts. His hair is washed and cut, and when he turns, I see that he's shaved his beard.

"Wow." I hide my grin with my hand. "Somebody cleans up nice." It's true. His brother might prowl my dreams, but Mikey's a hot piece of ass.

When his mouth's shut and he doesn't have a bottle of booze in his hand.

I glance down and feel heat and anger light up my cheeks. "What's that?"

Barefoot, he shuffles uncomfortably from one edge of the carpet to the other while his upper lip curls into a cruel snarl. It's almost enough to make me want to put space between us, but I hold my ground.

"Nothing," he says, lowering the bottle in his hand. Bourbon, I think, but I can't be sure. It's missing a label.

"Wow. You get thirsty on the walk upstairs?"

"Fuck you."

"Okay, then." Annoyed that I'm the one being nice when I should be punching the shit out of him for *daring* to bring a bottle of booze anywhere near me — despite the fact that I ran into him — I roll my eyes, cross my arms and head towards the door to my and Kane's room, which is right in front of us.

My hand is on the knob when he groans, "Wait." I turn and he holds the base of the bottle towards me. "It's for you."

Confusion mingles with my anger enough to curb the bite of the blow. "Don't you remember my last little encounter with that poison?"

Mikey smiles, and with his clean clothes on, I can smell peppermint and fresh cut grass. "You couldn't walk straight. I thought I was going to have to carry you the rest of the way to Seattle."

I start to smile until I refocus on the bottle. "That stuff really is poison, so I think I'll pass."

He doesn't lower his hand, but instead moves a half a step closer. "It's not to drink. It's a symbol." His bottom teeth worry his lower lip. It's crimson and full, rather than split down the middle as I'd last seen it. There's not a scratch on him from what I can tell.

"There was one other bottle in my pack that I didn't tell you about. I tried to drink it when you were out, in pain, but I couldn't. The taste in my mouth…" He sighs through his teeth. "It tasted like shame.

"I vowed that it would be my last drink, and so far it has been. I mean, that isn't saying much. It's been…" He pauses, then, "Ten days. Ten days sober." His gaze meets mine and there's a hopefulness in the darkness that makes my eyes burn unexpectedly.

A lump forms in my throat as I take the bottle from him. "Eleven, I think."

He smiles and turns bright red. "Eleven, then." He nods and without warning, turns and starts walking away.

"Mikey, wait." He flinches as I blurt, "Why did you do it?"

"Do what?" But I can see his back muscles bunch together beneath the thin fabric of his tee shirt.

"You know what. Why did you request the Tantalin? Why on earth did you try to fight your brother for me? You don't even like me."

"I like you."

I balk. "You don't love me though."

He opens his mouth, then frowns.

"I like you, but I love your brother. Even if you had won, did you expect I'd just let go of him?"

Mikey closes his eyes. His breathing is hard. "No."

"Then why?"

"Because it isn't…"

A long pause, and I push, "Because it isn't what, Mikey?"

"Because it isn't fair. He shouldn't get everything good. He shouldn't…" He covers his eyes with his hands.

I step forward and take one of his big mitts in both of mine. I clasp it to my chest fiercely. “I know you don’t want to hear this right now, but your brother isn’t a bad guy. But he also isn’t the only guy in the whole damn world. Heck — I know some people don’t even find him that interesting. I was just telling him last night how boring he is.”

Mikey shakes his head at his feet. “I’m sure that’s how the conversation went.”

“Of course it is.” I let go of his hand and cup his cheek. “My point is that you need to stop looking at Kane and look at you. Because you’re interesting too. And funny and witty and kind and even hot under the right circumstances?”

“You mean after a shower?”

I slip the bottle free of his fingers and hold it up. “I mean when you’re sober.” I pull back. “I’ll take this for now and when you can look after it yourself, I’ll give it back to you.”

“I don’t need it back.”

“Fine,” I say opening my bedroom door. “Then I’ll give it to someone who can look after it for you when and only when you find someone up to the task.”

“What is that supposed to mean?” He says as I shut the door between us.

“If you have to ask, then you’re definitely not ready yet.”

I close the door and leave him glaring after me.

Still barefoot.

Chapter Eighteen

"What are you wearing?" Ashlyn scrunches up her nose as she tries not to laugh.

I roll my eyes. "One of Tasha's contraptions. Now, shush. He can hear us from the driveway."

Kane's standing to my right, Ashlyn to my left, while a whole host of humans is spread out along the wall beside her. Mikey stands to Kane's other side, Tasha to his right. We look ridiculous, sixty plus people and aliens clustered in the freaking foyer, waiting for the Lavhe and his goons.

Ashlyn gives my skirt a tug and I rip the material free of her grip, feeling annoyed. Not at her though. Once again Tasha has poured me into a garment that's two sizes too small. Long, it trails on the floor when I walk, or would have had I not been in nine-inch platform heels that bring me up to Kane's earlobe.

I might be Sistana now, but I don't have the patience to stand up to Tasha when she traps me in these garments, and from the corner of my eye I can see her glaring at me. At my side, I see Kane fighting back laughter.

The tall, double doors swing open in tandem and fifteen aliens dressed in maroon uniforms walking in five rows of three move into the already crowded space.

This is utter nonsense.

I make a mental note to give the Lavhe a piece of my mind when I see him. And then I see him, and quickly lose the impulse.

He carries a cane, though he doesn't need it. It's thin and black, decorated with a silver handle that matches his fitted grey suit. His leather shoes click against the tiles as he walks and somehow that's all I can hear as I watch him. There is nothing else.

There's something sinuous in the way he moves, and something sinister in the way he stares. His skin is onyx and immaculately smooth, like petrified wood, and the bright whites of his eyes surround an even brighter amber.

Orange irises studded with two pinpricks of black, they land on me first and hit like a bludgeon before settling on Kane. I don't realize I've taken half a step back until Kane's hand on my wrist squeezes, trying to subtly hold me in place.

"Lahve," Kane says, releasing me and taking a single step forward to meet the presence that just entered.

There's no other way to describe him.

Not a man.

Not an alien.

Not an Other.

A *presence.*

He moves like he's dragging an imagined world with him and like that world's history is written in the margins of his coat and in the long, locked tendrils of his hair.

Kane holds out his hand and the Lahve suddenly appears before him. He doesn't move *fast.* I've seen bodies that move fast. He just *is.*

Not a man. Not an Other.

A presence.

I waver again, and this time I do take a half step back. The Lahve notices and his bright orange gaze slides slowly to meet mine.

I just about shit myself.

I don't understand how anyone can have a conversation with him, let alone a debate. A Notare is supposed to hold sway over this guy? How can they? He's not a guy. Not an alien.

A presence.

"Shit," I say out loud.

Kane speaks louder than I do as he clears his throat. "Greetings, Lahve," he says and I think he might be laughing at me somewhere in those gruff undertones.

The Lavhe nods, thin, tightly-knotted locks falling over his shoulder, just as dark an ebony as his skin. "Greetings to you, Notare."

His voice is soft, and yet the overlapping chords of at least three other voices can be heard when he speaks. Did he eat people? Are they somewhere in there still breathing?

The Lahve still hasn't looked away from me and I don't introduce myself. I can't talk to this people-eating presence.

Kane takes my hand and tries to gracefully drag me forward, but there's nothing graceful about it. I stagger forward one unwilling step.

"This is my Sistana, Abel."

"Sistana."

He inclines his head towards me and straightens, movements all slow and smooth. He extends his free hand towards me and I take it and it feels like I'm touching marble. Stone and hard and cool. Though his face isn't a day over thirty-five, there's something ancient in his aura.

"I have heard tales of your resilience. I believe you were recently involved in a brutal attack? This was just before you rescued Notare Kane from Notare Elise's illegal settlement?"

The words come at me three times, hitting me like fists from three different angles. I can't ward off the overlapping blows, and I grab Kane's arm so as not to stagger. I nod.

"Yeah." And then I shake my head. "No. I mean, yeah, but it was before Mikey and I rescued Kane."

The Lahve's orange gaze glows like the surface of the sun as it flashes momentarily to Mikey. "It is a wonder that he was not injured." His tone is filled with implication.

Kane must hear it as well, because he stiffens at my side and says, "Mikael has offered myhr both to myself and to the Sistana for his failure to protect her."

"Not a failure to protect. A total abandonment." He pauses. It takes too long. Way too long. Then he says, "I saw how he glutted himself on wine at Crestor's table and allowed himself to be dragged away while the Sistana was released."

He tilts his head from the right to the left as his gaze switches back to me, landing like a spotlight. "They thought you would leave, the guards. They prepared to hunt you when Crestor slept."

I can feel Kane tense at my side and it's my turn to grab his wrist this time.

Not sensing the danger, or unconcerned by it, the Lahve continues. "You were very clever," he whispers and it sends chills crawling like ants up my back. Like termites, they burrow.

"You distracted them with your sweetest blood, and then you freed the mutilated ones, even though it came at great cost. I watched you fight them. You were magnificent. I had not believed humans to be capable of such things."

He pauses again and even though the time stretches on forever, there's still no opening for anyone else to speak.

No one would dare cut off a presence.

"I watched you escape with Mikael and I saw as you attempted to persuade him to follow you to retrieve the Notare. I saw as he turned his back on you. His own Sistana. He ran through the woods away from you and when he found what it was he sought, he drank an entire bottle before thinking to go back for you. For a moment, it did not look like he would."

He straightens and suddenly everything shifts. He looks a little bit more like a person, like he had to remind himself to be less of a presence.

"Apologies, it would appear this information has upset you, Sistana. Would you prefer not to have known?"

"Yes," I blurt, tears on my tongue. I look past him at Mikey and try to remember that we're here and now and that it's all over, but it's hard.

I suck in a shaky breath and look away from Mikey's face. He says nothing. He just stares at me in a shock and horror true enough for me to know he did everything the Lahve accused him of.

"You saw all of this?" I say, feeling anger on the heels of this fresh betrayal. Anger at *him*. The presence who saw too much and flung it all across my foyer.

He nods. "I see much."

"How?"

"The Lahve has a gift," Kane says and he chokes and I can tell he's trying to keep it together just as much as I am. "He can read memories, among other things."

"It is well put, Notare." The Lahve speaks slowly, like he's got all the time in the world. "I read the memories of the survivors we found near Crestor's estate. A surprising number of accounts depicted yours and Mikael's movements, up until you were delivered into the hands of this human gang. I was not able to source them."

The Lavhe's body shifts ever so subtly and I can't get out what I was going to say next. He takes a step towards me until we're less than an arm's distance apart and I don't miss the way Kane angles his body in front of mine.

The Lavhe looks to Kane first, then says to me, "May I see your injuries, Sistana?"

"You want to see my scars?"

He nods. "It has come to my attention, during your wait for Kane's blood, your wounds left scars. I would like to see the extent of the damage."

"Why?" I say rudely and I can tell it's rude by the way everyone in the whole room stiffens — the mulberry guard in particular.

The Lahve doesn't answer right away and I wonder if he's waiting for an apology. If he is, he can keep waiting. Finally, he says, "I would like to fill in the rest of the gaps so that I may have a complete and detailed history of our Sistana. I will write these down in the books so that nothing is forgotten. No successes, and no failures." His gaze slides towards Mikey and I feel the irrational desire to protect him, even though he wouldn't do the same for me.

Not wouldn't.

Didn't.

Not when it counted.

"Fine," I blurt, hoping to hold his attention and spare Mikey the grief. I start to turn and raise my hands to the clasp at the back of my neck, but Kane grabs my shoulder.

"Apologies, Lavhe. I require that this conversation take place somewhere more private."

The Lavhe bows again. "Apologies, Notare, please lead the way."

Kane nods and looks out at the overfull room. "You all are dismissed."

He turns on his heel and I follow closely behind, gesturing for Ashlyn to join me. She gives me strength as she grips my hand, the clamminess of our palms acting as adhesive between us.

I can feel the Lavhe at my heels, following in long strides, each of which covers at least two of my own. I'm chased by the click-click-click of his leather-soled shoes on the marble tiles, and then off of the dark wood floor of the den.

Tucking his cane inside of his long cloak, the Lahve steps up in front of me as I stand in the center of the room. He lowers his gaze to Ashlyn beside me and I tense, fearing what he'll see about her too.

"I do not intend to offend, Sistana, but not even my guards have been permitted to enter the room."

"She stays. She's family."

The Lavhe waits. He doesn't move. He doesn't blink. He doesn't look like he's breathing, either. "Very well, then," he says rapidly.

"You wanted to see the damage?" I say.

"If it would not trouble you."

"No trouble. Ashlyn, would you mind?"

She unfastens the clasp at the back of my neck, then brings the zipper all the way down. With her delicate hands she pushes the sides of my dress apart and I don't miss the way she gasps. I imagine I would gasp if I saw me, too. Every time.

I can hear the Lahve approach, but before I know what he's done, a tremor ripples through me as his fingers touch my left shoulder.

His hand is ice and my body freezes over while I'm throttled back into the past. Into memories I never wanted to see again — memories I would unsee if I could.

Mikey in the woods, staring at me with one eye swollen shut, telling me he'll come back for me. The sickening sense of abandonment that grips me as I'm all alone, running for my life, away from Mikey. The first time I saw Jack and felt hope. The last time I saw Jack and felt hopeless.

Diego's hollow eyes, so full of pain.

I wish I knew where he was…

"Lavhe." Kane's voice snaps through the space like the tail end of a whip. With whips, I am all too familiar. "With great respect, you are in my house, in my territory, and while my Sistana may be generous enough to allow you the grace of touching her injuries, I am not."

Kane's face is blood red, though I'm distracted from the severity of his expression by Mikey at his side. Mikey's pale. Ghost white. His gaze pans to mine and he clenches his fists. His eyes genuflect, dropping to the carpet between us.

"Apologies, Notare. Curiosity led me to overstep," he says, without sounding sorry at all.

"I see now what caused the marks and I am sorry for what you endured, Sistana." When he says this, it actually sounds like there's some truth to it.

I turn and see him wiping sweat from his brow and wonder…he said *saw*, but did he *feel* it, too?

Quickly, he says, "These marks are unusual, even for a human." Ashlyn zips me back up, and I turn to see the Lavhe watching me with his head tilted askew.

"With your blood loss, I'd have assumed the marks to be more severe. You had little blood in your system and you were bled nearly dry. How did you survive?"

I look to Kane. "Kane gave me…"

Kane clears his throat, face betraying a nervousness that his tone doesn't. "I gave her blood from Notare Elise's lab."

The Lavhe doesn't move, not even on the inhale. *Is* he even breathing? "Do you know whose?"

A long silence lingers. Painful this time. Kane takes a few steps forward, coming close enough to take my hand. His fingers are so warm and familiar, his lips soft as he brushes his mouth across the backs of my knuckles.

"It is the Notare's," he finally says. "I gave her five drops of Elise's blood."

"And it was enough to save her?"

Kane nods and the Lavhe drags in a loud breath all at once, and I imagine that he's sucked all the air out of the room. I curl one arm around Kane's waist and drape the other over Ashlyn's shoulder. While Ashlyn takes my hand, Kane kneads the back of my neck as if to keep himself present, or to let me know I'm safe.

I wonder what he's feeling and what his thoughts are, because mine are entirely blank. I'm a goon now too, waiting for instruction, though the Lavhe doesn't seem to be in any particular hurry himself. Then again, he's lived three thousand years. What's another five minutes?

"Interesting," he says.

"Lavhe." Kane's voice is both a command and a question.

The Lahve nods and takes a slow turn around the room, unnaturally long fingers trailing the backs of the chairs and sofa as he walks.

"Crestor was not difficult to locate following the sacking of his estate by your hand, Sistana. My guards were able to effectively rescue those in his vault and those who wished to reintegrate into society are being rehabilitated, while those who requested release, were granted it."

I tense and Kane squeezes my neck reassuringly. I do the same to Ashlyn. While it hurts to hear that even those that escape may not have survive, it makes me feel better to know that some at least were able to live or die on their own terms. That they had a choice. That's all any of us can hope for in Population.

"Elise, however, has been more of a challenge."

Standing directly across from me, he grips the back of the armchair in front of him. His orange eyes glow fiercely against his skin and the even darker charcoal outline of the sky visible through the high arching window at his back.

"She is aware she is being hunted. Her compound in the Saltlands where you were held, Notare, have been burned beyond recognition. There is no memory there. She razed it out and surprisingly, I have not been able to locate her since."

"She must be brought to justice for her crimes," Kane bellows, taking a step towards him. "Have your troops been sent to Brianna? Root her out. She must have returned to her own territory."

The Lavhe waits to speak long after Kane has quieted. I can tell Kane has displeased him by the way the corners of his mouth twitch down, but that is the only reaction Kane wins from him.

"I understand your grief, Notare, but her territory has been thoroughly investigated and there is much terrain in this world — too much for my troops to cover inch by inch. It would be impossible, and Notare Elise is far too clever. But…"

He shifts and the light hits the hard angles of his face. He's built like a cut diamond. High cheekbones, pointed chin, straight nose leading to a broad, flat forehead. Only his mouth is human, and it's very human.

Lips full and rounded, black on the outsides, but when they part I get intermittent hints of pink.

"There is another way."

"No," Kane says before the Lavhe even finishes.

"I am relatively unfamiliar with the customs of humans, however, in our own culture, the Sistana has the right to speak for herself."

"You dare," Kane seethes, light flaring in his chest so bright it's visible through his blue shirt. "I could expel you now."

Quietly, the Lavhe says, "And neither of us would ever find the Notare or bring her to justice, and perhaps she would grow just clever enough to realize what a position those five little drops have put her in. Perhaps she would come to reclaim what is rightfully hers." His eyes move over me, and Kane positions his body squarely between us.

"I'm confused," I say, stepping around Kane. "How could Elise possibly know that Kane gave me her blood? And even if she did, why would her blood matter?"

The Lavhe tilts his head and stares at me like I'm half idiot. "It's not her blood that matters, Sistana. It's yours."

And then the wheels click all together now.

"Oh." I look up at Kane and he blushes. *Blushes.* "You don't mean that…it was just five drops."

"The quantity does not matter, Sistana. What matters is the effect. Five droplets of a human's blood would likely do little to a Heztoichen. Five droplets of my blood might, in fact, kill one of them.

"You received enough blood from her to affect your pysiology," he says, sounding impressed. "You healed faster. You remained alive.

"Kane had much of your blood in his system when he was taken by Elise. I do not doubt that you are just as bonded to her as you are to him."

Silence.

Nobody says anything. Not Kane, not Mikey, not the Lahve and not Ashlyn. I moan and sag onto the sofa. "I thought this was over, but you want to use me to find her."

"It *is* over. For you," Kane simmers. "I won't allow you to be a part of this."

"I'm already a part of this." In a moment, my life flashes in crisp images against the blackness of my eyelids, and I wonder how I got to this point. I went from a scavenger trying to rescue my best friend's sister from the Others to so deeply involved in their world that I'm a queen, attached to two of the most powerful amongst them. What fucking luck.

"We need you, Sistana," the Lavhe says, voice neither imploring nor desperate. He is simply stating a fact, and I can't shy away from it. "You have a blood bond with Notare Elise."

"We will find another way," Kane growls.

I shake my head. "Even if we could, she'd find me before we came up with a plan B and kill me. I put her at risk, don't I?"

Instead of answering my question, Kane says, "I will not allow that."

I look up at Kane and shake my head. "This is why you were so pissed? Why it was so personal?"

He doesn't answer.

I blow breath out of the corner of my mouth. "I'm sorry, Kane, but I've seen what she can do and I'm not interested in a plan B if plan A will do."

I look back to the Lavhe, whose face is stretched in what I think might be a grin. It's a grim thing, slightly softer than skeletal.

"What do you need me to do?"

The Lavhe quickly maps out a short-term plan which ends, rather than begins, with my locating Elise through our blood bond. The fear is that she'll be able to sense if I latch onto her location, and we'll lose our leverage.

He also forbids Kane from drinking any blood from me that isn't my sweetest blood. Blood from my veins has Elise's in it. He could bond with her, too, and if, for whatever reason, he drops dead and nobody else catches the Tare, then Elise could challenge me for his territory.

And I'd be doomed.

I don't know how many hours we're stuck in that room, but Ashlyn goes to get us all food *twice* and I couldn't say how many pots of coffee we finish. Ashlyn's asleep on the couch we share, her head in my lap. I don't blame her and could kiss Kane on the mouth when he suggests we get some sleep and finish going over the details in the morning.

"Do we have a strategy for transport?" Tasha says, entirely ignoring him.

She's joined us now along with several of the other Others and speaks says from her position at the brightly lit desk against the back wall.

Her hair has come undone from the braid it was in and falls around her shoulders in waves. She's been using her jade pin to point at everyone threateningly.

"If we aren't able to locate the Notare until the final hour then we'll need to have helicopters and cars ready so that we can access her location at a moment's notice. I mean, what if she's all the way in Tanen's territory? We'll never find her then."

"Tasha," Kane says gently, standing up. The Lavhe stands with him, and Tasha, flushing, rises, too.

"We can discuss transport in the morning." He looks to the Lavhe for confirmation.

He nods, face betraying not an ounce of tiredness. "There will be more than enough transportation options. Two of the Council members have even arrived by plane."

"Is Tanen coming?" Tasha says.

He shakes his head. "He will not attend, but this is not necessary. He has given me his proxy in this matter."

Kane sneers and shakes his head. "I'm glad they'll all be here, and that you have Tanen's proxy. It is imperative that we hold Elise for as little time as possible."

"Why?" I blurt, too sleepy to stop myself. "Worried she'll make a break for it?"

Everyone in the room looks at me like that's *exactly* the issue.

"I see," I whisper and when I stand, I drag Ashlyn up with me.

I'm almost at the door when a voice holds me in place. "Sorry. Kane, Abel, would you wait a second?"

I turn and rub my eyes at the sight of Mikey standing by the windowledge where he'd been sitting quietly this whole time.

"Sure. What's up?" I say as Kane slips an arm around me and holds me to his side.

"Though I have no right to speak here, I would formally request to be a member of the party that hunts down Elise. I was kept prisoner by her and her lackey, Memnoch, for over three years, and though my actions in Population towards the Sistana were criminal and wound me even now to think about," he says, gaze flashing to me and only me. It makes me feel good. Like he's learning to see past his brother.

"I'd like to help seek revenge against the one who threatens my Sistana." He bows to me and I feel totally weirded out by the gesture, more so than when Tasha or the others call me weird names.

To normalize the whole moment, I cast my vote right away. "That's fine by me. We'll need as many hands as we can get to take down Elise."

Mikey looks up at me and smiles a little when he sees me smiling. I give Kane a little nudge, hoping for him to respond, but he stays quiet.

It's the Lahve who answers. "Mikael must carry out his sentence and that may prevent him from functioning properly in battle."

"What sentence?"

"Mikael has offered you myhr as recompense for his moral failings, however his criminal charges must be dealt with by our Council."

I feel sick as I ask a question I don't actually want answered. "What's the punishment?"

"For drinking the blood of a Sistana, we will drain your blood from his system. To the drop. And for abandoning you in Population, he will receive one lash for each of yours. Salt will be rubbed into his wounds so that he does not forget what he has done."

"No fucking way."

"Sistana," the Lahve tries. Even Kane says my name. Even Mikey. Tasha, too.

I don't hear any of them. I don't have to. "Am I the fucking Sistana or not?" I shout. "Then let me speak."

I wait for the room to quiet. I wait beyond that, dragging time out in that horrible way the Lahve does, while I collect my thoughts.

"I don't know your laws. All I know is that it would hurt me to watch anyone go through what I went through. Is that your intent here? To torture me further after I've already been tortured, Lahve?"

The Lavhe's expression betrays nothing. Time stands still. Then moves on.

"I have seen his crime, Sistana. I have felt it."

"Then you'll know how much it will hurt to watch it happen again. Every scar you saw on my back will reopen if you do this to him."

He tilts his head to the side and squints, as if trying to understand a very complex mathematical equation when one of the variables is wrong.

He clasps his fingers carefully before him and watches me with compassionless eyes. "I do not attempt to understand your meaning. My species does not have the ability to empathize in the way you speak of when we feel the emotions of others directly. However, if you feel that this is a burden too great to bear, I can bring your wisdom before the Council and they can decide there."

"I'm telling you, I won't allow it. You'll have to take him somewhere far away and do it there, because if not, I'll break him out, or I'll die trying."

The Lahve smiles with one corner of his mouth, and it's the most *tangible* he's ever looked. "That is a noble gesture, Sistana, yet perhaps less than prudent considering your…mortality."

"I've never considered it in the past. Not sure why I'd start now."

"Interesting," he says. And then he looks to Kane. "I believe that, for your Sistana, you have chosen well. I shall take my leave of you and discuss the…suggestions made by the Sistana on the subject of Mikael. For now, he may join us."

Excused by Kane, the room empties except for Mikey, who lingers at the door. "Thanks for that, Abel," he says.

"Sure."

"You didn't have to threaten the poor bastard," he laughs like he just can't believe it.

"I wasn't threatening anyone. I was just telling him what I'd do to stop this from happening to someone else. I'd do it for anyone."

"Would you die for them, too?"

I pause, consider. "I'd try for them, too."

Mikey's smile carries just a hint of sadness. He says, "One day, I want to grow up to be just like you."

I laugh and throw a couch pillow at him and he disappears, closing the door in his wake, while Kane angrily closes me in a rough embrace.

"You shouldn't have spoken for him like that."

"Why not?"

"Because the Lavhe likely thinks you're insane."

"I am insane." I shrug.

Kane grunts, his lips coming very close to mine while the heat sparks in every direction between us. "Don't I know it."

He devours me and there's none of the same softness there was before. This is just heat and anger and fear and jealousy that moves us from the middle of the room to the bookshelves to the couch where I lower myself down onto my knees between his spread legs.

I grab his erection in my fist and watch precum bead along the slit. "You'll have to tell me what you like," I say. "I've never done this before."

Kane's jaw works, then clenches, as I lower my mouth over his straining cock. I lick and taste and suck, following the directions he gives until they become a stream of garbled nonsense and he's wrenching me up off my feet and lowering my body down onto the sofa beneath his.

"You better be careful with Tasha's dress."

I bury my hands in the thick mane of his hair, urging him to where he's headed.

He growls as his mouth works its way down my body, and the last thing I hear before my eyes shut to reveal an even deeper darkness is the sound of Tasha's dress tearing.

Chapter Nineteen

"It's time. Everyone out." Tasha claps her hands together and the room empties except for me.

The Lahve and me.

Kane is the last to leave. He hovers in the doorway in the same all-black outfit I'm wearing. It matches the combat gear the Lahve brought for us.

I'm not allowed to go after Elise myself — God knows I don't want to — but I'll still be joining the brigade and watching from the car with a satellite phone in case she moves and I'm able to sense it.

For now, we have to find her.

"No harm will come to your Sistana, Notare Kane," the Lahve says in that jarring, echoey voice he has. I don't think I'll ever get used to it.

"Kane," I say over my shoulder. "Really, I'm okay."

He grunts and doesn't respond, but grumbles as he finally closes the door, blocking out all sound so that the Lahve and I are in the den, alone.

I'm sitting on the couch and the Lahve is seated on the coffee table across from me. I have my hands on my knees and goosebumps prickle my arms and neck and calves. I curl my toes into my black boots. They're steel-toed and actually the right size for my feet.

"So um…how does this work?"

The Lahve is the only one *not* in combat gear. Somehow it's fitting that we're going into battle against a thousand-year-old psychopath and he's wearing a suit again, this one brown tweed.

Towering over me already, he scoots forward so that he's perched on the very edge of the table, his long, strong legs spread around mine, but not touching. He lifts his hand and traces the outline of my face, without touching. He's done this already three times.

"No distractions," he says finally, "There is not much of her blood to work with, so tracking her will be difficult."

"Okay," I say nervously when he lapses into another one of his impossible pauses.

His orange eyes flick to mine. "You were successful in reaching Kane when you had never seen the Saltlands before."

I nod. "Is this like that? I'm just supposed to like… search for her?"

He shakes his head no and his thin locks spill over his shoulders. Some locks hang even longer than his chest and stretch all the way to his stomach.

"I will search for her, but I will need your complete submission. Do not fight when I sift through your thoughts. You will need to give into the pain."

"Pain?"

He nods. "All of your thoughts are pain, short of a few."

I shiver. It freaks me out that he knows this. What's worse — or maybe better? — is that he's been with me there, in each of these moments, too. "You feel it, don't you?"

"Hm?"

"The pain."

His orange eyes blaze and shutter before I can read what lurks beneath. Emotion? He said he didn't have any of these. "All of it."

"But doesn't it hurt you?"

"Every time. That is the definition of pain, is it not?"

"But then…how can you stand it?"

"Because I must, just as you must, this time. Now, close your eyes," he says and I can feel the tender touch of his cool breath on my cheek.

My seat squeaks beneath me as my eyes shut and in that reverent darkness, I feel exposed. "What now?"

"Picture Notare Elise in the last moment you saw her."

Not a pleasant memory, I wince from it and nod. "I…I think I've got it."

His finger, just one, touches the space between my eyes and suddenly, I'm flying.

I'm in the cave and everything is dark and terrifying. The mountain is rumbling. My panic for Kane. The pressure of Mikey's mouth on mine keeping me alive — a moment he gets no credit for in any retelling of the stories. The light of her chest, winking out of existence.

Memnoch comes next and I hurtle backwards through memories and time until I start to make out the Lahve speaking to me.

"Picture her face and the light over her chest. Imagine you can feel the pulsation of that light in your own heart."

I'm sucked back down into the mouth of the mountain, rocks and boulders cascading, water and darkness consuming what is left, and yet just beneath the chaos I hear the thundering of two hearts. One of them glows fiercely, the other does not.

I shake my head, unable to place her. "I can't. Shit."

"Do not say can't. You do not know, Sistana, what it is that you cannot do."

And because I don't feel his presence shift in the slightest it scares the hell out of me when I feel his lips against my earlobe.

He brushes my hair off my shoulder and coos, "Elise…Elise…"

A wrenching on the front of my chest makes me waver wildly where I sit.

And still, he says, "*Tantena valys, Elise.*"

Boom. The sound isn't out loud. It isn't even in my head. It's in my body, in my chest, beneath my sternum hidden like a pebble. I look down and expect to see his hand striking my chest as if to reach the organ itself, but he isn't there and the clothes I'm wearing are no longer my own.

Panic grips me like a vice and I fly up onto my feet. Wait. I was already standing and when I move, all of my movements are filled with a strength that isn't mine. That isn't human.

I shriek words that I don't understand. I scream them at the top of my lungs. "Valyna Lavhe estilnotam etes. Vie gurys Notare."

And in my ears, distant words ring and repeat, "Tantena valys, Elise…"

I start to shriek and suddenly I'm running, rushing towards a huge wall of glass. My heels are thundering over the carpet and I have no problem running in them at all even though they're higher than any Tasha's strapped me into before.

I reach the window and for a second, think about running straight through it, but I don't. *I can't lose.* Is the thought mine? Are they words? Did I say them out loud?

I press my palms to the glass and feel the chill beneath my fingertips. Heat forms around them like a fog.

And then there are words spoken in English — a language I only learned a decade ago. They belong to the Lahve, the miserable, ancient relic, and they echo against the glass and concrete walls surrounding me. Caging me.

"What do you see?" The Lahve breathes and I can feel his cool breath on my cheek, making my heart beat faster and faster and faster…

"No!" I unravel from the center and the thing in my chest that should bear the light pulses once, and then not again for several breaths. I cannot die.

I will not die.

My fist pounds into the glass, shattering it, and cold air caresses my face. I pull the largest shard of glass from the floor and see my own reflection inside. Eyes as dark as coal, skin as white as death. I blink and the black eyes are gone, replaced by eyes that are blue.

She screams again. I scream again. The sound is horrible and I fight to past it. I'm shouting words now. Shouting as many as I can. I don't know what they are, but I keep shouting them until she takes that sharp shard of glass, brings it to her own neck — brings it to my neck — and slices sideways.

I scream as I die. Blood explodes over my hands. My whole body throws itself forward off of the precipice. I fall into outstretched arms. Reality shatters over me.

The sound of a door slamming open makes me blink. I see the city. I blink again. I see the rug beneath me. I blink and see blood and then I blink and there are hands pushing me up into a seat.

"What have you done?" Kane roars.

"Dying…" I say, but when I grab at my own neck, there's no cut.

"Lahve!" A voice gasps.

One of his guards charges into the room — a female with almond eyes, pale skin and jet black hair that falls past her shoulders in a straight line — and she approaches the Lahve standing at the window ledge, but does not touch him.

"Do you need a moment?" She says.

He doesn't answer, but I can hear him gulping in the same little sips of air I am. Coughing bellows out of me and I clutch Kane to me and for a moment, I watch the Lahve and feel…*bad* for him.

He died too when he looked through me.

Only now, here, among the living, he has no ability to receive comfort.

He straightens and turns and he's again this *presence,* that ethereal being. He looks down at me and swallows many times. His hand flinches as he touches his throat.

"Follow my breaths," he tells me.

I don't dare disobey and between his calm and Kane's gentle hands on my hair, I finally find something like normalcy.

Kane gently coaxes me into a seated position and, when I'm finally vertical, takes my jaw between his hands and tilts it left and right, inspecting my neck for damage.

"She slit our throats," I tell him.

Kane's eyes flare and he inspects my skin with his fingers, finding it uninterrupted.

"Not *really,*" I say, pushing his hand away. I shake my head and struggle up to standing. I don't quite make it and sink back down on the couch while Tasha appears with a glass of water in front of me.

She hands one to the Lahve as well who surprises me by taking it. He drinks. I drink. We watch each other drink.

Kane says, "I don't want you reaching out to Elise, again."

"You know," I say, lowering my glass and breathing hard around it, "you're going to have to stop being so paranoid one of these days."

He doesn't smile. He sits down on the coffee table where the Lahve sat moments before and his fingers continue moving across my face as if searching for seams.

"Only when I figure out how to put a force field around you." His lips brush my forehead and his warmth eclipses mine. "Are you sure you're alright?"

"Yeah. I'm fine. I just…" My gaze switches away from Kane's face, past Mikey and Tasha and two more guards who have joined the first.

"That was crazy," I say on a laugh and I'm rewarded when the Lahve smiles with just one edge of his too-human mouth.

"Yes, it was."

"It really felt like she was killing me. Killing us. You felt it too?"

He bows his head forward. "All of it."

"How did she do that?"

"She is a powerful female, and now she knows where we are, so we need to move."

"But we don't know where she is," I say, but the moment I say it, my face scrunches up and my mind flashes and I remember all the words I shouted when I was her.

"Shit!" I jump to my feet, then fall into Kane's arms when all the blood rushes to my head at once. "I do know where she is. It worked."

"It did."

"So where is she?" Mikey says, looking like a menace with twin handguns already strapped to his either hip.

"She's in an apartment building between a…a movie theater and a super tall building with a green…greenish roof. It has a dome on the top." My gaze snaps to the

Lahve's and I gasp as he lifts just one eyebrow higher than the other. "Holy fuck. She's in Vancouver. She's in the freaking Diera."

"Yes, she came back," he says slowly.

"But why? What for?" I gasp, so confused.

He smiles again and this time, it's a terrible, terrifying sight. He breathes, "Sistana, she came back for you."

Chapter Twenty

"What did you tell her?"

"I told her to reveal herself."

"And what did she tell you?"

"That she is not afraid you," the Lahve told me. "It is her mistake, just as it was Crestor's."

"What do you mean?"

"Underestimating you."

We drive in silence while I turn the Lahve's words over in my mind. Kane sits beside me, two guards in the front, two guards in the back. To my left, Sandra holds a bright blue box in her lap. She clutches it like a first-time father might hold a newborn.

I try to make conversation, but all the words are lodged deep in my lungs. Vocabulary ceases to exist as the bright green signs beckon us forward. Vancouver, B.C. eighty-five miles, then thirty-four, then suddenly six.

Bienvenue à and *welcome to* are stacked on top of faded ivory lettering that reads, 'VANCOUVER!'

We drive into the city limits and Kane has to remind me to breathe — twice — before we take the next left and pull onto West Pender Street.

West Pender and Abbott. Those are the cross-streets that I remember from a memory that isn't mine, but belongs to someone else.

Someone who wants to kill me. Or, at best, torture me and use me as leverage.

I inhale sharply and Kane asks me what's wrong. "I can feel her," I answer, clutching his hand when he offers it. "I couldn't before."

Kane nods solemnly and ducks his head, staring out of the window. "Good. Then she's still here. She wants to make her presence known to us."

"That's a good thing?"

He doesn't respond. We drive down the narrow city streets, and I imagine that at some point they had been broad. Now nature has overrun the city, brambles and overgrown tree roots preventing us from moving forward in places.

Where the debris can be cleared, it is, and where it can't we find alternate paths around.

We're a total of six huge SUVs and four pickup trucks. Seems like overkill for one woman…but I've been thinking about what the Lahve said and I know that the reverse should also be true.

We can't underestimate her either.

Power lines and bus cables drip from old utility poles, dangling in the wind. A building with a circular satellite tower passes on our left. It looks like the Space Needle I saw in Seattle.

Salt wounds heal, but they leave scars.

I can feel them on my back now, like nightmares glowing on my flesh, bright and luminous and a frightening reminder of all the places I have been. I get the feeling that we're nearing some kind of end when we pass by the broken sign for the Ramada — the RA and the final A are missing. I smirk at the remaining letters.

It's all gone mad, hasn't it? Me sitting with the enemy going to kill a shared one.

The enemy sitting with me going to kill one of his own because of the risk it places to me.

The love.

The car slows, and it isn't just because of the fallen tree branches that crunch beneath the tires, or on a cause of the roots as thick as steel that disrupt the asphalt.

"The movie theater." The one from my memories. From her memories.

Cineplex Odeon passes on our left. Its bottom floor has been decimated, windows all broken so that their frames hang like open mouths with shattered glass shards for teeth. But we slow nonetheless, because just across the street is our final destination: the apartment building.

It's abutted by the tower with the green dome on top. The air is cold when the car door opens and I shudder looking up, up, up. There's something menacing about that tower, even though it's the apartment building we're after.

Maybe when we're done here, we can just torch the whole block. Just for fun, you know?

Ducking my head, I glance past Sandra out of the window, scanning the apartment building in search of signs of life. I don't see any, but I feel them. One strong one that absolutely refuses to die. She isn't going down without a fight.

I guess she read the same rule book I did.

"Where the hell do you think you're going?" I grab Kane's arm when he starts to get out of the car, and feel the muscles in his bicep bulge beneath my hand.

His gaze is apologetic, though his words are pure heat, giving little in the way of concession. "I have to do this."

"We agreed that we would *both* stay in the car. Or did you lie to me again?"

"I never agreed to that," he says, and I think back to the whispered promises me made me while he was between my thighs, milking me for every ounce of pleasure he could.

Whatever he thinks he said, I heard something else.

"You're being an ass again. She could kill you."

The Lavhe's guards have already exited the car and the trunk is open. I can hear them whispering in alien as they distribute weapons.

Kane's name is called, followed by, "Notare, we must go now. Her guards are on the move."

Kane nods, sparing them a glance over the backseat. He opens his door and I hit him as hard as I can in the thigh.

"You're going to get yourself killed."

When he dives back into the car, coiling his thick fingers through my hair and crushing his mouth to mine, his kiss is full of desperation. He knows I'm right. I can feel the thrumming of his heart beneath my bulletproof vest and I can barely breathe.

"Why are you doing this?" I gasp when he pulls back.

"Because I have to be sure."

"Have to be sure of what?"

"That she dies. Every second she's alive is a risk to the only thing I can't live without." His gaze flares and heats and I grab his bullet proof vest at the collar. I wrench him into me and bite his lower lip hard enough to draw blood.

I lick a droplet away greedily and he shudders in my arms.

"Come back to me. Or else."

He smiles at me very slightly while the wind whips his hair across his forehead in clean black lines. "For you, always." He begins to shut the car door, but hesitates and lifts a single brow. "I don't need to repeat myself, do I?"

I roll my eyes. "What trouble could I possibly get into staying here in the car?"

He narrows his eyes. "That wasn't what was promised."

I remember rolling him over and straddling his hips. Whatever he thinks I said, he must have heard something else.

"If you're in trouble I'll know."

"Abel," he growls.

"You're *coming* back. Even if I have to reach through the gates of hell and pull you out myself."

"Abel…"

"Notare," the Lahve's voice calls over the whipping wind.

I grab the car door handle and shut it between us. There's nothing left to say.

Kane glares at me through the tinted windows, but he doesn't try to argue with me.

The locks all click into place a moment later and half a dozen guards take up posts around the outside of the SUV. Beside me, Sandra sucks in a breath through her teeth. Her fingers are white around the edges of the box, but I don't offer her any encouragement.

Instead, I watch a line of guards move down the road, to the apartment building. Mikey, Kane and the Lahve jog after them in a second wave along with other guards.

The Lahve looks completely absurd in his suit and cane. Feels like he should have a top-hat or something. I snort at the image and Sandra jumps in her seat.

"Sorry," I whisper.

"None needed. Just jittery."

I nod. "Same."

This time, she snorts. "You hide it well."

"Saltlands isn't a place for nerves."

"This isn't Seattle," she tells me, but she's wrong.

I shake my head and touch the window. "Yes, it is. She brought it with her."

And even though another dozen guards hug tight to the Lahve, Kane and Mikey's backs, it still doesn't feel like enough. It feels, rather, like there's a picture in front of me, but it's turned down at one corner. There's something there and it's important, I just can't see it…

What don't you want me to see, Elise?

Low, imagined laughter floats through my thoughts as the contingent of warriors enter the apartment.

We wait.

The moments that follow drag on and I count the seconds in my head until I lose count and have to start over again. I do this a few times, the silence really grating. Sandra's breath sounds so loud. Or maybe it's mine. Or maybe it's someone else's.

I flex my one good ear forward, trying to hear… something. For now silence a good thing. Silence means no shots. No shots mean no deaths. I can track the pressure of Kane's pulse in my own wrist, though the other heartbeat that should exist right along there with it has flat lined again. But, like the stillness of the outside world outside of these windows, it feels forced.

I press my fingers to the cool windowpane and watch the moisture of my fingers form condensation against the glass. I breathe, and in the fog, draw a flower.

Sandra says my name, but her voice sounds like she's talking through water. Turning to face her, I feel my face scrunch up when I see that she's still sitting right next to me.

Her eyebrows knit together over her nose and she touches my arm. I can see her fingers on my skin but I feel nothing.

"Are you ready to watch him die, Sistana?"

The voice *consumes* me.

It's everything. Every sense. Every thought. Every feel.

I tighten, but I can't *find* her. I can't react. I can't move. It's like she reached in through the roof of the car and slipped into my skin without my permission.

Sandra's fingers press against my jugular, trying to get a pulse. Can she feel it? That third heartbeat pounding like a battering ram throughout my whole body?

Where did Elise go? Where was she before?

"What do you want?" I blurt out loud, unsure how she managed to communicate in intention, rather than in breath. She seems to be able to hear me nonetheless. Where is she?

"I want what everyone wants, little Sistana. I just want it more," Notare Elise's voice whispers through my thoughts, consuming me like a disease that corrupts the body from within. *"Immortality."*

I blink and see the city skyline, the grey looming so ominously above it, a blackened concrete building and a suite of cars parked just beside it. *Our* cars, from above. The top of the apartment building.

She can't be inside if she's looking down.

"So very clever you are, Sistana." Her voice fades to laughter and my hands fumble with the blocky yellow phone tucked into the back of the front seat.

I grab it and press the speaker button since it only connects to one other number.

"She's in the tower. Up in the green dome," I tell Kane on the other end of the line, but there's no answer. "Get out of the apartment. Get out of there!"

Sandra is panicking and the guards on the other side of the car door are shifting restlessly now. I bang on the window and a guard — the female with the dark hair from earlier — opens it just a crack.

"Why aren't they answering?" I shout.

"Why do you think? He's already with me. Why don't you join us, Sistana?"

Elise's voice grips my thoughts and makes it hard to think. I see images of Kane and he's hurting, but I don't know what's real. I picture his blood dripping into a drain…but that was from before. What's real? What's happening?

"She has Kane." Or she's pretending she does. "It could be a trap," I tell the guard. "But I'm sure of one thing. She's *not* in that apartment. She's in the building next to it. We need to go there and get her before she does something…"

And I can feel her doing something.

I just don't know what.

"If you're not going to do anything, then I am," I shout.

"I was ordered not to allow you to leave your vehicle, Sistana."

"And as your Sistana, I command you to open the door."

After a moment of uncertainty, the Other wrenches open the door and I stumble out into the cold. "She's up to something," I tell her and Far, who looms up behind her, looking concerned.

"You cannot trust what she tells you," the female says.

Far counters, "How much can be falsified through the blood bond, Laiya? I hear nothing from our guards when I reach out to them."

"We have orders to keep the Sistana safe, Far," the one called Laiya answers, but if she says anymore than that, I don't hear it.

I'm falling down, down, down until I'm hovering inches above my head.

I can see me up close even though I'm standing up above in the green dome, so far away.

I blink and then there's a second image. I'm back in that glass and concrete room again, only this time I'm focused on the wiring covering the ceiling, hard beige bricks being connected to timers and triggers and I understand. Finally.

"She wants me alone," I say, lurching out of Elise's mind. Out of her many, many wants.

"She wants me alone or she'll bring the building down on all of them. She wired the whole thing with explosives."

"Good girl," she whispers to me alone.

I glance up the length of the old building again, noting how it's managed to withstand the elements far better than the apartment next to it. The younger, newer, modern apartment.

Of course she'd want to finish things here.

"Now come and finish this."

"We should send someone in for the others," Laiya says.

I shake my head. "We don't have that kind of time and there are enough of us out here to be able to take her into custody. Aren't there?"

Inside, I feel rather than hear, as Elise laughs.

Laiya looks at Far. Far looks at me.

"Morithan," he barks and another guard jogs over to him. "Alert the Lahve that we have gone for Elise. The rest of you, prepare for war." As Morithan takes off, Far returns his gaze to me and as it settles, I feel sure.

We're going to take her ass down. I grin as the laughter dies in me.

"We look to you, Sistana," he says.

I reach, not for the gun strapped to my chest, but to Diego's knife in my pocket. I wish I had Kane's sword, but last I saw, Mikey had it. The dagger'll do for now.

I look at the aliens — the team — before me and nod once. "I guess we go through the front doors, then."

I look back at Sandra. "Stay here," I tell her. "And if Kane comes back, tell him where I went."

She nods, looking terrified, and I'm surprised when the female called Laiya unstraps one of the handguns on her belt and hands it to Sandra. "Take this," she says. "Stay safe."

Sandra's cheeks darken, her eyes widen, but she still nods.

I slam the car door shut and take off at a light jog, the pounding of feet echoing behind me. They sound like thunder, moving in unison in a way I find both soothing and frightening.

The glass doors are broken in and nip at my skin as I step through the open frame. A fire has claimed the lobby, though a single sign still hangs on the scorched walls. I'm still able to make out the words *Vancouver Sun Tower* in blackened flowery lettering covering the back wall.

"She's near the top floor. I can feel her." She's waiting. "We'll take the stairs."

When I take a step forward, Laiya pulls me back with a curt apology and heads towards the heavy wooden door first. Swinging her automatic rifle around, she places her hand on the knob. Black comes off on her fingers when she pulls it open, revealing bronze.

We step into a hollow stairwell, and a spiral staircase made of textured white marble leads in only one direction.

Up. Black fissures run through it like life lines and I trace the crisscross patterns they make as we ascend.

We climb side-by-side until we reach the fourth floor and my legs start to tire and she starts to pull ahead.

She whistles through her front teeth and six of the twelve Others with us now surge ahead of me while the rest form a line at my back. When we take the next curve, I look back and see that Far and another male are actually climbing backwards, their hands on the triggers, ready.

They don't use them, though. Because no one attacks. In fact, the silence is pervasive, all but for the sounds of our boots on the dusty marble. The fire made it inside of the stairwell, and though the walls are charred, nothing burned but bodies. It must have happened a long time ago, because the smell is gone and all that remains is the dust they left behind.

We're on the fourteenth floor and my thighs are burning with the effort of keeping up when Laiya whistles again and all the soldiers around me come to an immediate stop. Must be another six or seven floors to go. We're most of the way there.

And then Laiya and Far and the soldiers at the top and bottom of the stairs turn in unison to face the doors in front of them. They start shooting just as the first bodies barrel through the wood and the abruptness of the attack and the roaring sound of bullets blazing leaves me stunned.

Laiya returns to my side while soldiers battle on the tenth floor and the twelfth.

Eleven.

This was Kane's floor.

And that's the last thought I have before the door in front of me flies open.

A soldier fires, but Laiya throws her body in front of mine and withdraws a short sword. In one swift motion, she decapitates the female warrior in front of her.

Far, below, shouts another order, which Laiya repeats and suddenly we're moving again, pushing and fighting our way up.

I try to find a target, but I'm a weak shot, and there are too many friendlies between me and the ones we're fighting. The Lahve's guards are also a formidable force. Shell casings twinkle against the marble far, far below as Laiya pushes me up, up, up.

I'm half-falling, half-walking. The heat from so many bodies is suffocating. When a door flies open to my right, the Other standing there levels her gun at my chest. I point my gun at her head and fire, taking the top half of it off before she manages to do whatever it was she was going to do.

She wasn't aiming for me, though. None of them are.

They want me alive.

Laiya grabs my arm. "Sistana, we cannot rise higher. There are too many of them."

She shoves me through the rusted metal door marked by blood spray and a faded number fifteen without waiting for my consent, and I stumble out onto hard concrete. In addition to Laiya, three Others from our side follow me.

Planting my feet firmly, I pivot, waiting for the first assault, but this floor is empty — under renovation, perhaps, and never completed. Now it's just desolate, full of an eerie silence that's broken up only by the sounds of the battle raging in the stairwell.

I can tell by the expression on Laiya's face as she moves past me that she's just as apprehensive as I am. Turning to face the Others that have followed us onto the empty floor, she rattles off a command and all four of them close in around me.

The door slams in its frame as bodies fall against it. Gunshots ring muted through the walls, and at the same time, a small earthquake shakes the foundations of the building.

"Kane," I breathe, taking off at a sprint to the east-facing windows, Laiya and the others holding that impenetrable square around me.

I press my face to the glass as I stare, horrified, at the demolition job happening next door. She said she wouldn't…if I came alone.

Grief grips my chest as chunks of concrete fly. The whole building collapses in its center, forming a black hole that sucks in everything. Would they have survived?

I feel Kane still there, but maybe I'm confused. Maybe it's Elise again trying to torment me…

"Sistana, do not panic," Laiya breathes into my ear. "Look."

She points towards the street and a subtle movement catches my eye. Black-clad guards move swiftly towards the tower. They hug the sides of the buildings, sticking to the shadows until they become mere shadows themselves.

"And there, Your Grace."

She points and I follow the line her finger creates. The Lavhe in his stupid tweed suit is climbing in through one of the ground floor windows, and a swell of hope fills my chest when I see Kane with him. I smile down at him while the apartment building finally settles in a thick pall of dust and smoke. Looks like they were warned in time. Looks like Elise's leverage no longer exists.

"We should wait for them here, Sistana, before seeking out Notare Elise."

"It's a little late for that, don't you think?"

I blink and see me tucked safely within a ring of guards. I see my face, blood spatter on my cheek, gun clutched in my fist.

I blink and see her standing in the center of the empty room, dusty tarp billowing at her back like a curtain. She steps through it with her arms crossed wearing a dark and lovely blue.

Wordlessly, the guards create a triangle around me. Only Laiya remains at my side, gun trained on the Notare's chest, which glows so subtly I almost can't see it.

"You have something that belongs to me," she says, gaze locking with mine and making me feel small and stupid. She planned for this. Every move.

I knew that and I walked into it with more confidence than I had. Maybe I did underestimate her. Or maybe I overestimated me and the Lahve and Kane and everybody.

My mouth is dry but my hands are warm. I pull out Diego's dagger and hold it in my free hand. Her gaze flashes to it and she grins.

"You here to arrest me all by yourself, Sistana?"

"Yeah."

"Interesting."

"Yeah, I think so too. You ready to give up, yet?"

She actually manages to look surprised by that question. Surprised and annoyed. "You are a stupid human."

"Yeah. Definitely. But I've got your blood in me and rights to all your lands." Her face hardens. Her eyes narrow. "So if you want your blood back, you better come and get it."

Elise's chest pulses once with light before it fades and she moves and the guards begin firing as one.

I don't even get a shot off before Laiya grabs me and runs. The other guards stay behind — not to win, but to give us time. They're fighting though, holding their ground. I hear Elise hiss as bullets hit her stomach. She surges forward and a guard ends up fighting her hand-to-hand. The female falls and Elise reaches down and yanks her head off her neck while another guard stabs her in the back.

The door to this floor flies open and I'm shocked and thrilled to see Far standing there, Others I recognize behind him.

They start firing too, and soon Elise is surrounded.

But she's laughing. "Is this all you've got, Lahve?" She screeches, but I can't hear his answer if he gives one.

Instead, Laiya has my arm. She's pulling me across the room to the far wall and pushing me through the shattered opening of a window. I think she's killed me until my feet hit the unsteady foundation of a fire escape.

Holy freaking frick.

We're high up.

The tree house I fell from with Drago was nothing compared to this. This fall won't kill me, it'll *eviscerate* me. There won't be anything left but mush and blood.

I take an unsteady step down, but Laiya grabs me and shoves me up. "Up, Sistana." Her body presses against mine as she climbs after me, forcing me to go the opposite direction that all my instincts scream to move.

"Up?" I shout, but I've got no other choice with her boxing me in. "Up!"

Wind whips its ferocious fingers through the fabric of my shirt, though it doesn't manage to pierce my bulletproof vest. The vest insulates my heat and, with my adrenaline thickening the blood in my veins, I've begun to sweat. My feet hit the rusted stairs, but Laiya's still grabbing the back of my vest and shoving.

"Apologies, Sistana," she says, though she doesn't mean it at all.

"Don't think you can outrun your fate, little Sistana!" Elise's voice echoes up from three floors below.

My toe catches the bottom slat of the next step and I stumble while behind me gunfire reigns. I can feel Laiya's back press against mine as she urges me upwards until there's nowhere left to go. We've reached the dome and these stupid stairs just *stop* at a small, square window.

I grab hold of the open frame and am shocked that what I thought was a copper dome is actually just painted concrete. A prop masking something perfectly ordinary.

I smile just a little as hope flowers in my stomach. *Fitting that it should end here for her.*

"Move!"

I wriggle into the dome and Laiya falls into the space after me. Taller than I am, she has to duck low to avoid hitting her head on the yellow beams that crisscross overhead. Above us are a series of suspended metal walkways and in front of us is a bunch of industrial equipment. Large metal squares with cranks and dials and buttons, and beyond them a metal panel in the ground. Even though elevators haven't functioned in a decade, we've found the elevator room.

"Sistana, up." Laiya points to the metal stairs leading up to the very top of the dome.

I don't get this as an exit strategy, but I don't question her and move onto the scaffolding. I climb up the ladder and am halfway there when I feel it. No — when I smell it.

Her perfume.

"Laiya, behind you!"

Elise must have climbed around the dome like a spider because she's coming in through the oculus *behind* Laiya. I point and fire and even though I miss, the split second distraction is enough to pull Laiya — and the barrel of her gun — around.

She fires, missing nine times out of ten. The shot that meets its mark hits Elise in the leg and she staggers but only for a step. She reaches Laiya before I can get my second round off, and grabs her by the neck.

Laiya's body looks far too much like Becks's did as Elise throws her across the room and into the equipment against the far wall. She advances on Laiya while Laiya struggles to drag what looks like a shattered femur beneath her, and punches her fist through Laiya's stomach.

"No!" The word is mine, and I fire until my clip is empty, hitting Elise in the back twice. The force is enough to drop her to one knee, and she roars as she flips her hair back and turns to face me.

Sensing her intention, I stagger backwards as she jumps up onto the scaffolding in front of me. I fire, but my clip is empty. I chuck the gun at her and it hits her in the forehead and she gapes at me, like she's really shocked.

"Stupid human," she seethes.

I brandish my dagger at her and prepare for the end.

She raises one clawed hand, but it never falls, because as she focuses on me, a body slams into Elise sideways and with enough force to rip through the metal railings on either side of this narrow walkway.

Elise screeches as she plummets off of the scaffolding and lands at Laiya's side, Kane straddling her waist. He has his hands on her throat and I whoop with glee, but Elise isn't down like I'd hoped.

She releases a shriek and grabs Kane by the right shoulder and hip. She throws him into the concrete wall, which cracks dangerously beneath him.

She advances on him, but he's got blood on his mouth and determination in his eyes. He punches. She ducks. He kicks, nailing her in the chest and throwing her off her feet and into metal panel covering the elevator shaft. It buckles and starts to cave, but she manages to scramble off of it just before it gives completely.

It takes forever for the crash below and in that time, Elise staggers back to her feet. She dusts off her pants and sneers, "I was wondering how long it would take you to come for your queen. What did you do, scale the outside of the building?"

Kane doesn't contradict her. Nor does his gaze leave her face. As he rises to standing, he doesn't so much as blink.

"Very well, then. I can assume that reinforcements aren't far behind, giving me little time to savor this moment. Are you going to attack or should I?" She wipes the back of her wrist across her mouth, the crimson standing out vibrantly against her porcelain skin.

"Go up," Kane says, and it takes me a moment to realize he's talking to me as the two predators begin circling each other in that small, crowded space.

"Fuck that," I say, nearly shaking with rage. "I'm not leaving you alone with this crazy bitch."

"And I wasn't asking. I can't fight if I'm concerned for your life. You being here is a risk to us both." I've only ever heard Kane's voice like this once before. When we were in that cave and he was begging Mikey to save my life over his. Furious, I don't delay. I know we only have seconds as Elise's lips curl up.

She watches me run across the scaffolding, and as I reach the ladder, coos, "Fly, little bird, fly."

"Go!" Kane's voice is murderous and a very potent rage tickles the backs of my palms as I stow my dagger and climb the ladder up through a small opening in the concrete that leads into an even smaller concrete room, just big enough for a body or two.

Like mine and Mikey's.

I throw my arms around his neck and he hugs me back and lifts me all the way into the cupola. "Sorry I didn't give you this," he whispers against my throat at the same time that he presses my sword into my hand.

I zip Diego's dagger back into my pocket as I smile down at the sword, like I'm revisiting a familiar friend. "Thank frick. We have to go back and help him…"

He grabs my arm and shakes his head. He presses a single finger to his lips, then points that finger down. I follow the line it makes past the scaffolding, past Kane, past Elise to the broken opening of the elevator shaft just as the Lahve climbs through it.

He moves so quietly, I can't hear him at all. I wonder if the others can, but when Elise keeps her attention fixed on Kane, I feel the most overwhelming relief.

Mikey covers my mouth with my hand and pulls a pad out of his pocket. On it, I see words scribbled.

The Lahve planned it this way. The only ones who knew were Laiya, Far and him.

Bastard.

I laugh against his palm while tears prick the backs of my eyes. I remind myself that we are still in the Saltlands, so tears aren't yet allowed. But they feel imminent.

Just like the end.

He flips to the next page.

We never even into that apartment building. The Lahve knew she'd try to get you alone and was waiting. Everything else was just a diversion. Not even Kane knew. And yes, he's pissed. I am too.

It suddenly feels like we're all pawns in an elaborate game of chess only the Lahve and Elise are playing. I shake my head, not caring at all if it means we win.

He flips to the next and final sheet.

He needed her to think she had the upper hand in order to beat her.

I nod, but as I listen to the silence radiating up from below, I can't help but think, *How can we be sure that she doesn't?*

We lower to our bellies now so we can peer out at the scene below and I pump my fist secretly as the Lahve launches himself at Elise in the same instant that she launches herself at Kane.

He reaches her first and tackles her to the far wall and a pained scream wrenches out of her.

"It's over, Notare," the Lahve says, easily holding her in place. "Yield."

She starts to thrash and cry and shriek and…and laugh.

She's laughing now and the sound is blood curdling. "Oh Lahve, I will admit, you did surprise me there. But did you truly not think I wouldn't come with surprises of my own? Or that I would let you take me breathing?"

The floor beneath my belly begins and I glance up at Mikey to see if he feels the same thing. His gaze meets mine and suddenly, he's got me in his grip, trying to wrap his whole body around me.

"Fuck!" He screams and it seems like he knows what's happening better than I do, because I'm still surprised when the concrete beneath our bodies is wrenched out from beneath us.

Smoke rises up and pulls me down into the elevator room below. I don't know what I hit, but it hurts *almost* as much as the concrete that falls onto my face and chest and tries to bury me alive.

Mikey's shouts are muffled and his arms are on my arms, but I'm being lifted through the rubble away from him. My whole body is in motion and I yelp in pain as I'm dragged from the aftermath by the hair.

I blink and gasp.

The entire roof of the dome has been blown open, bits and pieces of the cupola scattered in the wind. I'm freezing, even crushed against the warmth of a body…and it isn't Kane's…

"You didn't think I wouldn't come with my own surprises!" Elise roars again.

She's got blood on her mouth and her right arm hangs at her side at the wrong angle. She keeps me trapped against her chest with her one good arm. Her hand cups my throat. She supports my entire weight as she edges back, my boots dragging limply against the rubble.

What happened?

Mikey roars, though he's buried in debris up to the waist. Most of the elevator room is too. Only Elise managed to escape it. She knew where to stand. Where to go. Where to duck.

The others didn't.

Kane is wedged between two huge machines. His eyes lock on me as he tries to free his legs from a mass of metal, and his eyes are screaming.

The Lavhe stands from underneath some scaffolding that managed to stay put. He's got crimson on his knuckles but is otherwise untouched. He rises to his full height still holding his cane. He twists the handle and removes a thin sword, which he points at Elise.

"Elise, unhand the Sistana." The inflection he carries suggests the first hint of emotion I've heard from him. Irritation. Maybe also surprise.

Elise staggers to the left, edging her body behind some of the equipment, closer to where Laiya lies crumpled in half, knees tucked to her chest, black hair frayed.

She's still alive, though.

Her face tilts up to mine and I wonder if Elise notices the way her slanted eyes watch us with hate and promises of revenge.

I meet her gaze and hold it and without words, I try to say, *Take it.*

The dagger's still in my pocket, but I struggle with the zipper that I need to open to free it while Elise coils herself around me. She presses her face close to mine, silken tresses tickling my cheek as she uses me like a shield.

"That doesn't seem like a fair deal to me," she says, licking a line up my throat that makes me shudder. "I'm going to need something in return."

Kane roars, freeing himself from the metal caging him and staggering to Mikey's side. He slips his shoulder beneath Mikey's armpit and hauls him free of the rubble. Both of them are panting now.

"Release her and I will give you what it is you seek…"

The Lavhe hisses in overlapping notes though when he speaks, his tone is even again. Even, but *loud*, like he's talking through a speaker.

"You dare make requests of the Notare? You dare blackmail me? You dare hold the Sistana captive? You will die for your crimes, Elise."

Elise's pitch rises to a shriek. "For all your glory, you cannot touch me! You are *just* the Lahve. I am a Notare. You do not hold the light…"

The Lavhe tips the point of his blade to Elise's chest, only just visible around mine. I crane my neck so I can look down, but over the red and white swell of Elise's forearm, I don't see anything. Nothing at all.

And that's the point.

"Neither do you, Elise."

Elise's light is gone.

Elise screams and as she screams, her hold on me lets up just the inch I needed to reach my pocket, free the dagger, and toss it into Laiya's waiting fingers.

She jolts up without hesitating and plunges the dagger into Elise's back.

Elise falls forward, voice cutting off with an abrupt gurgle. She roars and it's a piercing blood-curdling sound that's equal parts maniacal, hysterical, and defeated.

Her hands clench around my arms and I'm suddenly sailing through the air. My shoulder hits a pile of concrete, spinning me around, but I don't stop.

My fingers can't seem to catch on anything as I skate over the dusty floor, which abruptly gives out.

Mikey yells. "No!"

Kane charges towards me.

The Lavhe has Elise's hands pinned behind her back, her body pressed flush to what's left of the concrete wall. His orange eyes widen as they meet mine and without knowing him at all, I'm sure he's never been so surprised as this.

That can't be good.

I'm reaching up. Kane's so close to me now. His fingers touch my fingers but the slippery blood lubricates the contact between our hands. Our palms glance off of one another and then Kane's shouting and I'm falling backwards through the empty space of the elevator shaft.

Chapter Twenty-One

I'm still falling.

It takes longer than it should.

Because while I fall, I panic, imagining what it'll feel like when I reach the bottom and what it'll sound like to Kane all the way up there at the top.

I'm pretty sure he wanted to jump after me, but I saw Mikey's body tackle him across the opening shortly after I started falling.

Kane is screaming as if mortally wounded and Mikey is shouting and the Lavhe is speaking and Elise is laughing until all at once, her laughter is cut short. A scream echoes down the hole that's taken me. Her scream. She sounds like she's in pain and a fleeting smile moves me.

One of the heartbeats I carried fades while the other continues to beat brutally in my ribcage willing *something* to happen that can't happen anymore. Because when I hit the bottom, there's no coming back.

It's just a split instant of pain. A jolt to the back of my head. My eyes close. My heartbeat jolts to a stop, and the last thing I feel is the will of a stronger heart.

And then not even that.

I die.

Until I remember…

Rule number one.

Chapter Twenty-Two

Waking up after I die is strange, and not just because I do. It's because of the smell. Blood and perfume.

My stomach lurches, but I don't retch. Instead, I just lay there, idling at the crossroads of life and death.

God?

There's wood at my back and against the outside of my arms that splinters my skin when I shift against it. My mind flutters and I recall some of my life's final events. In them, I was wearing a bullet proof vest and a shirt — two things I'm not wearing now — though I can feel the fabric of the same pants scratch my legs when pain shoots through them.

It ebbs and flows in time with the weird energy blowing through my bones like breath through a flute. I definitely feel like I'm being played.

For a fool, likely.

Because I'm *pretty* sure I died, and I'm a hundred percent sure that this is a coffin.

Fucking fantastic.

I wonder if they buried me alive, until I realize that doesn't make sense. I can't be buried when there's light and there *is* light. An intense radiance illuminates everything — the surface of the box inches away from my nose, the bloody fingerprints on the insides of the wood where hands closed the lid, sealing me in.

But why would they have left a light in here if they thought I was dead?

God? I ask myself again. But God doesn't answer either.

Instead, I look down, trying to root out the source of the light and gasp.

"Holy freaking crap."

The light is *me*. Am I on fire? No. There's warmth but it's the good kind, the bathtub kind. Not the Trocker kind. And there's light, but it's not the blinding kind that filtered in through the helicopter windows.

This light is like Kane's light, maybe even stronger. It blazes all the way across my chest, from nipple to nipple, collar bone to collar bone, all the way down to my ribs. coming from me.

I jolt back like I'll try to get away from it, but my feet kick the wood above me and I realize they're bare again when I stub my toe.

"Fuck!" I can't even move my fists up to touch my chest and investigate the light because the space is too narrow. "Fuck! Get me the fuck out of here!"

All at once my body slams into the wooden wall to my left. I hadn't realized I'd been in motion up until that point, but the stillness overtakes me as I keep kicking and fighting against my cage.

Sounds soon start to become more distinct. Voices are talking nearby and one's screaming louder than the rest. A female voice. I recognize it as Tasha seconds before talons dig through the center of the coffin, shredding the wood at the expense of slim fingers and manicured nails.

I see her face as she pulls the last board away. Her eyes are red like she's been crying, but right now she just looks stunned. She's staring at my chest.

"Howisthispossible…" The sentence comes out as a single word on her breath.

A voice behind her shouts, "Is it true? It can't be. She's dead!"

Tasha is immobile, and gargoyle isn't her best look. Clearing my throat, I have to swallow a couple times in order to remember how to talk.

"Get me the fuck out of this box!" I shout.

"Abel," she blurts, coming forward, but she seems hesitant to touch me. "Are you sure it's…safe to move you?"

"I don't want to be in here anymore. It's creepy. Get me out."

She grabs me and hauls me up into a seated position, and the moment I'm upright, I'm overwhelmed by the scent of clean air as much as I am by the reaction of so many beings — human and Other alike.

Calvin shouts my name, Sandra begins to sob uncontrollably, and the guards standing just behind them all take to one knee. They're standing beyond the edge of the open trunk, car tilted askew making it look like we've run off the highway or *been run* off the highway.

My legs fumble for the ground and I have a hard time walking for the first few seconds. Tasha holds my hand as I stretch out my legs and plant my bare feet on the cracked asphalt. I expect to feel chill in just a pair of pants, but all I feel is warmth.

"Stop that," I snap when I notice that even Calvin and Sandra are kneeling now. "Get up!"

They amble to their feet and I hug Sandra first, then Tasha, then go to Calvin, but he just stares at my chest — no, at my tits.

"Um…" He shoves his hand between us and I can't help it. I laugh and give his hand a shake.

"Where is everyone? Where's Kane?" I say, looking down the road towards the next SUV, but there's only the one.

Tasha's lips fumble and she seems to struggle to make sound as wind pulls her hair across her neck. "Notare," she says, as if testing the word on her tongue like a beginner taking a stab at a foreign language.

"You are Notare." This time she sounds sure, but I don't get how she can be.

"I…Notare? What? Where's Kane."

"You are a Notare now. You have the Tare," she says, voice getting louder and louder.

Sandra is either laughing or crying or both and Calvin's started clapping now. A couple of the other guards clap too, as if unsure about how to handle this.

Well, me too.

"Holy fuck," Calvin shouts, "Abel, how the fuck? We all watched you die. You were dead for more than three hours. You died…and now you're…you're a…I need to sit."

Calvin starts to sink down, but Tasha grabs his arm. "No time for that. We need to get you to Kane."

"Yeah. Where is he?" I say while she shoves me into the front seat of the SUV and gets behind the wheel. Sandra doesn't even have her door closed before she takes off, going zero to sixty in seconds.

The tires squeal. She keeps glancing over at me frantically.

"What happened, Tasha?"

I say, breathing hard as I try to keep my tits covered. Maybe some of the brightness, too. It doesn't help. I need a shirt. Or maybe a parka. The whole car is filled with my glow.

Tasha licks her lips and adjusts her rearview mirror so she can see me better. "You died and Kane killed Elise. The Council is trying to determine how to proceed. We haven't had murders like this between Notare in recorded history. But you get a vote, no matter what they decide."

She looks again to my chest. The light pulsates in time with my heartbeat, though I no longer feel Kane's.

I knead the skin of my pectoral and try to keep my voice steady as I say, "Why can't I feel him anymore? Is he okay?"

Tasha shudders. "He most certainly is not okay. He loves you and you died today. Blood bonds can be broken through death. And you died today," she repeats, "you died." She shakes her head and a smile plays out across her lips. "How many angels watch over you, Notare?"

We drive past that faded blue sign demarcating the entrance to Vancouver, race through the city block Elise leveled, and as we pass by that concrete tower, I think of Elise.

She spent hundreds of years trying to discover the key to Tare and died without knowing that she got something right.

How? I don't know. And I don't need to. I'm just a human with a serious mortality problem, but a knack for coming back.

The tires squeal as Tasha brings the car to a stop in front of a low building that might have, at one point, been a library. Calvin is outside wrenching my door open and pulling me out into the grey.

Tasha grabs my hand as we climb the concrete steps to meet a row of guards who don't even notice me. "Only Notare and the Lavhe are permitted from this point forth," one of the guards says.

Tasha straightens, looking a little insane with her hair and clothes all disheveled and my blood covering most of her arms. Still, she's in fine form as she points to my chest. "You *dare* address a Notare like this? I could have you exiled, soldier."

The alien steps back, eyes widening as he finally registers me. I try to cover my chest, but Tasha holds my arms down and prods me in the back so I'm just standing there, tits out, proudly.

"I…you…you're human," the guard shouts as loud as he can.

"Uh yeah," I answer.

Tasha steps within an inch of the guard, eclipsing his height. "Escort the Notare inside at once or I will be forced to report your actions to the Lavhe. Go!" She shouts when he still doesn't move.

The poor bastard jumps and bows to me deeply, so the others do, too. Tasha hangs back as they guide me inside through a set of heavy wooden doors, down a hallway lined in books.

The room opens up and there they are — the Council — looking rather unimpressive sitting in the middle of a rather immaculate library at a long wooden table.

Guess people didn't feel the need to loot books when the world ended.

The guard standing beside me clears his throat. "Uhm…I." He tries again while faces begin to turn in our direction. "The Notare is here?"

The Lahve sits at the head of the table facing me. His eyes find me and my chest and I reach up and cup my boobs and step forward.

Kane's sitting at the end of the table closest to me, but he still hasn't turned around. Can he feel my presence? Is he scared to look?

"Kane?" I say and he stiffens like he's been electrocuted.

"No," he whispers. "Kane, it's me."

One of the female Notare rises from her chair, looking lovely and ancient. "This is not possible," she says simply. She presses her fingertips into the table and looks to her left. "Lahve, please. An explanation for this."

He stands and when he moves, his chair thwacks to the floor. He holds his cane stiffly in his hand and takes one meaningful step forward.

"I have none, Morgana. It would appear that Kane's Sistana has been resurrected as Notare."

"That's not possible," Morgana repeats.

One of the males says, "Do you believe her capable of deception?" He smirks. "She does not appear it."

They launch into a debate after that, but Kane still hasn't spoken. I step forward over the faded dark blue carpet. It's hard and my toes curl up into it. I cover my boobs as I walk until I reach the back of his chair.

I place my hands on his either shoulder and I notice that the room has gone completely quiet around us.

Kane jolts under my touch, but his hand still reaches up to touch my fingers. He holds them in front of his eyes, looking at the blood crusted in the grooves of my palm and around my fingernails.

"Kane," I whisper. He shivers visibly and I step up behind him and press my lips to the top of his head. "This isn't a dream," I tell him.

He tilts his face back and up at the same time that he pulls me in front of him and onto his lap. His heat washes over me, and I notice that, at no point, does he look at my chest.

"Leave us," he whispers.

"We came all this way and now you're ordering us to leave?" The other female says. "I don't think so. We need to get to the bottom of this."

"Alright," Kane answers, voice deceptively even. "Then you can stay and watch."

"Watch?"

Kane stands, bringing me with him, throws back his chair and lowers my body down onto the table. He arches over my torso and kisses the light flaring between my breasts before his mouth works to the right, finds my nipple and sucks.

I yelp as excitement flashes through me, far hotter than any embarrassment I might have otherwise felt. I'm with Kane and he's here and we're both alive.

"I want to feel you," I gasp as his mouth moves up to my throat, biting and pulling at the skin there.

"I'm going to open you now," he snarls.

"Please." I grab his hair and yank his head into the curve of my throat, exposing it to him.

"First from me," he moans, and before I know what's happened, he's got a knife in his hand and he's dripping blood from his neck onto me.

The chairs at the table are all being pushed back now. I can hear voices arguing shrilly as Kane lowers his neck to my mouth and I suck while his hands move to the belt at my waist. He breaks it in a single pull and by the time I'm full on the taste of him, he's pushing me back onto the table and pushing himself into me.

He breaks the skin at my neck with his teeth at the same time that his erection plunges past my lower lips and fills me with a fullness that I hope to feel every day for the rest of forever.

His hips smack into mine with abandon and we find our first shared release on the table. But it isn't finished. Not by a long shot.

Kane carries me onto the floor where he turns me onto my hands and knees. I'm shaky and I feel strangely vulnerable in this position, not because I can't look into his eyes, but because of what he can see.

"Kane, are you sure? The scars..." I breathe.

He bends over and I see the glow of his chest burn a slightly darker orange than the lighter yellow of mine. Both just as intense. Both just as angry and consuming and tragic and whole and wonderful and, in this moment, one.

He kisses my shoulder. And then he kisses the back of my neck. And then he spends the next hours kissing every single scar Jack branded me with.

His cock lines up with my opening and as he kisses the side of my face, he enters me and moans my name. "I love your scars, because they are you."

He slows and I sit up and we somehow manage to have sex like this, front-to-back and seated. There are so many positions, so many possibilities for pleasure I would have never even thought of.

"I want you to show me," I whisper as I lean back and lick the blood from his cheek.

Misunderstanding my meaning — or maybe understanding it perfectly — he says, "I will show you everything."

He slides his hand between my breasts and my Tare shines around his fingers like a torch and in my ear, he whispers, "But you will never leave me again, and this is my command to you."

I nod as he picks up speed and the incredible pressure in my body builds as he pounds into me from below and my legs shake, fighting to keep up.

"I don't make a...a very good ghost."

"No, you don't." He barks out a desperate laugh and a moment later, he's releasing into me, and my insides are clamping around him.

I fall forward onto my hands and he falls on top of me, pressing me into the carpet so that I'll definitely get rug burn all over my elbows and knees.

As the tremors fade, I feel his lips on my scars again, then on my back of my head. He tilts my face to his and touches my chest, dragging just the tip of his finger through the light.

"You don't give up."

"Not even when I'm dead." I shake my head and laugh. "I think you're stuck with me, Kane."

"Good," he sighs, hanging his head forward and I get the feeling that I wasn't the only one who came back to life tonight. "Good."

"I love you forever," I say.

"And you might just get that chance, *Notare*…"

Chapter Twenty-Three

Stepping through the front doors of Kane's house, I'm inundated by hugs and gasped congratulations.

I guess because the Lahve and the Council voted that I get to keep Elise's lands? Or maybe simply because I lived.

Laiya survived too, and stands next to me now as the foyer fills with people. Well, she stands as next to me as she can given that Kane's still stalking me like a shadow.

Ashlyn bounds out of the hall and wraps me up in a hug that nearly takes me to the ground. I'm breathing hard when she makes room for others.

"Are you alright?" Kane says, for the hundredth time in the past twenty minutes.

I roll my eyes. "Feeling better than the average corpse."

Kane drags his heavy hand through my matted hair, fingers tangling in the knots he finds there. Abandoning the gesture altogether, he smirks. "Good."

Gabe and Calvin crack jokes in the open doorway with a couple of the alien guards. Sandra's managed to coax Laiya into a wheelchair and is determined to doctor her, despite her best efforts to resist. Sandra asks Ashlyn to get sutures and a first aid kit and Ashlyn's off again.

"Where's Mikey?" I ask when I don't see him in the crowd.

Kane grimaces. "He didn't take your death well. He ran."

"Ran where?"

"Here."

"Here? By himself? Where is he now?"

"I don't…" Kane cocks his head, then looks up at the stairs. "Here, it would seem. Your Sistana's gone and made herself a Notare now, brother. What do you think?"

I follow his gaze to see Mikey standing at the top of the staircase. He's got a bottle of booze trapped in each fist and both are nearing empty.

He doesn't react to anything Kane said, just stares like he's looking at the ghost of a lost relative. I guess, in a truer sense, that's exactly what he's looking at.

"You're *dead*."

He points one of the bottles at me and it falls from his grip onto the marble floor below, narrowly missing Tasha. She frowns up at him before rolling her eyes, and as she makes her way into the recesses of the house, she pulls the pins from her frazzled hair so that it tumbles around her shoulders.

"Animal!" She shouts over her shoulder.

"I was, but I decided I could do better than that," I answer.

Mikey shakes his head in shock, staggers, then runs. He takes the stairs two at a time, half-falling to arrive at my feet.

"You're drinking again," I say, reaching to take the remaining bottle from him. He gives it to me willingly while a blush ravages his already wind-chapped cheeks.

"You weren't supposed to die," he whispers, "that wasn't the plan."

"I don't think it was." I pull down on the collar of Kane's shirt and light spills out and over Mikey. "I don't think anybody could have planned this."

Mikey gawks, freezing in place.

"Easy, brother," Kane says, reaching around me to hold Mikey away from me by the shoulder.

"Easy?" Mikey doesn't seem to understand and scrunches up his bearded face. "Easy? How can I take this easy? She's a fucking Notare." I fleetingly expect anger — jealousy — but then a grin splits his face so wide, he looks a decade younger.

He grabs me away from Kane and wraps me up in one muscular arm. My feet leave the floor as Mikey tosses me over the shoulder and begins spinning wildly in the foyer.

"She's a fucking Notare!"

He shouts and I laugh and people are laughing and cheering and clapping, even as I drop the bottle of booze in my hand and Mikey slips on the spilled liquid.

I land with my knee on his neck and Kane scoops me up to stand before I can properly suffocate him.

"You did it," Mikey says, slowly staggering up after me. He grabs my head and gives me a noogie. "You beat Elise."

"*You* guys beat Elise," I counter, holding onto Kane's arms. I'm still dizzy from all the spinning.

"Mikael, for fuck's sake, be careful with her. She just *died*," Kane tries for light, but his voice breaks.

I grab his hands in both of mine and lean on his chest. There, together, he sighs.

Mikey's dizzy, too and Calvin jolts with laughter when Mikey trips and falls back on the stairs. He looks up at me grinning, still and then switches his gaze to his brother.

"So what now? Does she get Notare privileges and Elise's territory?"

Kane nods, but I'm the one who answers. "It looks like all of her territory passes to me."

"And?"

"And what?"

"What's the first order of business, captain? Or should I say, Notare Abel?"

Leaning forward, he props his elbows on his knees and looks up at me raptly. That's when I notice that the room is pretty much silent, bodies all leaning forward, listening to my answer.

I cling to Kane's hand in mine. He's my pillar of strength — one I'll need as I move forward with the crazy plan brewing inside me. "Elise's territory is now mine. It's called Brianna, with two Ns, I guess."

I inhale deeply as more than forty sets of eyes focus on me, waiting to hear what I'll do with this power, this responsibility.

"I've decided I'm going to try to rebuild. I want that land to be safe human territory. Others — Heztoichen — are welcome, of course, but there's not going to be any cannibal Saltlands gang crap anymore. It's gonna be safe.

"I want to canvas Population for survivors once I make sure basic things like infrastructure and water and all that are up and running."

Ashlyn is beaming at me from only a few feet away, on her knees in front of Laiya's wheelchair, and I can see Becks in her face, smiling too. Would she be proud? I think she she would.

Nerves make my stomach flutter as I continue. "The only thing is, I'll need some help. Kane said he'd help me get started, but he's got a lot on his plate, you know…

running a seventh of the world. And I'll need humans of course to help me integrate the other humans from Population that haven't been as fortunate as we have.

"It's going to be dangerous. Really dangerous. And it won't be easy and it won't be comfortable. I know this isn't a great sales pitch and I don't know if now's the time to ask for volunteers, but I don't know what the hell I'm doing and I could really use your help."

The minute I stop talking, the chorus of competing voices that shouts back makes me laugh. My eyes blur but I blink the wetness away and focus on Calvin as he steps forward.

"No way in hell you could stop me from following your crazy ass across the continent."

Gabe, at his side, agrees. "I'm in, fearless leader."

"I'm coming too," Ashlyn chimes.

Sandra, still focused on the shears in her hand as she cuts through Laiya's pant leg, says, "And since there will be quite a number of humans, I think two doctors might be required." She shoots Ashlyn a conspiratorial wink.

Surprising me, Laiya places her hand on Sandra's and says, "And if you would need additional protection, Notare, I would be more than happy to join your guard."

Three of the other black-clad guards step in line beside her and, when she bows, they drop to one knee.

"And heaven forbid you should to dress yourself on this voyage."

I turn and see Tasha reenter room, looking like she just got back from vacation. She's in an entirely new outfit, skin clear, hair braided like a zipper down the back of her head.

"I'll help as I can, Notare." She nods and I nod back.

I turn then to Mikey, but he just grins and shakes his head. "Don't insult me by asking if I'll come. You need all the help you can get with your mortality rate."

I grin and feel the reassuring pressure of Kane's hand on my waist as I glance around at my friends, my community, my family. A rush of warmth swells in me that has nothing at all to do with the bright flares of light that ripple across my skin, but everything to do with this newfound feeling of hope. I rub my cheeks roughly and laugh as a small chorus of cheers echo across the walls.

Cutting through them, I say loudly, "Well, then, it's settled. We are generation one."

New Rules for the World After

Rule 1 *(aka the only rule)* — Never give up. Not even when you're dead.

~~Rule 1 Never hope~~
~~Rule 2 Pack light~~
~~Rule 3 Don't get personal~~
~~Rule 4 the BIGGER the badder~~
~~Rule 5 Run~~
~~Rule 6 Always trust your gut~~
~~Rule 7 Never drop your weapon~~
~~Rule 8 Don't help strangers~~
~~Rule 9 No talking in the grey~~
~~Rule 10 Don't start a fight you can't win~~
~~Rule 11 Double tap~~
~~Rule 12 Don't talk to the Others~~

Thanks so much for submerging yourself in the battleground that is Saltlands! Book three continues the trek to Brianna and is told from the perspective of a new character (that you've already met!) — Get Generation One today!

To get early access to future books filled with hot, possessive alphas and the resilient, warrior women they worship *not to mention a free ebook* feel free to sign up to my mailing list at www.booksbyelizabeth.com/contact.

Thanks again and happy reading,
Elizabeth

Generation One *preview*

Abel should have let me die. Jack should have killed me. Now I'm stuck trying to keep this band of humans alive, including the insufferable Pia — the one who makes me want to live.

Generation One: An Alien Invasion SciFi Romance
Population Series Book 3 (Diego and Pia)

Available anywhere online books are sold
in ebook and in paperback

Chapter One

Listening to the sound of voices, I wonder if I'm dead or asleep. It's the same question I've been asking myself for days now. Or has it been weeks? It doesn't much matter. Time doesn't exist. There's only pain. A bright, effulgent agony. It cuts across my skin, burrowing deep into my flesh, finding home near my brittle bones. The wind whistles through them these days, sounding like sand pattering against paper. I'm just dissolving away.

The hurt hurts worse against my face and chest…but also across my back and shoulders…and also, mostly my right leg, which has been partially flayed.

The bastard enjoyed doing this to me. I wonder if I was wrong in thinking that I'd escaped. Maybe Jack let me get away. Just so I could die like this. *Of course I did, Diego.* Fucker. His voice is all I can hear as I lay dying. That low, demonic chuckle.

My mouth is dry, lips cracked and bleeding, but I can't taste the blood. There's only ash as I lie on the side of the road like something discarded, the slow wheezing of my breath and Jack's ringing laughter keeping me conscious.

I wish I wasn't.

Wish I wasn't alive, either.

I want to die. I've wanted to die from the beginning, but instead, I clawed my way across this wasteland, moving from one water source to the next.

I thought finding the highway might lead me to some town where I could find medical supplies and recover but in the middle of the crumbling asphalt was where my body stopped working and I decided I'd rather let the crows and the carrion take whatever trash Jack left.

The brutal way my body was built was the only part of me with any purpose anyway, and there's no saving it. So there's no point to salvaging something worthless. Fuck it. Let the carrion creatures come out to hunt.

That's the spirit.

A sound in the distance grows louder as everything else begins to fade. Sounds like thunder. A lady once taught me about thunder. Said it was the cough of some great big man who lived up in the clouds. She called him The God. She also called herself mother. I didn't believe her when she said it, and I didn't believe her about that big man either. Nobody treats their kids like that.

Not her.

Not *him.*

How could you think that, my sweet, sweet Diego? I loved you. I love you still.

Another stretch of time passes before the coughing starts up again…then continues, pulling me out my drunken stupor and into the world of pain I thought I'd been lucky enough to leave behind.

The sound persists, forcing memories on me. Memories of big, fat trucks on heavily trafficked roads while me and the other kids running under Jack try to lift merch from them. We succeeded more than we didn't. Jack gave us each fat cuts. I was thirteen? Ten? Younger than that, maybe. But I was a prince to Jack's king. And he's right, I did love him. *Do, Diego, you* do *love me.*

Maybe he's right now, too.

But here and now, it's the sound that's wrong. I can't be hearing the groan of an exhaust pipe. The last time I heard that sound was a decade back, when eighteen-wheelers still ran. They're too big and too slow for Population though, because they present a moving target for gangs — gangs like Jack's. The one I joined sometime after the one called Mother.

When he found me, I'd been on the streets and I was convinced that he was The God she'd spoken about.

Shouting words sound over the thrum of the truck. Some of the voices are deep and distinctly male, but others are lighter, operating at too high a pitch. Kids or women? And that's surprise number two, because kids don't exist out here and the women that do wish they didn't.

I remember the last woman I'd seen on the road, strung up in a kill box. She'd been bloodied worse than anybody I'd seen in a long while, but she held out. She kept fighting. It'd been hard to watch — not the torture, but her spirit slowly evaporating into the sky. With those injuries, she wouldn't have lasted more than a few hours after I cut her down and let her loose. Whatever Jack didn't do, Population woulda done the rest. She'd a died just like I'm doing now. Broken and bloody and in pain. Alone on the side of the road. Road kill. Wearing her insides on the outsides.

Except I'm not alone. Not anymore. Because there are murmurs belonging to voices that belong to the people whispering them. Distinct words peel apart from the whooshing sound that's filled my ears. I hear "can't" and "Sandra" and "save him."

Don't, please don't.

Wishing I had enough strength left to slaughter one last person — whoever talking about trying to save my skin — I try moving my arms. My left hand twitches, but my right is numb, paralyzed up to the shoulder. It's been that way since I swallowed mud two days ago. The closest I could get to water. I'm just rotting now…rotting from within.

"Hey, hey!" Fingers slap my left cheek, the one that isn't a raw, pus filled lesion, then pull up on my eyelids.

Colors blur and swim, making it impossible for me to see the face looming above me as more than just a muddy smear against a darker light. The sky. It's hideous. But that doesn't matter, because I've seen the sky everyday, but I've only heard that voice twice.

"I know you," she shouts, voice too loud and too close and too fucking impossible. The woman from the kill box. The one who I cut down. The one who's dead.

"I know you and you saved my life. Remember? You fought your brothers for me."

I remember. How could I forget? The one halfway decent thing I've done in the past thirty-two years was what landed me here, strung out on the side of the road wearing my insides as a blanket. The irony is as tragic as it is hilarious.

Good men die in this world. Brutally. In piles of piss and shit and blood.

I'm a bad man, so how is it that I'm here, dying like one of the good ones?

My senses grow distant, numbing out into numbness, until I feel pressure on the open wound that rips down the right side of my neck. I hiss, my body writhing, trying to distance itself from the pain. I can't get up. I can't get away. My chest constricts as I push stale air out and I can tell this will be one of my last breaths. Finally.

"Hey!" The voice roars. "You're not allowed to die yet. I won't let my debt go unpaid. Just hold on. I've got a doctor here and she's going to work her magic. Isn't that right?"

I redirect the last seconds of willpower I've got to my eyelids and blink once to clear them. A brown woman sits at my right side, watching the dead one. Forehead wrinkled, lips turned down at the corners, her expression isn't one I've seen a lot, but I'm still human enough to understand it. She's sorry. She can't help me. Thank fuck.

"Abel," the woman speaks quietly, but I can hear her just fine. I'm dead, not deaf. "The most I can do for him is ease his transition."

"No no no no no." The dead one shakes her head, looking just as fierce as I remember. Just as obstinate, too. Her will to live must be stronger than mine because I don't understand how she could have survived the beating and the lashing and the smoke from the Other's immolation unless she had their blood in her system. A lot of it.

"There has to be something you can do," the corpse says to the breather. "You're a healer. *Heal* him."

The woman doesn't respond right away. After a moment, she coils a piece of rubber around my left bicep and inserts a needle somewhere in my arm. Not that I can feel it. I can't feel anything at all. "Ashlyn, bring me the morphine."

I feel her hand on my skin as if there are layers of dirt separating us. Rick told me that when you die, you hallucinate in your final seconds due to a lack of oxygen in the brain — that was a few days before I killed him. Is this an atrophy of the mind? Am I already six feet under?

A small blonde child comes up behind her, but the specter called Abel holds her back. "No! No, fuck that. Sandra, that's too much." Abel grabs the Sandra woman by the wrist. Clear globs of liquid drip from the needle's delicious tip.

Sandra meets my gaze. I stare up at her listlessly. She whispers, "I can end his suffering."

"No. Don't you fucking dare disobey me." Abel points a finger threateningly at Sandra's nose and shoves her shoulder. "I'm the *Notare*, goddamnit! If I can't exercise my power to save this one man then how am I supposed to save the rest of humanity?" A Notare? Sounds like Other speak. I wonder if I'm not hearing her incorrectly.

"Relinquish the few to save the many," Sandra counters diplomatically. But that's fine. I'm happy to be a statistic.

Abel surges forward when Sandra raises the needle a second time and shoves the woman's shoulder. Seated on top of her heels as she is, Sandra falls onto her ass. There are people — men *and* women — standing in the background, watching. None intervene.

"Don't give me that battlefield triage bullshit. I wouldn't be here right now if it weren't for him."

Sandra doesn't seem to rise to Abel's challenge, but instead retreats further into herself. Her hooded gaze looks off into the distance, anywhere but at my face. "If you had been as injured as he is now, then it is likely, Your Grace, that I wouldn't have been able to save you either. It was the blood."

My eyes close and open and behind Abel's frustrated expression I see the tops of heads and above them, spindly boughs crawling up the grey mist, looking like desiccated fingers desperately seeking salvation.

Abel turns to me, places her hand on my good cheek and says, "I'm going to give you my blood."

I gargle up blood and saliva when I mean to attack her. The hell she is. I've lived this long without their shitty alien blood in my body. I'm human. *All* human. One of the few left.

Her wrist comes towards me and I writhe — in my head — because outwardly, I'm not sure I move at all. Castrated by blood loss and incapable of rebelling, I'm grateful when a man steps up behind this dead bitch and grips her shoulders. For a moment I hallucinate Jack. How the fuck did Jack find me? But then I blink.

This guy's not Jack. He's bigger than Jack was — than Jack *is* because it's clear that fucker won't ever die. This guy's bigger than any human I've seen. He's got Jack's dark hair and Jack's green eyes but there's a slight orange pulse around the collar of his shirt that makes it look like he's smuggling a flashlight under his black tee. Huge? Glowing? Nah, he's definitely not human.

So he's a fucking alien Jack. How ironic. All of my favorite fucking things. *You know you could never get rid of me, sweetie.*

My outside shell is immobile though my insides scream as Abel says, "What's the point of *this*, if I can't save him?" She yanks down on the neck of her own black thermal and I see an orange glow pulsing in time to a quick, steady beat. I thought she was human. I was *sure* of it.

I must already be dead and already dreaming.

The other Jack — the Jack Other — shakes his head. "As my Sistana, I can't let you give him your blood. It puts us both at risk."

His voice is even though his eyebrows are pulled together, as if concerned. He watches the human with the glowing golden heart with a fondness that makes me think that he somehow *cares* for her. Jack would never wear an expression like that. He would slice that expression off of any of his dogs' faces if he saw it. He did once.

"Come, Abel. Let Sandra help him." He pulls Abel gently to her feet.

A second male that I recognize as equally inhuman steps into my line of sight. My optic nerve has all but incinerated with the effort it takes to keep my eyes open. I want to close them and fucking die, but curiosity holds my attention just enough to keep me anchored to the hard concrete at my back and the cold breeze nipping at my front like the cruel edges of small, sharp teeth.

"This is the guy?" The blonde Other says. His chest doesn't glow, or if it does, I can't see it underneath his sweatshirt. He's got on black basketball shorts and his hair is tied up in a knot on top of his head. He looks fucking stupid — aside from being nearly too big to take.

"Yes," Abel says, voice pleading and haunting. Not the melody I wanted to die to.

Her fists are wrapped in the glowing Jack Other's shirt. She's pulling. He's staring. They're all fucking staring. "He's the one who cut me down. I thought I was dying — hell, I thought I was already dead. But he fought off Jack's men — his war dogs, or whatever he called them. I was all by myself and *he* was the one who protected me before Mikey showed up." She looks to the blonde. "Before *you* showed up and carried me into the river."

But I'm still stuck — protected her? Is that what I did? Evidently in unknown coordination with this big, blood-sucking idiot.

Confusion puts a clamp on my throat. I'm not breathing. And then I'm seizing. My teeth clench together and my eyes roll back. Pain stabs its fingers into my wounds, whittling down through the diseased and rotten flesh until it scrapes bone with its nails. This is it.

I'm covered in pus and mud and blood and a shadow appears before my eyes where that fated fabled tunnel should have been. I'm dying until I feel a hard, warm object against my mouth and pungent heat dripping down the back of my throat that tastes like metal and eggs. A hand shifts behind my neck, tilting my head up at an angle and I cough as my tongue swells up in my mouth, fighting not to swallow.

"Come on man, you want to live or not?" The blonde fucker speaks to me in a low growl.

No, I don't. I really fucking don't.

But I can't speak and he doesn't hear me and the smell of piss is suffocating and the taste in my mouth is like sucking on pennies and shit. When he withdraws a few moments later, a tingling sensation sweeps my body and is followed closely by an unnatural euphoria. Drugs. Other blood and human drugs. They're working together to fuck me over by keeping me breathing.

Death was so close. I was almost there…

"Thank you, Mikey." Abel's voice whispers as sleep and I war with one another. Her low pitch and the Mikey Other's burn and blur together, becoming a thick haze. "Thank you so much."

"I owe him. The debt you sought to pay was mine."

I've never met the alien, but he sure as shit owes me now. He owes me a death. Because as air comes more easily to my scorched lungs, I understand that I'm not in hell but somewhere much worse. Instead of that easy slip into nothingness, I've been condemned to life.

Chapter Two

"Diego...Diego, can you hear me?" The words are faraway but coming closer, like a train from the World Before and I'm tied to the goddamn tracks. She calls me Diego. How in the hell does she know to call me that?

As if I asked the question out loud, she answers, "I remember your name from before. The murdering asswipe from your gang called you that, so I'm going to assume it's correct. You'll have to tell me if it isn't."

Her hand touches my forehead. I want to get out from under it. So hot and heavy and disgusting in the comfort it tries to provide. I don't need comfort. I don't need anything or anyone.

Suddenly another voice cuts in. I know it too. Sandy or Sana or Sancha something. "Diego, if you can hear me we've stopped moving for the night. I'm going to put you under again. I need to keep you sedated and tied down so that I can work on cutting out the scar tissue.

"Mikey's blood has rid your body of infection but the wounds were severe and, left to fester, his blood won't be able to heal your face so that it looks like it did before."

She doesn't apologize, but instead says stiffly, "I am going to see what I can do to minimize the damage."

I say nothing and relish in the numbness that creeps over me in the seconds before I pass out. It's as close to good as I've ever felt, so I take it without complaint once, twice, a dozen more times until finally I wake and somebody that isn't the blessed Sammy hovers over me.

The corpse is back.

The dead woman that is definitely no longer dead is sitting up, looking down her nose at me. Infrequent shafts of light hit the right side of her face. It's brown, like the skin on the backs of her hands and her throat. Darker than mine is. The same color as Santana but just… different.

Her hair is dark, maybe black, unlike the medium brown fuzz that grows out of my head and that I usually raze down to the root. Her hair is clean, too.

I don't see clean hair a lot in Population, so it distracts me. Little feathery wisps touch her jaw in curls. I think it might even be a little longer than it was the last time I saw her.

Now, definitely not dead, I find the way her dark blue eyes watch me annoying, but perhaps it's only because she reminds me of someone I knew once. Someone I liked. Or maybe hated. Is there a difference?

I think about Jack. I wanted him dead — to die suffering — but at the same time, I'd have done anything for him. I loved him with the entirety of my black, withering soul.

Corpse scoots towards me until I feel the warmth of her hip against mine. The first time I've been made aware of my own body in days. As she moves, something beneath her rattles. Metal on metal on wood. It takes me a second to understand, but I'm on a cot and there's another identical cot stacked on top of it. Above me, slats stare down. Bunks, but where?

The Other who gave me his blood sits on the cot across a short aisle, his sneakers propped up on the bunk I occupy. Abel pushes his shoe away when it brushes her other hip. It's a damn tight fit in here. Like army barracks. Except I can feel the rumbling beneath me and hear the humming of that fabled exhaust pipe and ever so often, the battering of the wind against whatever structure covers us.

So we're in some kind of moving army barracks. I'm alive. The corpse is alive. The Other who looks fucking stupid and stares at her like she's the sun to his universe isn't trying to kill me, but save my life. A blanket covers me. Beneath it, I'm naked. And Sansan's wonderful drugs are numbing me, but not enough.

"How do you feel?"

I don't want to feel. That's what I'd tell her if I could, but I lack the voice. Instead, I turn my head away and close my eyes and try to push back the sensation of sandpaper sheets rubbing like little razorblades against my too sensitive flesh. I focus on the sensation of air flowing in and out of my nostrils. The smell of a canvas tarpaulin. Grease. Metal. Human sweat.

"Diego, I don't know if you remember me, but my name is Abel. You met me a few weeks ago when you and the members of your gang trapped me and a Heztoichen named Trocker." I'd never fucking forget it. "You saved my life after Jack beat and whipped me. I can only assume that you got at least some of your injuries shortly after that."

She pauses again, as if waiting for me to say something. I don't and I won't.

I feel her shift on the cot beside me. I wish she'd just get the fuck off and go away. Die like she was supposed to.

"We found you on the side of the road five days ago and my friend Mikey gave you his blood to keep you alive. He's one of the Others. So is my husband, Kane, and so are my friends Tasha and Laiya and the Lahve.

"The Lahve isn't with us, but some of his troops are. They're here to protect us as we cross Population. The rest of us are human. There's a long story here that you probably aren't ready to hear now, but I'll give you the bullet points.

"The system of governance for the Others is based on which among them carry light, or glow in their chests, like Kane does and like I do now. These seven Notare have divided up the planet. They each rule a different region and the grey area we humans call Population is what was left to us."

Yes, I know Population. I know it well. My jaw ticks, and so do the muscles in my forearms as I remember years and years of pain and suffering. Not mine, but that which I delivered. So. Much. Pain.

"Through a series of events, I ended up bonding to another Notare when we swapped blood. She killed me and when she was killed in retaliation, her light passed on to me. That makes me one of the seven rulers of the world now, in the Others' eyes.

"I'm taking over her lands and making them a human sanctuary. Heztoichen won't be barred from joining us, but there won't be any more of this cannibalistic shit. There won't be any scavenging, no looting, no robbing, no rape, no killing. There won't be anymore gangs.

"It's going to be a helluva lot of work getting there and it's going to require a lot of man power and I know it's a lot to ask of you right now, but I'd love it if you stayed with us.

"I don't have a lot of warriors on my team and I could use someone with your skills. It's going to be at least another two months of hard, deep trekking across Population before we get there, and that's only if everything goes well. The plan is actually to try to find people on the road. We want to bring them with us, if they seem…amenable to it."

What a fucking joke. Jack laughs.

I agree with him. What a fucking joke.

Her tone is higher and more severe as she says, "We want to rehabilitate those that can be rehabilitated, both physically and mentally and we want to be able to give everyone we meet the same choice I'm giving you now. I've got Sandra and Ashlyn here as medics, and some of the humans who've spent more time out in Population can act as sort of…mediators. They'll try to help.

"But what I need now are contingencies. It's not going to be easy to convince people and it'll be harder to get gangs to disband and to absorb them. I want people on my team there for when things don't work out. I need warriors to defend us in case they attack and I've seen you in action."

Her voice trickles away as she asks me to give her something so many others have tried to take. That Jack took with love, with psychological fuckery, and with force.

My obedience. My free will.

"Would you consider it?"

"Because we could always just drop you off on the side of the road, like we found you," a hard male voice cracks. The blonde Other. The one with the stupid haircut. Mikey, she called him.

"Mikael," a deeper male voice reprimands. Who the fuck is this now? Fuck if it's that Fake Alien Jack.

You know you miss me with all your bloody soul.

My muscles twitch with an eagerness to smash my fist through Fake Jack's teeth in an attempt to reach the back of his skull. I'm weak though, arms too heavy to lift.

Of course they'd ask me now when I'm at their mercy, because that's what the hungry do when they finally achieve power. They make slaves. They devour.

I clench my teeth together and close my eyes, blocking out the light as I struggle to shut out the other sounds. Whispering nearby, loud talking just a few paces off.

In the seconds that I wonder what they're saying about me, my self-hatred grows. I don't give a fuck. I don't need this woman's protection. I don't need another Jack, even one with tits on her.

"Diego?"

I twist away from the sound of her voice until I feel the stitching on my neck begin to tear. Let it. Who fucking cares?

"Look, you don't have to answer now. I'm just excited to have you here and happy that you're better." I hear her rise to leave and the sound of heavy shoes hitting the ground beside her.

"Just to let you know, Sandra's managed to cut out most of the excess scar tissue. You'll still have some, but it's better than it was." Sandra. The docs name is Sandra. I hate myself for registering it. For caring.

"I'll get you some food and water. Sandra and Ashlyn have been keeping you on an IV but it'll be good to replenish the old fashioned way, chewing and swallowing and shitting. All that fun stuff."

She whistles, then shouts, "Calvin, would you bring Diego some grub?"

"Sure thing, boss," comes the faraway reply.

I wait for her to leave, but she doesn't. Instead the bitch fucking touches me again, this time my shoulder. I *hate* the feeling of it. I hate being touched. The stress of it brings a cold sweat to my armpits, my hairline and my crotch. It's a contrast to the ferocious and unwanted heat of her right hand on my exposed shoulder. My sternum shudders. I'd have broken her wrist with my own hands if they weren't under the drug-laced spell Sandra put them under.

So instead, I snarl up at her, "D-d-d-don't…fuck-fuck-fucking t-t-touch mmme."

It's been a long time since I've been forced to speak. A long time. Jack and his war dogs knew better than to try. The words come out more mangled than they usually do and I watch the frame of her eyes widen until I can see white on all sides of the iris. She sees me for what I am. Pathetic. And she pities me. And I hate her for it. She looks away and opens her mouth.

"D-d-d-d…" Don't. The word forms perfectly in my mind, repeating itself over and over. But the stutter is like a fucking intruder breaking into my home. I try to push him out the door, but the harder I push, the harder he digs his heels into the carpet. I'm sweating. Fucking convulsing. My face feels hot. My chest feels cold. My palms go clammy. And he's laughing the whole time.

"It's okay," Abel says without giving me a chance to speak. To try.

I'd cut the tongue out of her mouth for it. I've done it before. Jack approved. He held the boy down while I heated the knife, then whittled it in past the kid's teeth.

Jack wouldn't let anybody talk shit about my stutter. He never finished my sentences. He always waited. Patient. Tender. *Because I love you, Diego.* He did. And I worshiped him in return. Let him enslave me. It hurts knowing that he still does.

"Don't," I choke out, the word arriving minutes too late.

Abel nods once, hard, eyebrows knitting together severely over her well-shaped nose. "Calvin'll be over in a second with some food. Just rest up. You've got nothing to worry about while you're here — from any of us," she says, though both of the Others at her back look like they might disagree.

They follow her down the narrow walkway to a bunk bed three over where they whisper and throw uninhibited glances in my direction, judging me, debating their stupid decision to keep me alive and so close to the rest of the innocents.

Of the twenty some beds in the space, most are empty. A few aliens sit near the open entrance of the barracks looking old world stormtroopers, dressed all in black. They look lethal and are watching me like I'm a threat. *Let them come. Let them see what I made you.*

Only two humans sleep within one set of bunks from me. Sandra and, above her, a blonde woman. She doesn't seem to notice me, the blonde woman. The only one who looks over me and sometimes meets my gaze and no matter what, maintains her naive, stupid smile. I hate it. I hate her. I look away.

Coming towards me now is a blonde human man holding a plate and bottle of water. Like all the others *but the stupid, moron blonde chic* his grin fades when he looks at me. Probably because of the scarring, but maybe also because of the twisted expression on my ruined face — a face Jack ruined.

No, I didn't ruin you. You were born ruined.

I turn away from him and close my eyes, sparing him from the burden of having to look at me. Because I know the truth. I'm the most monstrous fucker here, alien or not. It's what Jack made me.

No, Diego. You were born a monster. I merely unlocked the cage and liberated you.

Population Series

Population, Book 1 (Abel and Kane)
Saltlands, Book 2 (Abel and Kane)
Generation One, Book 3 (Diego and Pia)
Brianna, Book 4 (Lahve and Candy) — *coming 2021!*
Book 5 (Constanzia and Tanen) — *coming 2021!*
Book 6 (Mikey and Sung) — *coming 2021!*

Series by Elizabeth

Population: Post-Apocalyptic SciFi Romance
Population, Book 1 (Abel and Kane)
Saltlands, Book 2 (Abel and Kane)
Generation One, Book 3 (Diego and Pia)
Brianna, Book 4 (Lahve and Candy) — *coming 2021!*
Book 5 (Constanzia and Tanen) — *coming 2021!*
Book 6 (Mikey and Sung) — *coming 2021!*

Xiveri Mates: SciFi Alien and Shifter Romance
Taken to Voraxia, Book 1 (Miari and Xoran)
Taken to Nobu, Book 2 (Kiki and Kinan)
Taken to Sasor, Book 3 (Mian and Neheyuu)
Taken to Heimo (Svera and Krisxox)
Taken to Kor (Deena and Rhork)
Taken to Sucere, Book 6 (Halima and Jakka) — *coming 2021!*

Brothers: Dark Romantic Suspense
The Hunting Town, Book 1 (Knox and Mer, Dixon and Sara)
The Hunted Rise, Book 2 (Aiden and Alina, Gavriil and Ify)
The Hunt, Book 3 (Charlie and Molly, Anton and Candy) – *in the works*

Find out more at www.booksbyelizabth.com.

CPSIA information can be obtained
at www.ICGtesting.com
Printed in the USA
BVHW031344141220
595686BV00008B/112